NO BROKEN BONES

Gail Morellen

ISBN 0-7414-4995-1

Cover art by Levi Thompson, http://www.ruraldesigncollective.org

Published by:

INFI∞ITY
PUBLISHING.COM

1094 New DeHaven Street, Suite 100
West Conshohocken, PA 19428-2713
Info@buybooksontheweb.com
www.buybooksontheweb.com
Toll-free (877) BUY BOOK
Local Phone (610) 941-9999
Fax (610) 941-9959

Printed in the United States of America

Printed on Recycled Paper

Published September 2009

Dedicated to my mother,
who showed me how it can be

Acknowledgments

I give my compliments to Gay Holland, who made my first experience of working with an editor surprisingly easy and rewarding. May our friendship continue.

To my pals, Rosaria W., Nancy A., Terry M., and Nanci J., I give my greatest appreciation for their advice and praise when I needed it most.

To members of the best writers group on the West Coast, Anne, John, Joyce, Lily, Martha, Mary, Mike, Mimi, and Sharri, I give my humble thanks for their invaluable, kind-but-honest criticism. I promise something more fun next time.

I give writer Jayel Gibson my gratitude for teaching me the fundamentals of publishing and reminding me to have fun.

To all of my family, I offer my admission that too many important things go unspoken, and too many complaints get voiced. I'm pretty lucky to have you all.

I give my greatest love to my husband, who not only endured this book's completion but encouraged it. I've always considered him the exemplification of a good guy, and now he's exceeded even that.

And to our unnamed supporters who helped us get through it all, I return their compassion. Take care.

Table of Contents

PROLOGUE: SUNDAY, APRIL 7TH 2002, 2:02PM

"Hello. It's Carley."

Your call is right on time, for a change, just like the court order says, but your voice sounds like you don't really want to talk. Though I've never seen the inside of your tiny house, I've formed an image from previous conversations. I picture you there at the kitchen table, the digital clock placed in front of you deliberately. The TV is on in the background, so your Gramma and Grampa are on guard in the living room, close enough to hear your conversation with us.

"Hi, Carley! How are you doing? We've missed talking to you. It's been over a week."

"That's 'cuz we just forgot to call you and Gran'daddy last time."

"That's okay. I'm glad to hear you now, but you don't sound well. Do you have another cold?"

"No, I just have the sniffles 'cuz I been crying a lot an' I couldn't stop an' I got the sniffles."

"Oh, that's so sad. What's wrong?"

"I started crying 'cuz I got two swats from my Grampa when I didn't get out of the tub when my Gramma said, an' I hadn't gotten swats in a long time so it surprised me an' took my breath an' I started crying. I couldn't breathe right for a minute an' that made me cry harder."

"Oh, sweetie, I'm so sorry. I wish they wouldn't spank you."

"It's okay, it's just 'cuz I didn't get out of the tub when I was s'post to. I didn't obey them. It says it's okay in the Bible."

"But I know you understand things when they're explained to you. I'd hoped they would talk to you instead of hitting."

"No, it says in the Bible to spare the rod an' spoil the child."

"What do you think that means?"

"It means to not use a stick."

"You okay now? Can we talk about some good things?"

"Yeah, what good things?"

"How are you doing with your reading? Are you practicing?"

"I do at school, but I don't want to talk about that."

1

"Do you read at home, like you read with us when you're here?"

"I read the Bible, but I get to words that even my Gramma and Grampa don't know."

Again with the Bible.

"I bet. That's a very hard book to read. What about other books? I know you have some there that you told us ... Sweeney, no! Spencer, get the cat! He's got a bird! I'm sorry, Carley. Your stupid cat just caught a bird on the stump outside."

"Did Gran'daddy get him in time?" Your voice has gained its smile now.

"Yeah, can you hear him?"

"I hear him yelling at Sweeney, and laughing."

"Yeah, it's funny when the bird gets away, not nice when he brings it in the house. Spencer says that's a trick you taught Sweeney. Is that right, Carley?"

"I just taught him to sneak up on them and scare them. Put Gran'daddy on."

Obeying your command, I move the phone away from my mouth again to call him.

"Spencer, Carley wants to talk to you. She says Sweeney isn't supposed to catch them, just scare them."

He's eager, as usual, to pick up the other phone.

"Oh, is that right, Carley?" he says, ready for play. "Something must've gone wrong with that trick."

"That's 'cuz you told him to do it," you counter.

"Oh no, YOU told him to."

"Unh-uh, YOU did."

So for exactly seventeen minutes, we get to enjoy you.

You impress us with your bravery when we tell you the bad news that the vet had to put Rosie to sleep. Our basset hound was a good companion to you when you were here, and I know you've lost too many friends already. I remember how sad you were when your favorite teacher moved, and when an old woman from your church died. But you evade the sorrow now, not willing to give in to the tears still so near the surface.

As I try to help you understand "putting to sleep," you begin telling me, as if you are the doctor, about how the shot worked. We let you tell us, because it's diverting and because we really love to hear how your imaginative, scientific mind works.

At one point you look at the clock and, after asking the adults there to do the math, say that we have six minutes left. You and Spencer tell stories about Rosie, making stuff up and saying, "remember when Rosie ..." When you check the clock again, after they tell you to hang up, you're surprised that we got seventeen minutes.

PART ONE—BIRTH

(1984—1993)

CHAPTER 1

When Spencer and I first became friends and then fell in love, in our mid-twenties, it came as a wonderful surprise that we both had the same wish to adopt children. We felt like fate must have truly thrown us together. The more we talked about it, the more it felt like the consummate plan, that it couldn't be easier.

We spent five-and-a-half years just being in love, together and having fun. Somehow, we knew that the time was right for changing, for growing up a bit. That's when we got in touch with the State Children's Services Division, or CSD.

We hadn't bothered to get a legal marriage yet, believing that it wasn't the state's business to tell us whether we were married or not. Our commitment was our own, voiced and more real than any official paperwork could validate. We had taken care of details like putting health insurance and property titles in both names (by checking the "Married" box on all the forms) and hadn't encountered any problems. But the state definitely needed to see our marriage licensed and sanctified, so we did it.

Exactly two years and nine months later, we got a call from our caseworker, Margie, with news that she had two girls that she thought would be right for us. We thought the timing was funny, because two years is what the state required to ensure that the marriage would take, and the nine months was just like a pregnancy.

It's hard for me to relate to women who feel the need to bear children. Not that I find fault with their feelings, but in conversations with them, I've been treated as if there was something wrong with *me*. How could I want children and not want *my own* children? I've tried explaining that I knew I wanted children, I just never felt the need to reproduce. From the time I was a teenager, I told them, I knew there were lots of unwanted children in this world, and why should I add children when there were already too many to go around? It sounded naïve even to my ears. By the time I turned twenty-five and still had not felt any flutters of reproductive longing, Spencer and I knew what we wanted. How he came to his decision I don't know, but I was glad he'd had a vasectomy and there wasn't anything more to consider. I do know that neither one of us has ever regretted our decision.

The *choosing* of children, however, is not as easy as one might think. After passing all the tests the caseworker put to us (she established that we were financially capable, emotionally stable and non-criminal), we had to state what kind of children we wanted, or perhaps easier, what we did not want. We knew we wanted two because we lived on an isolated farm in the rural town of Belleville. It would be unfair to have a lonely child with no one to play with, and three was too many. But, boys or girls? Racial or ethnic background? We didn't have a preference. How about disabilities? This was an extremely hard factor to consider. After heart-searchingly honest talks with ourselves, we came to some conclusions. We could not have a wheelchair-bound child because of the rough ground on our farm. That was fairly easy to get to. However, it was harder to admit that I couldn't handle a severely retarded child. I felt it would be too hard, too painful to know that there was never going to be any improvement; I had to have hope.

Spencer had one limitation of his own—no fire-setters.

So that was it, and Margie did the rest. When we got the call, it was to tell us that she would send photos and brief descriptions of each girl, and that we should think it over before replying. She told us they were Kim, age nine, and Tisha, age six. They had been in protective custody for three and a half years, most of the time in the same foster home. They were sisters, but, their caseworker told us, Tisha was obviously the product of a "one-night-stand" because she was brown-skinned and the mother, legal father and Kim were white. The biological mother had to sign a statement that she didn't know who the father was, and we had to answer whether that was important to us. We said, "No."

There wasn't much else to go on. Then Margie told us about the problems "Hard-to-Place Children" face when they've been in the system so long and they finally get a chance at adoption.

"You really, really don't want to build their hopes up and find out later it's not going to work, Gail," she said. "If you tell them they're going to a new home with a new Mom and Dad, and then tell them no, there's been a change of plans, it's very damaging. In this case, it has happened already. A family was selected a year or two ago, and then backed out."

We understood that these girls could not go through another rejection like that.

It consumed us for days. We got the photos, Polaroids taken against a dark-paneled wall. The girls looked as if their caseworker had posed them for the occasion, dressed in their school clothes, their cute, eager faces smiling at the camera. No one could resist. The written descriptions didn't tell us much that we couldn't see from the pictures—blond, blue eyes, right-handed, favorite color: purple—black hair, brown eyes, hand proclivity not yet determined, favorite color: pink. We thought they must be kidding. What possible difference did right-or-left-handed make? This was not information on which to make life-altering decisions. Spencer wanted to know why it didn't say anything about whether they had a sense of humor.

But we made our decision, and once we did, it became the right one. That's the way it happens. At least, I think it must be the same with all people who have to make serious choices. You weigh the pros and cons, examine your deep feelings closely, and then you go for it. Once you've stepped off the edge, your heart is calm with the knowledge that you made the right decision.

Our family started with what Margie called a long honeymoon period. For two years we were the happiest family that could ever be. The girls laughed and grinned and loved everything in their new world. We didn't notice when the honeymoon ended, because the problems came so gradually. There were little fights, then they grew into big, door-slamming, sister-punching, scary fights. Neither Spencer nor I had experienced such anger with our own siblings, and we weren't prepared. Our friends that had children told us it was normal, but the descriptions of their household battles didn't sound like the same thing. We felt there was something frightening just under the surface.

Thus began our education into the science of abnormal behavior.

CHAPTER 2

Along with the legal documents we needed for adoption of Tisha and Kim, we received background information including psychological evaluations. The earliest report dated back to when Kim was six; there was a suspicion of sexual molestation, reported, but not substantiated. When we read phrases such as "no evidence of insertion," "incomplete police investigation," and "concern of possible 'seductive' and sexually precocious behavior," the red flags went up. It was obvious to us that whatever had happened to this young girl, and to some extent to her little sister, the damage was not controlled.

Despite the inadequacies of their previous environment, we still had faith that things would work themselves out. As we read the reports, the alarm signals going off were partially absorbed by our dreams of the loving family that we would become.

The concurrence of opinions was that Kim was exhibiting unusual behavior as a result of family dissolution and living with too many different care-givers. The parents lived a chaotic life and were unstable, at least in terms of living arrangements, if not of a more temperamental nature. Those were broadly hinted at, but not tested. The father was a roadie with a rock band and, when he was in town, lived with the girls after he and the mother had split up. When not in town, the girls were left with friends or relatives described as "dysfunctional" by the caseworkers. There was evidence in the reports that the father had tried to care for them, but was too impulsive to follow through with recommended parenting classes. He had appealed the court's decision to terminate parental rights, so at least that showed that he wanted his children. We hoped that he was motivated by love and not a claim of ownership.

The information on the mother was that she was intellectually limited, and that she could not take care of herself, let alone her children. That struck us as a strange thing for a psychologist to say. But we supposed courts making decisions about children's lives need to have hard facts without any sugar coating. At any rate, she was out of the picture.

We pored over the psychological evaluation of six-year-old Kim, since that was the crux of the court's decision to take custody. Much was made of her evasiveness when talking about her feelings, and that she exhibited coquettish behavior for attention. It said she did not easily acknowledge that her parents were divorced, and she missed her mother. She was mad that Dad had spanked her for some things Tisha did. The good doctor made an attempt to find out about the sexual abuse, but could not elicit any details except that Kim experienced frightening nightmares and was apprehensive about being physically touched.

Kim and Tisha had been placed in a children's residence and treatment center for further assessment. This was documented by a social worker who recorded specific behaviors, including daily routines and activities with the other children. Kim's most obvious problems, according to this professional, centered around her habits of procrastination. Yet the social worker listed the dates and details of Kim's temper outbursts.

In one week: Kim hit three girls for not sharing, pushed Tisha out of her chair, hit the social worker and an aid with a jump rope, said she hated another worker, stomped off and slapped a smaller child.

The list went on. The Summary Impression at the end of the report stated that Kim was learning to verbalize her feelings and express pent up anger.

What had the biggest impact on us, though, was the description of Kim's bedtime routine. She told them about monsters and witches, and the fear of being alone in the dark. She whispered to herself nightly, and awakened early in the morning and talked to herself. We felt that the so-called professionals were missing something big.

Almost everything in the evaluations came to the same, simple point: both girls had lots of potential, given the appropriate adoptive family, one which was sensitive to their special needs.

They got us.

CHAPTER 3

Our family doctor was also a psychiatrist, which made it easier to describe symptoms of physical ailments that were tied to family strife. My physical examinations for everything from strep throat to pap smears were ministered by the doctor with words of comfort; he knew our family was suffering from emotional strain. At different times, Spencer and I needed counseling sessions to cope with infrequent bouts of depression. Talking individually like that probably didn't do much to heal the family, but we managed to feel better and keep going.

Kim was fourteen the first time she was seen by the doctor for psychiatric counseling. She wasn't agreeable, though, and it was obvious that the time was not right. The doctor told us that if she wasn't ready to be treated, there was no point in trying to force it. It took another year and a half for Kim to acquiesce.

Tisha, meanwhile, was being treated for Attention Deficit Disorder. Her behavior in school had been deteriorating, with increasingly disheartening remarks from her teachers. It was apparent to them that she tried with all her might to complete assignments and to stay out of trouble with the other kids, but her inability to stay focused caused disruptions, in her academic work and with classmates. Trouble with other kids began, as far as we knew, in Tisha's fifth grade, at age ten. This rural area bred its share of bigots, and Tisha had her first real experience with racial bullying. When teachers weren't looking, kids called her names and ostracized her. The principal said he couldn't do anything about it if no one saw it. She had started school as a bright, pleasant and joyful little girl, then she learned meanness. She adapted quickly to the school's divisive culture, and the citations began coming home.

Our doctor felt it was a good case for a trial dose of Ritalin. He said we would know quickly whether it helped or not, because the symptoms would respond to the drug if caused by damage in her brain. If the cause was due to nervous anxiety, we had other problems. The Ritalin helped almost immediately, and regardless of

12

its reputed misuse, I don't know how Tisha would've lasted without it.

With Tisha's improved behavior, it almost felt like the turmoil in our house had subsided. But with every step forward for one child, there were gigantic steps backward for the other.

One evening, the four of us were eating dinner while watching a TV-movie about Gloria Vanderbilt. It portrayed young Gloria as a spoiled brat given to vicious temper tantrums. From out of the blue, Kim began one of her own.

"I WILL NOT SIT UP AND EAT! I DON'T LIKE IT AND I'M NOT EATING IT!" she burst out with hands slapping the table next to her plate.

We thought she was joking at first. Not a very good joke, and I let her know that I didn't appreciate it. "Knock it off, Gloria. You're not funny."

Spencer tried kidding her out of it. "Oh, I don't know. I thought it was pretty good. Do you think you can do it any louder so that they can hear you across the street?"

Kim did yell louder. "NO! NO! NO!"

She put her hands under the seat of her chair, so that she could lift it as she pushed off the floor with her feet, bouncing the chair and herself as one piece on the hardwood floor. The racket accented her screams and made us all freeze our movements. Tisha had been sitting very still since the first outburst, but now she looked at Spencer and me in alarm. This was not Kim's usual display of teenage anger. We were face-to-face with a Kim we hadn't met before. Or she might have been there all along and showed herself infrequently, but we had ignored her.

My patience was the first to go.

"Okay, okay, that's it! Go away. We're eating and we don't want to put up with your dramatics. Go to your room, go outside, I don't care. But GO!"

Kim glared at me from across the table, her arms crossed, her teeth clenched and her chin jutting. I looked back, trying to assess the direction her anger was going to go next. It was a stalemate. No movement. I got up from the table, crossed to her and took hold of her bent elbow and stiff shoulder with both of my hands. Because she wasn't ready for it, a swift motion brought her to her feet and propelled her towards the stairs without resistance. Spencer and Tisha looked back at their plates. The TV-movie's tragic music and droning dialogue filled the silence.

13

Kim found her voice again and shrieked, a child's high-pitched wail, as if she had just gotten swatted on the behind for disobeying. At the foot of the stairs, I pushed her ahead of me, my hands putting firm pressure on her lower body. I tried to step up and keep her moving upwards, but she caved in as if her body had deflated and she lay sprawled on the carpeted stairs. Her long legs and outstretched arms covered at least six steps. When she reached out with her right leg and planted her foot on the wall under the railing, her left foot holding her weight on the third step and her strong arms gripping either side of the staircase, I was blocked.

Her bawling cries now were indecipherable. There was no reasoning with her. It was going to take physical power and I knew I was outmatched. It struck me that the only way I could move her was to use leverage, a tool short people know well. But there was every chance that I would break her arm.

It had come to that. Parental control, when limited to might-makes-right methods, can be bested by the growing child. Causing pain or using weapons can win a fight, but this was my child, not a thug.

My voice was calm. "Help, Spencer. I don't want to hurt her."

He moved quickly. He had been on the verge of moving all along, but had to wait. Our rule was, whoever started it had to be given the chance to finish it. Now he slipped past me and grabbed Kim's closest leg, swinging it forward so his foot had room on the bottom step of her spread-eagled entrenchment. With one motion, he grabbed her arm on the same side and kept climbing the steps.

Kim screamed even more defiantly, recognizing defeat. Still her fifteen-year-old body fought with a toddler's willfulness. Spencer kept pushing-pulling, using his own long-legged strength and leverage, until they were at the end of the hall and Tisha and I heard the slam of Kim's bedroom door. The wailing continued, but we were glad to hear only Spencer's determined footsteps coming back down the hallway.

CHAPTER 4

In her mind, Kim had gained power from the fact that she was bigger than I was; whatever influence I'd had to control her temper outbursts was lost. Our doctor agreed to begin psychotherapy sessions with Kim. For months, the terminology he listed on the evaluation sheets gave us new concepts to consider: socialized-non-aggressive adjustment anxiety, borderline manic/depressive, schizophrenia and split personality. He settled on major depression and borderline multiple personality disorder, for which anti-depressants and continuing psychotherapy were prescribed.

Kim and the doctor worked together for the next year and a half. At the very least, the counseling gave her someone to talk to, an ally who expected nothing from her. The medication worked its magic and gave the appearance of calm, even if we all suspected Kim's balancing act would not last. Spencer and I thought it was the best we could do.

Most of the time, she was in therapy sessions by herself, but occasionally one of us went in with her. I was there for the one and only hypnotherapy session. Nothing much came out of it and the doctor later said it might work better at another time. He had hypnotized Kim in an attempt to reach the "controlling others," one or more hidden personalities that the doctor believed were there.

*   *   *

I sat quietly to one side of the therapy room while the doctor talked softly to Kim, who was showing no fear. She treated the situation casually and agreed to listen to whatever the doctor told her. Though I tried to reflect her attitude, inside I was half-expecting shocking disclosures, obvious voice and character changes that would scare the socks off me. The other half was skeptical.

The doctor described to his sleeping patient a safe place for her to feel comfortable, a big, soft chair that she could sink into and feel protected. Then he instructed her to go backward by years to age four.

15

"What's there, Kim? Where are you?"

"There's a house, and a room." She sounded cautious, hesitating, and I desperately wanted to believe that my daughter was really asleep, not pretending.

"What's in the room?" the doctor asked.

"Nothing. It's just a big, empty room. It's dark," she said.

"Is there anyone else there?"

"No," she answered. "I'm not even there."

There was nothing more. No angry, dominant personality spilling contempt and vengeance. There was only Kim's lost and frightened little-girl self that spoke.

Multiple Personality Disorder put a label on the problem, made it somehow less frustrating for us to deal with. It put new light on previous incidents that had completely bewildered us.

There was the time Kim was baby-sitting for our neighbors. She was around twelve, and the mother across the street felt it was safe for Kim to watch the two-year-old and four-year-old while Mom worked out in the garden. There was a pot of hot stew on the stove and Kim was warned to keep an eye on it so the kids didn't reach for it. The mother came in after finishing her gardening and found Kim gone. Kim had walked out and left them without telling anyone. I heard from the furious neighbor when I got home. Kim had no explanation, and said she didn't remember leaving or walking home. She just remembered being home.

Her school reports ranged from "a wonderful, gifted student, a joy to teach," to failing grades due to missed assignments and "poor classroom behaviors." We saw suspension citations stating that Kim had gotten into a fight because another student had teased Tisha, and others that said she had hit her sister and called her a dirty name.

I had read about MPD, and it had crossed my mind that aspects fit Kim's behavior, but I hadn't mentioned it to Spencer. It seemed too remote, too bizarre. After the psychiatrist put it in writing, we kept our minds open.

Given that the hypnosis was anti-climactic and the doctor felt he had gone as far as he could, we were indecisive about what to do next. We tried to look for cause-and-effect solutions, but our skills were limited. I wasn't ready to give up on the professional approach. Our next try came two years later from a different direction, a social worker in behavioral sciences. Whereas the psychiatrist had been an intimidating, large man in a white lab coat, almost everything about Jean was medium. She was middle-aged, with medium build, coloring and style, and a moderate voice. One aspect of her passive

16

appearance that stood out was a face that expressed sincere empathy. It made her the perfect listener and Kim took to her right away.

I was excited after one session in particular in which I had been invited to participate. Kim had revealed much of her past anger and confusion with the torn life she had lived. When we came home I asked Kim to help me tell Spencer about it. We looked at her, waiting for her to relive the session's moments of discovery and relief that I had witnessed.

The frightened look of panic on her face was real.

She said, "I don't remember."

"What do you mean? What's the matter, sweetie?" I went to her and held her hand. She looked at me and then into the distance.

"I remember going in to see Jean, but I don't remember anything else until here."

*   *   *

Jean taught us that forgetting is a child's best salvation. She hadn't accepted the MPD diagnosis; in fact, she said, there wasn't anyone in our area with the professional credentials to make that call in such a rare and specialized field. Instead, she chose to call it Disassociative Disease, and described it as the ability to mentally and emotionally leave a situation that was too painful and scary. Because Kim was intelligent and highly creative, she most probably developed an extraordinary skill to disassociate from her early childhood reality of abuse. It becomes a disease when the child is so good at it that the salvation later turns into a self-destructive pattern. A child's normal lying goes way beyond self-protection to stay out of trouble; perception of truth can be altered without knowing.

Whether there were multiple personalities in Kim or not, disassociating explained why she was unable to see the truth when we were holding it in our hands. She could tell us the unfinished homework was left at school even as we held it up to her face. There was no hole in the wall where her boot kicked it, her teeth were brushed even though her toothbrush wasn't wet, there weren't dirty dishes in the sink because she had done her share of the chores.

At fifteen, she suffered a broken leg when she walked straight into the path of a car as she crossed the highway to get the mail. Though she passed the driver's exam, she couldn't drive because she couldn't tell how she had gotten to any location when in a car; she couldn't see that you pass through Doolin to get to Camas City.

Kim had so many blank periods in her life, we could understand the explanation that it was like having a different reality. If she didn't like the reality in front of her, she changed it. She wasn't lying; it existed for her. The usual parenting tools, like The Carrot or The Stick, didn't work. How could we discipline bad behavior when she believed that she wasn't guilty? If we tried to encourage good behavior with rewards, she discarded her favorite things because the price was too high. We had no carrots left to offer.

After countless searches, Spencer discovered one method of discipline that got us somewhere. He had heard her door slam one too many times, so he took it off. He got the tools out and took the door off its hinges right in front of her disbelieving eyes.

Privacy, we learned, was Kim's one irreplaceable reality.

CHAPTER 5

At eighteen, Kim believed she had achieved adulthood, and everything that was supposed to come with it. She had learned some of the behaviors but none of their meanings. Moving out of our house was her big statement, but she had to disguise her shame that she couldn't get by without our help. While she was forced to accept money and rides from us, she would hate us. It didn't matter that we loved her and treated her with respect and kindness, she saw us only as the enemy, out to destroy her freedom and happiness.

Dewayne Wall was the boy Kim decided she'd fall in love with. Before meeting Dewayne, she had been on only one date with another boy, whom she accused of rape. The charge could not be substantiated, but we had her talk to the Victim's Assistance counselor as a matter of course. We had honest talks about friendships, love and sex, but like most parents, we had no idea what was getting through. When the relationship with Dewayne started, we tried to hold judgment while still keeping an eye on them when we could. It was obvious that Kim was impressed with Dewayne's tough-guy looks, how he could sneer with a cigarette hanging out of his mouth while he leaned on other people's cars in the Safeway parking lot. They were odd together, looking like a bad reenactment of an old James Dean movie; they both recited script but showed no emotions. He was a year and a half younger, and it was clear that Kim could dominate him. Since he still lived with his parents, we hoped things would move slowly.

Kim told us she'd found friends to live with in Willows, a community halfway between Belleville and Doolin and not within walking distance of anywhere. Her story was that she could continue going to school on the bus because that's what Nadine did. Nadine was the girl who lived there, with her mother and her mother's boyfriend. Kim would allow us to take her to therapy sessions but didn't want us to contact her for anything else. Even so, it didn't take long to find out that she'd stopped going to school, that the man living there was having sex with both Nadine's mother and Nadine, and that Dewayne stayed there more often than he stayed at his parents' house.

Within months, Kim informed us that she was moving out and wanted our help getting her stuff. The smell hit us before we were even in the door of the place, and then I saw the dog manure incongruously piled in a plastic tub on the living room floor. I couldn't count the dogs, rodents and birds that seemed to be everywhere. The two adults sat on a couch covered with dirty rags and papers and watched TV, not bothering to look up. I tried to say something, but it was hard to look at them through their cigarette smoke and the overwhelming filth. They were obese, their hair was so greasy I couldn't tell the color, and they seemed to be covered in the same rags and clutter as the rest of the room. We had to go through the kitchen to move Kim's boxes, and the cupboards were open and empty, but every other space in the room was covered. The sink, counters, table and the floor were loaded with dirty dishes, crusted pots and pans, animal cages and trash. I stopped and gaped, not able to understand what I was seeing—heaps of empty, dirty cages on surfaces that were supposed to be for food. The fact that there was no food in sight seemed somehow a blessing, and I kept moving.

Kim had a mattress on the floor at one end of the attic, Nadine had the other end. It wasn't nearly as dirty as the rest of the house, but we quickly packed things out of there as if breathing the air might poison us. Kim handled herself with quiet efficiency, as if it was someone else's stuff. Spencer did, too.

Some of Dewayne's clothes were mixed up with hers, and it was obvious that they slept together there. We might've been embarrassed for her, if we hadn't known she was pregnant.

*   *   *

We had expected it to happen one day, but there was nothing helpful we could've done to prepare ourselves for the blow. The visible pain in Spencer's face when she told us was like nothing I'd seen before. I realized then that our dreams for our daughter had no chance of ever coming true. She was going to suffer more, maybe more than she'd ever suffered before. Or, she'd stop feeling anything at all.

We worked, then, to try and help these kids with their new dilemma, which meant dealing with Dewayne's parents. We knew from Kim that Walter Wall, known as "Buck," was a mechanic with his own shop in Doolin, and his wife, Mara, did the bookkeeping.

Kim thought that he was probably a few years older than us, and Mara was about my age. Other than talking to them on the phone, we hadn't met them. Both had Southern accents, but not Deep South. Mara talked in a little girl's voice which struck me as phony, and it fit the talk around town that she liked to wear tight sweaters and was an obvious flirt. People told us Buck had a good reputation as a mechanic, but no one really knew him. We had no reason not to expect a sensible discussion about our joint responsibilities.

We first met them at their house, an old, small three-bedroom on one of Doolin's back streets. Someone had made an attempt at a flowerbed so the house and yard were distinguishable from the empty lot next door, and there weren't any old car parts or other junk lying around. A dog was tied up on the porch, and another one greeted us inside. The front room was small and crowded with furniture, but well kempt except for the dirty ashtrays and the heavy smell of cigarette smoke.

The Walls were friendly enough, maybe slightly embarrassed, but weren't we all. They made a big deal about Dewayne's and Kim's sloppy birth control efforts, and they voiced some hope that the drug-store pregnancy test was wrong. In the half-hour we spent there, we didn't come up with any plan besides my getting Kim to a doctor for a real examination. And they insisted that Kim stay at their house. That seemed like a bad idea to us, seeing as how it was cohabitation with Dewayne that got her pregnant, but Kim wouldn't come home. She didn't want us making any of the decisions.

The next encounter was with Buck, who called and asked if he could come to our house by himself to "discuss the situation."

"Excuse my work-dirt. I just come from the shop," he said from the door.

"Come in and have a seat, Buck. Can I get you something to drink? Beer, soda?" Spencer asked.

"I'd take a cold beer if you got one, but I better not sit on a chair. I can stand." Buck made a helpless gesture at his dirty coveralls.

"Here, sit on a barstool, you're fine. What's goin' on?" Spencer sat on the other barstool in the kitchen and I opened a bottle of Bud for Buck and a Pepsi for Spencer. I thought it would put him at ease if I let Buck deal with just Spencer, so I stayed in the background.

"Well," Buck began after he sat down, "this is kind of awkward, me coming here without Mara an' all. But I figured I'd better talk to you. Mara—she's not thinking this out. She's just thinking about having another grandbaby, ya know? She's happy as all-get-out!" He took a desperate breath through his mouth and looked away quickly. "Look, I don't know how you folks feel about Kim and Dewayne havin' this baby, but I gotta tell ya. I've been livin' in the same house as them for the past week," Buck shook his head and gave a short laugh, "and they can't do it. They have no business trying to raise a kid. I mean they're just a couple of fool kids themselves, and they can't even take care of their selves, let alone a little baby. I don't know how they think they's gonna do it!"

He stopped talking all of a sudden and took a long drink of his beer, appearing depleted. Spencer responded quickly, giving the poor guy a break.

"No, of course they're not ready to be parents. That's exactly the way we feel. Kim's eighteen and most of the time acts thirteen. She's got emotional problems ... you know she's working on that, and we're trying to help her, but there's not much we can do if she doesn't want us to."

"No, I know." Buck said, more easily now. "Dewayne is barely seventeen. He's not gonna finish school. He don't know what he's gonna do and I try to tell him he better come up with something. I sure as hell ain't gonna support him forever!"

"No kidding," Spencer said. "They don't realize Mom and Dad aren't going to be there all of the time to take care of them. They're supposed to be the Mom and Dad now. I mean, this is a big responsibility. I'm sure they're not fully aware of that."

"We talked to Kim," I said, "and we've been talking to her every chance we get. I think she knows we will help her through this, whatever she decides. But we want her to know her options."

Buck looked up quickly from his bottle, nervous again. I didn't know whether it was because I spoke for the first time, or because of what I said.

"What do you mean by 'options'?"

"We're going to talk to her counselor with her," Spencer spoke up again. "Like I said, Kim is having some trouble and she's been seeing a therapist, whenever she lets us take her."

I added quickly, "She told me she'd go this week with us."

"And she can't make this kind of decision by herself," Spencer said. "The therapist knows her, has been working with her for a couple of years now, and will be able to help her."

"What do you folks want her to do?" Buck asked us. His tone was flat but his face twitched as he looked from Spencer to me and back to Spencer.

"We're not telling her what she should do. This is a big decision, like I said, probably the biggest decision she'll ever have to make. We're not going to make it for her."

"But we are going to make sure she knows what her choices are," I said.

"That's right," Spencer said, looking directly at Buck, but saying no more.

Buck stood up as he finished his beer. He put on his cap that he had kept hold of for the whole conversation, and said, "Okay, well. I don't know yet what we're gonna do, but I thought I'd better come down here and discuss it, being's how we're all in this together." He started for the door, and we followed him, but he wasn't finished yet. "I'm just so damn frustrated with this whole mess! And I don't know how much longer they're going to be living at our place." He went on to tell us about the fighting between Dewayne and himself, something Kim had already told us about. It never went beyond yelling but it was apparently violent and getting more frequent with Dewayne's refusal to get off his butt. Kim blamed Buck for being too strict and unreasonable, and said she and Dewayne were looking for somewhere else to live.

Spencer and I stood at the door watching Buck drive up the driveway, and then exchanged a look of skepticism. I said, "Well, I guess it took a lot of guts for him to come talk to us."

Spencer sat down tiredly on the couch. "Yeah, but does he have enough guts to go up against his wife?"

CHAPTER 6

Life for Kim and Dewayne in 1993 became a series of convenient stops along the way after they left his parents' house. The fighting there had escalated and Kim said they decided to move in with some friends. Never looking further ahead than a week or two, they took hand-outs from one friend after another, without gratitude or reimbursement of any kind.

As Kim's pregnancy continued, she kept her agreement with us to get counseling. She went with me to the Christian adoption advocates and to our family doctor. I asked the questions that she didn't know enough to ask, but otherwise offered no advice. From her comments, it seemed there were moments when she understood that abortion was sensible, but I could see her struggling. Our drives back from counseling sessions were opportunities for me to see Kim as herself. She sat with a look of great consternation, asking a question every once in awhile with a seriousness and intelligence that I'd forgotten she had. But her deeply rooted desire to please was overpowering. It was clear that all three of the Walls had told her to have the baby.

The term "open adoption" had surfaced from somewhere, and it was something she kept returning to. She wanted a deal, a solution that made everyone happy.

Mara, meanwhile, had moved to Camas City. According to Kim, Mara needed to go to the psychiatric clinic there several times a week for therapy sessions, so she rented an apartment to be closer to the hospital. We couldn't get a clear story regarding Mara's need for that much therapy, but it became evident that she and Buck had separated. As we later discovered in a review of court documents, Mara "left" him in April of 1992. I didn't understand that, because we saw them together in January, 1993. Spencer had an explanation; if she was not living with her husband, she was eligible for welfare housing and mental health treatment. It was a scam.

Mara decided that Kim and Dewayne should take the empty apartment next to hers. As they asked us to share with the rent, she and Buck explained to us that this was better than Kim and Dewayne living with "scummy" friends, not knowing where they would be from day to day. Though this made sense, we were uneasy about Mara being close at hand for the delivery.

When we saw the apartment Kim was moving into, more red flags went up. The neighborhood was well known to all local police departments as a big drug crime area. Some of the low-rent shacks were home to the local chapter of Gypsy Jokers and other motorcycle hangers-on. Kim became acquainted with a couple of young mothers and one middle-aged woman known as "Ma." On meeting her, I couldn't say who scared me more, "Ma" or Mara.

Spencer and I had no way of coping with the bleakness of the situation. All we could do was try to talk with Kim to let her know we loved her and that we would support her, no matter what. But we had to wait for her to feel like calling us from Mara's phone, and that was only when she needed money. She and Dewayne were smoking heavily, and they couldn't get cigarettes with Food Stamps. We didn't yet allow ourselves to consider other drug habits they might have.

Discussion with Buck Wall went nowhere.

"Kim and Dewayne's baby is going to be our flesh and blood, and we're gonna do what we can to take care of it," he replied.

We were sick of hearing it. Dewayne recited the same line, though less practiced. He was compelled to add, "My brother had a baby taken away from him by his girlfriend, and we're not allowed to see it ever. That's not gonna happen to me!"

We were beginning to understand the depth of Mara's power, and perhaps the direction of her mental illness. Kim didn't stand much of a chance. She had left our influence, physically and mentally.

The focus of our attention would shift to the baby.

CHAPTER 7

Kim phoned us on September 9th to tell us that she had her baby early that morning. She had gone into labor the night before and called Mara, who had taken them to the hospital. There were no complications and Carley Rebecca Wall was born a normal, healthy girl.

Because Kim didn't say it, I did. "We're coming to see her. We'll be there as soon as we can."

Spencer and I got off work and went separately to the hospital, so we didn't see each other until later. Sitting on the barstools in our kitchen at the end of the day, we shared our misgivings.

"It's wrong, Gail," he said, shaking his head slowly. "Something... I don't know what it is. I looked at Kim's face and there's nothing there." He pushed his stool back, stood up abruptly and paced two steps, turned and sat back down. He spread his hands in exasperation, then set clenched fists on the bar, facing me.

"I'm completely baffled. You know what I mean? Did you see?" He let out a deep sigh. "It's bizarre. That's the only word I can think of."

I knew. We both had seen the same thing and shared the same conflicted feelings. It's wonderful to have a granddaughter, and we were so scared for her.

*   *   *

Mara was standing holding the baby when I came into the hospital room. Kim was sitting up in bed, fussing with a cup of ice chips with a straw. Dewayne rocked in a rocking chair, not paying attention to either one.

Mara said, "Hi. Come see my new little precious girl. Isn't she a doll?" She swayed back and forth, cooing at the pink bundle in her arms.

Oh, Mara. No surprise you're still here, I guess. I went to Kim and hugged her. "She's beautiful. I'm happy everything went okay. How are you doing?" I asked.

"Fine," she said. "I asked for more pillows, but the nurse hasn't come back yet." She wiggled her shoulders to show her discomfort, her eyes not making contact with me.

"Can I hold her?" I looked from Kim to Dewayne, who was now gawking at me with smugness, and to Mara.

"Oh, sure." Her high-pitched drawl gave the word two syllables. "He-e-e-re ya go."

I should probably excuse your baby-talk, Mara, under the circumstances. But, man! It really grates on my nerves.

The exchange stirred the tiny bundle awake, and as I whispered into it, I was immediately captivated by the impish face.

Well, there's no denying that Dewayne is the father; she has his high, wide forehead.

But the instant Carley's eyes opened and her puckering mouth made the shape of a smile, I could see the best of Kim looking back at me. I tuned out Mara's continuing claptrap while I gave my feelings time to sink in.

Then the nurse came to the door and told Kim she should try to feed her baby again.

"Where's my extra pillow?" Kim asked coldly, almost commandingly. The nurse was clearly taken aback and we exchanged a look.

Oh no, Kim. Don't do this now.

I had heard Kim talk to nurses like that once before, when she was fifteen and had broken her leg. We had been ashamed of her rudeness. At the time, it was a personality of Kim's that we hadn't met yet.

I handed Carley to Kim. "Come on, Mommy, this little one needs you now," I said lovingly. The nurse left and returned with a pillow, giving me another uneasy glance. She helped Kim to arrange herself and Carley's head, and gave Kim kindly instructions about breastfeeding. I watched Kim move with abrupt awkwardness, a blankness to her face that contradicted the scene.

This isn't right. The nurse sees it, too. Kim, what's the matter with you? Why aren't you looking with loving adoration like all mothers do when they hold their infants?

The nurse kept up her encouragement and Carley finally worked her mouth around to suck at the breast while the nurse's hands held her to it. The nurse looked up at me, but I didn't know what to say. Kim stared out the window.

"Well, you'll get the hang of it." The nurse forced a smile and gently pressed Kim's hands to Carley and removed her own.

As she left the room, I started to take note of what Dewayne and Mara had been gabbing about.

"I called them already this morning to tell them she was born, and now all they need is a copy of the birth certificate. Carley Rebecca's Indian card should be here in a week or two," Mara was saying.

"Does that mean she gets her share of the Indian money, or do we get it?" Dewayne asked.

He was leaning against the windowsill with his hands in his pockets. Mara had taken the rocking chair, sitting on the edge of it with her hands clasped between her knees like a kid.

"Well, there won't be no money, at least for the time-bein', 'cuz the Mukilki aren't a rich tribe. But there's college money for when Carley's eighteen, and benefits for her insurance and stuff. But it don't hurt to get her enrolled in the tribe right away. And I sent for your card, too." She reached over and patted Dewayne's thigh.

"What do we need to do?" Kim asked, distracted from the activity at her breast.

"Dewayne just has to sign the form, but he should wait till after his birthday next week so he's eighteen and considered an adult."

I asked, "So he's not a member of the tribe now?"

"No. I got one for myself a while back, but I never applied for him or his brother and sister."

Mara's face showed how pleased she was with herself.

"But now he can do it, and he can get Carley's application in. Like I said," she turned to Kim, "you just have to send in her birth certificate and sign as her mother….er, as her father. Dewayne has to sign." She looked at Dewayne and he stared back blankly. "Well, it will come to me anyways, so I'll just bring it over and get the signature and copies and such."

I saw Kim nod her head slowly, as if she was following the plan.

The nurse came in again, followed by another woman in scrubs. I was still standing by the bed, watching helplessly as Kim handled Carley dispassionately. *This isn't like bottle-feeding one of those puppies you took in. It's your baby, for Christ's sake.* The new woman went over to the window to close the curtain, moving Dewayne unceremoniously.

"You don't need to expose yourself to everyone on the opposite wing now, do you?" She turned to smile at the new mother as Kim was casually handing the sleeping Carley off to the first nurse. *Wait, Kim. Hold her close, gently. Take your time.*

There was a long silence as the women looked around the room. I could feel their confusion, as if they were trying to sort out the family dynamics. *Yes, it is as bad as it looks. Help me, please. I don't know how to fix this.*

I asked if I could hold her again.

The nurse placed Carley up to my shoulder in the burping position, making sure the blanket snugged all around her. I rubbed the tiny backside lightly. The two women left the room as Kim, Mara and Dewayne continued talking about Indian benefits.

I took the moment to hold Carley close, and wished that with our touching she'd somehow know my promise to her. *Carley, we will do everything we can to protect you. I promise.*

CHAPTER 8

Shortly before Carley's birth, Mara went back to Buck. She told Kim and Dewayne, "You kids need the bigger apartment, and I'm done with my therapy anyways." The police report that we obtained later indicated the move was to save her marriage.

People we knew in the legal and social service circles were aware of certain disclosures before we were. On the advice of one of those friends, we got all public records concerning the Walls from the county clerk's office. There were the predictable reports of Dewayne's delinquency and some small claims and bankruptcy papers. Then we found the revelations that would strengthen our resolve to fight.

Buck had filed for divorce August 19, 1993, citing irreconcilable differences, stating that Mara had moved out in April of 1992 and had not returned. A paralegal from their attorney's office, instrumental in drawing up the divorce papers, was Sandra Ryan. On August 31st, she reported to Camas County Sheriff's Deputy Anthony Romano that Walter Wall had assaulted her.

Officer Romano's report read:

<u>Observations</u>—Upon my arrival at 0950 hours on 08-31-93 at the doctor's office, I was informed that Miss Ryan was undergoing examination and X-rays. When she was available, Miss Ryan informed me that she had gone over to Walter Wall's residence to talk to his wife. She stated that Walter Wall then came home and physically threw her out of the house.

Miss Ryan did not appear to have any type of serious injury. She instructed me to go and arrest Mr. Wall. I informed her that I would make that decision after I talked to all parties.

<u>Statements</u>—Sandra Lee Ryan stated that she went to Walter and Mara Wall's residence at approximately 8:30 a.m., to see Mara Wall because she is concerned for the well being of Mrs. Wall due to the fact that Mr. Wall is abusive to her. Ryan stated that she had walked through the open front door without knocking, that she

knew that Walter Wall was not at the residence at this time, and that she had called out hello but received no answer.

The substance of Miss Ryan's further statements is as follows: After approximately five minutes Miss Ryan heard Mrs. Wall say, "I'm fine, leave me alone." She then called out to Mrs. Wall, "Please, just talk to me." Mrs. Wall then said, "I don't trust you."

Mrs. Wall then phoned Mr. Wall and he showed up a few minutes later. He told Miss Ryan, "Get off of my property," and she then said, "No, I am talking to Mara and it's her property too." Mr. Wall then grabbed her around the neck and drug her to the front door and pushed her out of it, at which time she fell down. She stated that Mr. Wall continually pushed her until she was off of the property, telling her to never come back.

Miss Ryan states that she had slept at the residence many nights last November and December, that they all have been personal friends for about two years. She stated that Mrs. Wall is seeing psychiatrist Dr. William Brown, and therapist Judith Edwards, who is giving her information regarding Mrs. Wall's condition. But Mrs. Wall went yesterday and told Judith Edwards not to give Miss Ryan any more personal information. Miss Ryan stated that she knows Mrs. Wall is mentally incompetent to make decisions on her own.

At approximately 1150 hours, I contacted Walter "Buck" Wall at his place of business, Wall's Garage. He said he was willing to give me a statement. While I was taking Mr. Wall's statement, his wife, Mrs. Mara Wall, arrived.

Walter "Buck" Wall stated to me the following in substance: He received a call from his wife telling him that Sandra was at the residence banging at the bedroom door. He stated that when he arrived he told Sandra to leave and that she refused, telling him that he is trying to con his wife out of not filing for a divorce. He knew that the only way he was going to get her out was to push her, and he admits to giving her a little shove at the door, and that she did trip over something on the porch. He stated that he pushed her off of the property, told her to leave and never come back. Then she tried to pick up some sort of stick or something to hit him, but she couldn't find anything big enough. He stated that he and his wife are currently separated; they were going through a divorce but are trying to get back together.

Mara Rose Wall stated to me at approximately 1153 hours, the following in substance: She had arrived at her husband's residence the day before to do laundry, with his permission. Miss Ryan showed up and said, "What are you doing here?" After some discussion, Miss

31

Ryan informed her that she didn't think she was competent to make decisions about going back with her husband, and that if she did not leave with her, Miss Ryan would go to her (Mrs. Wall's) brother-in-law to have her declared mentally incompetent. Miss Ryan left then, but returned on 08-31-93. Mrs. Wall then went to her bedroom, shut the door and phoned Buck.

Mrs. Wall stated that when she first separated from her husband, she was living with Sandra. Mrs. Wall does state that she is seeing Dr. Brown and Judith Edwards, and that she has multiple personalities. She states that one of these personalities is male, and that Sandra is in love with this personality. She states that she and Sandra have had sex together, and that Sandra has also had sex with her husband while staying with them. She believes that Sandra is still in love with her. She stated that she wants to get back with her husband, that he has abused her but only verbally. Mrs. Wall stated that she just wishes that Sandra would leave them alone.

Narrative—I later made phone contact with Miss Ryan and informed her that my findings did not constitute a criminal assault. I informed her that I would not be arresting Mr. Wall, but I would send a copy of the report to the District Attorney's office. When I asked Miss Ryan if she ever had sexual relations with either Mr. or Mrs. Wall, she became very upset, stating that she wanted Mr. Wall arrested and that she felt that she was being treated like a suspect and did not like it. I informed Lt. Pritt of the situation. He informed me that he had already received a phone call from the Walls.

*   *   *

On September 2nd, Sandra Ryan made a report to the Doolin Police Department that subject Mara Wall had taken some of her belongings when she moved. Officer Richard Nelson reported that he had made contact with Mrs. Wall, who said she would return the vacuum cleaner and the keys, but that the furniture was a gift from the reporting party. The subject said that she gave the reporting party a dog and that if the reporting party wanted the furniture back, she should give the dog back. The subject claimed that she could get statements from witnesses. Officer Nelson reported that he advised Miss Ryan that, in his opinion, it was a civil matter and she should consider civil litigation.

On September 8th, Mara made a complaint to the Camas County Sheriff's office.

Officer Romano's narrative concluded:

The reporting party, Mara Rose Wall, states that she is being harassed/stalked by subject, Sandra Lee Ryan. Both parties contacted by phone. No crime has occurred (yet). Parties referred to "Judge Wopner" of the People's Court. No further action.

On September 9th, Carley was born. On September 19th, Buck and Mara filed for dismissal of Buck's petition for dissolution of marriage. On September 27th, the District Attorney's office issued a letter agreeing with Deputy Anthony Romano.

Case Status: Closed.

CHAPTER 9

"This is crazy. I mean, what are the odds—Kim and Mara both with Multiple Personality Disorder?" I said to Spencer.

"What a 'kawinkidink'!" He mocked surprise. "Maybe it's contagious."

We had to laugh, because it helped us to find humor where we could, however short-lived. Considering the remark the cop made about TV's Judge Wopner, obviously we weren't the only ones that thought it funny.

I was, nevertheless, still struggling with Mara's latest announcement.

"But Kim was diagnosed long before she even knew Dewayne, so she didn't get the idea from Mara. Mara must've gotten it from her."

Spencer's voice now rose with frustration. "What does it matter? They're all a bunch of liars and morons."

"Only Buck is a moron. Mara is a nut case, and Dewayne is an idiot," I said, trying to make us laugh again. But I couldn't. "And I don't know what Kim is."

People told us that it was just a matter of time before Kim felt motherly instincts and bonded with her baby. It wasn't happening.

We tried to keep in touch, calling to ask if we could come to see them once or twice a week. When we were allowed in, neither Kim nor Dewayne would be holding Carley. It was like watching two uncooperative children playing a game of house; if Dewayne was there at all, he would leave as soon as we arrived. Kim was always awkward and nervous. Sometimes there were two or three neighbor girls passing Carley and puppies back and forth like they were interchangeable. There were always puppies or kittens, which made the apartment smell terrible. We gave them a vacuum cleaner for Christmas, but that only pissed Kim off.

I still tried to get her to appointments with Jean, her therapist, but Kim usually canceled them. When we did make it there, Carley went with us since Dewayne was never around to take care of her.

Maybe seeing Kim interact with her baby was helpful. Jean first focused their conversation on Carley, then tried to steer it towards drawing out Kim's feelings. Unfortunately, Kim was regressing, either because she was overwhelmed with responsibility or filled with even more hatred for those she blamed.

I, too, was overwhelmed. One time, Kim forgot Carley's bottle and didn't realize it until Carley was crying for it. It took us an hour to return to the apartment, and then Kim had me drop them off at a neighbor's house because she didn't have a key to her own door. Dewayne was nowhere to be found. Kim assured me the neighbor would have a bottle for Carley, but she wouldn't let me go in to find out. I left them there, a house I'd never been to before, with a yard full of motorcycles and barking dogs and no sign of the woman Kim said would help her out till Dewayne got home.

Spencer and I made the decision to ask State Children's Services for help. Because we'd adopted our children through that agency, we knew that they had established programs that could help Kim get on her feet. We thought it was a fair agency, with people trained to provide these services in a regulated, uniformly mandated way. At the time, Spencer was working as a home remodeler just a few blocks from the Children's Services office, so he persistently dropped in and asked them to look into Carley's welfare. Finally someone listened to him, a caseworker named Emily Sanchez, who quickly agreed that there was negligence.

Dewayne ran crying to his mother immediately after he found out what we'd done, and Mara was outraged. Dewayne told us later that she said the State had no right to poke its nose into their business. Apparently she had no qualms about Kim's and Dewayne's parenting skills. Her way of helping them cope was to pick Carley up and take her to her own home almost every weekend, where she had already turned a bedroom into a nursery stocked with baby clothes and bedding that she'd been collecting for months.

Emily Sanchez told Kim the same as she told us, that Children's Services Division (CSD) would not take their baby away from them as long as they provided adequate care and protection. We all met and heard her explain the concerns and how they could be resolved. Kim and Dewayne signed an Initial Service Agreement that said CSD would assist with transportation to parent training classes, and provide a Resource Worker and case management services to help them reach their goals.

The expectations spelled out for Kim and Dewayne were:

Maintain appointments with Resource Worker Susan Chesley and cooperate with recommendations made during her visits in the family home.

Kim will continue group and individual therapy through County Mental Health.

Kim and Dewayne will attend and complete a parent training program, and be able to demonstrate an understanding of what is being taught.

Kim and Dewayne will move their dogs and cats outdoors within two days. No pets will be allowed inside the family home.

The family home will be kept clean and sanitary for the safety of Carley. Susan Chesley would not make unannounced visits.

No other adults or children will be living in the family home. No overnight visitors without authorization of the caseworker will be allowed.

*   *   *

The agreement was to last a year, with further intervention assured if the parents failed to make adequate progress. Emily Sanchez communicated to us that she wanted us to phone her at any time if we felt Carley was not getting the care she needed. Over the next few weeks we developed a trust between us; Emily knew that we would do what was best for Carley even at the risk of losing the love of our daughter.

At first, Kim tried to meet the demands. Dewayne went to one parenting class with her, but they had stupidly left Carley with a neighbor because they didn't think it was important to take her. He didn't go again. Kim's attendance was sporadic for a few weeks then eventually stopped. In that time Susan, the Resource Worker, had made weekly or biweekly visits to the apartment, getting less and less cooperation. We saw for ourselves that the house was still dirty. Kim appeared to be in a trance most of the time, and admitted to me that she once woke up on the floor, Carley beside her, without knowing how they got there.

The County Mental Health sessions didn't seem to be doing much good, but Kim liked going. She was getting a lot of attention. Her new therapist didn't have the same occupational ethics and restraints that Jean had. This woman didn't hesitate to diagnose Multiple Personality Disorder and listened to Kim describe the personalities in detail. Kim told me that, at last count, she had seventeen different people living inside her. She could name them all, tell me their ages and their particular characteristics. Surpassing

Mara's story, two of Kim's personalities were men, one was a blind girl, and one woman spoke French.

We made the decision to not concern ourselves with Kim's mental health; it didn't do any good, and Carley's welfare was absolutely more important. Emily agreed that there were many concerns. She knew Kim sometimes left Carley with neighborhood babysitters that were suspected drug addicts, and Dewayne hung out with the drug crowd regularly instead of looking for employment.

We tried to keep our relationship with the Walls amenable so that we could take Carley home once in awhile. It was on those precious occasions that our emotions hit their highest and inevitably fell to their lowest. For a day or two we could enjoy cuddling and playing with our baby granddaughter as if everything was right in her world. We were typical grandparents, sharing the feeding, diaper-changing and dressing duties like they were coveted turns on a backyard swing. We handled the usual, new-baby urgencies as they came up, and we quickly learned how to read the signs of hunger and discomfort. In the daytime, it wasn't often that Carley cried.

But the worst came when she was fighting sleep. We'd made a bed for her on the window seat in our bedroom, thickly rimmed with protective pillows, but as soon as she sensed bedtime approaching, she screamed. We tried all different approaches to comfort her: caressing, holding, rocking, talking softly, singing, walking, and both extremes of ignoring her or taking her to our bed.

Listening to her wail her heart out tore at us. We didn't want to imagine the terrors that nighttime evoked for her when she was at home.

PART TWO—LOSS

(January—May, 1994)

CHAPTER 10

From the beginning of CSD's involvement, Mara had been seeking help from the Mukilki tribe in Oklahoma, of which Carley was an official member. The legal affiliation worked this way: Mara said that her grandfather was 3/4 Indian, which made Carley 11/128 (Spencer figured out that you could actually get to that fraction by going back a minimum of eight generations) and this tribe considered you a member if you could trace any heritage at all.

We first heard the name of their agent, Mr. Tracy Faulkner, from Emily Sanchez. Emily wanted us to fully understand the impact of the Indian Child Welfare Act of 1978 (ICWA), a federal law created to protect Indian tribal heritage. Mr. Faulkner had phoned her to say that, as the tribe's ICWA Specialist, he approved of leaving the decisions of Carley's welfare in the hands of CSD, under her direction. Emily called Spencer at work immediately, and gave him her candid, off the record opinion.

"She says she doesn't believe Faulkner's going to stand behind anything he's saying," Spencer told me later that evening. "He's telling CSD everything they want to hear—'yeah, yeah, our tribe's going to look into this carefully, and we'll work with your agency to follow your usual procedures'—but Emily thinks he's just giving them lip service and will fight the state's involvement."

"And he's the only one we can deal with?" I asked, not following this new connection. Who were these people, the tribe, and how would they help Carley?

"So far, Emily can't get past him when she contacts the tribe. She sees him as an egotistical micromanager that we shouldn't trust at all. But she has to be careful because her boss, Cowan, is intimidated by ICWA and told Emily to back off. I told her not to put her job in jeopardy, but she wants to see this through, not give up. She considers her job is protecting children, and Cowan is just a paper-pusher who doesn't ever handle actual cases with children."

I said, "Yeah, but if she loses her job by pissing off this paper-pusher, Emily won't be around to help anybody."

"She kind of touched on that. But she wants to help us all she can, so she said she'll still keep communications open by phone and not let Cowan know she's working with us."

We knew then that Emily Sanchez was an exception, a compassionate, reasonable person in a bureaucratic world where the wrong people have the power.

*   *   *

We got the name of a lawyer that was recommended by friends. It was a woman who was serving as chief counsel for the local confederated tribes, and was an authority on ICWA. She told us that ICWA language protects the best interest of the child, and shouldn't apply in Mara's case anyway because it speaks for tribal parents, not grandparents. It was her opinion that if CSD wouldn't argue for Oregon's jurisdiction and fight for custody, we should. She recommended we retain Jason Norden, as he specialized in family law.

After listening to our concerns, Jason Norden told us that we would probably be heading for court, so we should start keeping very good records. It was that advice that helped me keep my sanity over the next few months. Somehow, knowing that everything was documented in black and white made the gut-wrenching bewilderment easier.

We started copying and filing every letter we sent and those we got in return, faxes, and notes we jotted down from phone calls. We both even started writing down our thoughts that possibly could be used somewhere later. We didn't know what would be helpful, so we kept track of everything.

Spencer's first approach was to introduce ourselves to this ICWA specialist, and make sure he knew we were here.

*   *   *

Letter to Tracy Faulkner, Mukilki Tribe of Oklahoma, 1/13/94:
Dear Mr. Faulkner,

I'm writing to you regarding my granddaughter, Carley Rebecca Wall. I understand from Emily Sanchez, Oregon Children's Services Division, that you represent the tribe's interest in ICWA cases and are familiar with the involved parties. My wife and I are the maternal grandparents of Carley, and our primary concern is for her welfare. We may have been characterized as meddling grandparents whose only desire was to remove Carley from her biological parents, but that isn't true. We're involved because of concern that she is not

42

receiving the nurturing human warmth and love that any infant deserves.

At yesterday's meeting at CSD, Emily told us that you authorized her to protect Carley's interests. I asked Emily to request that in writing from you, with a copy sent to Dewayne and Kim, because it's probable that he won't believe it otherwise. Dewayne has told us that the tribe will tell CSD and us to stay out of his life and let him raise Carley as he sees fit. He and Kim were supposed to attend that meeting, but chose not to.

I can give you some background on our daughter. We adopted her when she was almost ten. In her birth home she had suffered some sort of serious trauma, which she has yet to confront and deal with. She hasn't exhibited any apparent emotional ties with anyone. Her relationship with Dewayne is one I would characterize as symbolic: that is, she is fulfilling what she sees as a need, but is still not making an emotional commitment. Her decision to keep Carley can be characterized in the same manner. Emily has also noticed that Kim cannot make any emotional bond.

We suspect that Dewayne is going to tell CSD to leave them alone, and tell us that we can no longer see Carley. Kim has turned over her decision-making to Dewayne. She is not exhibiting any natural mothering instincts, which may cause Carley some long-term emotional scars. Dewayne doesn't exhibit any kind of fathering skills; he doesn't know anything about changing diapers, preparing bottles or what kind of schedule Carley requires for feeding, changing, or sleeping.

Emily is concerned that their living condition is unfit for Carley. However, Kim and Dewayne reject any help from the agency or from us. The situation here is that they are under no formal obligation to follow the directions or mandates from CSD.

Is it possible to use tribal influence to force them? As I understand ICWA, the tribe has as big an interest in the care and raising of its children as do the parents. Does your tribe get involved in these types of cases before any termination proceedings are initiated? What, if any, investigation is done by your tribe to help make these decisions?

Please contact us at the number and address listed below if you have any questions, comments or guidance.

*   *   *

43

At first, I felt awkward writing down stuff that was probably inconsequential, day-to-day life. I tried not to be paranoid, but at the same time I worried that I might be ignoring a crucial turning point.

Journal entry: 1/16/94—Sunday

I went to Kim's. A neighbor told me they went to stay at a friend's farmhouse. I got the location and called the Camas Co. sheriff's office, explained my worries and asked them to check on Carley's welfare. They called back that Kim and Carley were okay, and that Kim told them she was having "problems with her mother."

1/31—Monday

Kim called on Friday to ask us to take Carley for the weekend because they're going to paint the apartment and Buck and Mara weren't available. We told her we were going to Portland, but she said, "No problem." So, we took Carley on our overnight trip and had a great time visiting with Spencer's brother, his wife and their baby boy. They were surprised that Kim let Carley go, and that Carley showed no separation anxiety. For four months old, she was <u>too</u> adaptable.

2/3—Thursday

Our friend in the courthouse told me of an Incident Report from the sheriff's office showing 15 counts of telephone harassment over a 3-month period charged by Sandra Ryan; suspect listed as Mara, calling herself "Jane," one of Mara's personalities. Officer reported that when contacted, Mara denied the accusation and said to tell Sandra that soon "it will all come out."

2/11—Friday

I stopped by the apartment—Kim says Mara took Carley for a few days because Kim couldn't cope, says she and Dewayne are fighting too much. Nothing I say helps.

*   *   *

There was nothing to do but keep going; Spencer and I at our jobs, and Tisha in school. On weekends, we did the bare minimum to keep our home livable. Our friends weren't around much. Maybe they were busy with their lives too, or maybe we were uncomfortable company. Tisha, at sixteen, was getting in trouble at school on a weekly basis. She started fights with boys, mouthed off to teachers,

44

and was sent to detention for swearing in the halls. Except for mealtime, at home she kept herself in her room. When we checked on her, she was doing homework. Her grades were okay, so we consoled ourselves that at least she still had some interest in classes. We knew she was hurting, but neither Spencer nor I had the capacity to reach her.

CHAPTER 11

Journal entry: 2/17/94—Thursday

Kim called me at work to tell me that she and Dewayne are going to go work for the carnival. She said, "I know what you're thinking and it's NOT like my birth parents being roadies. Buck gave us a van and is paying for the insurance. And we're giving Carley to them with *'papers'* so it's legal."

As I listened on the phone at my desk, I tried not to cry because there were people working around me. She was right; my mind immediately went to the disturbing thought that she was going down the same road as her biological parents. I was trying to focus but I couldn't keep up as Kim explained the plan—the carnival was in town now and Dewayne was getting a job with them, then they would leave to travel with the carnival in two weeks. I tried to persuade her to stay, to make another effort, that she could make it with CSD's and our help, but she said Dewayne doesn't do anything and she knows she can't do it alone. Buck and Mara have had Carley since last week.

Kim said, "You guys can't have Carley because you wanted her aborted in the first place. And besides, you guys work all the time." Before I could argue, she went on. "We are going to go make some money and eventually we'll come back and get her."

I worked to keep my voice calm and to reason with her, but she wouldn't hear me, like her mind was on one track and she couldn't stop until she was done. I finally got to ask her how we would ever see Carley again. She was convinced that nothing would change for us, that Mara would let us have Carley once in awhile if we asked her.

*   *   *

I got through my day in a stunned state. When I finally met up with Spencer at home, I was wound up.

"Spencer, Kim is talking like a puppet, like she's just mimicking whatever Mara and Buck have told her to say."

"I know, Gail, I know." He kept his cool by soothing me.

"She's just done in, and doesn't have any idea what's going on. She's been out-manipulated."

"What do we do now?" I asked him. In our practiced way, we took turns steering each other through each crisis.

"I'll talk to Emily tomorrow. She wasn't in her office today, but I faxed her a letter explaining what was going on, saying to call me."

I calmed down and got it together enough to phone the Walls. Buck answered and said everything was fine, except for Carley's "tight stomach." They'd been feeding her solids for a month and giving her prune juice. Now, he said, they thought she had the same "intestinal tract problems that Dewayne had when he was a baby." Mara got on the phone to tell me she and Kim were taking Carley to a pediatrician.

I asked her if she knew what Kim was doing about custody of Carley.

"Oh, Terry Faulkner said for us to get the local Indian attorney to draw up papers for temporary voluntary custody, I think he called it, to prevent CSD from forcing Kim to give up her baby."

Spencer saw that I was about to lose control, so he took the phone. Although at first they were against it, he convinced them to let us have Carley for the 3-day weekend. We were to pick her up at their house at 5:00 Friday.

*   *   *

Journal entry: 2/19/94—Saturday

Before we went to get Carley yesterday, Kim called me to tell me that the pediatrician wouldn't give Carley an upper/lower GI like Mara wanted him to, but prescribed water, Pediolite and burping. Kim knew we were getting her, so she wanted to make sure I knew what to do. Mara gave us the same instructions when we picked Carley up.

Spencer had reached Emily and told her we were allowed to have Carley for the weekend. She phoned last night to make sure everything went alright, then said to stall the Walls on Monday, tell them we can't come into town and would keep Carley until Tuesday. We're not sure what Emily is up to—we assume whatever it is it's without the official sanction of her bureaucratic kiss-ass boss.

Today, we're just having fun being grandparents.

2/21—President's Day

Called the Walls—they argued a little that we needed to bring Carley back to them today, but finally gave in. Buck sounded goofier than usual. Sometimes I think he is relieved to not have a kid around.

2/22—Tuesday

In the morning, we got a phone call and a fax from Emily telling us what she'd done. The petition she filed states:

"In accordance with ORS 419.569, the minor child named below is being taken into protective custody by the State of Oregon Children's Services Division, in that the child's condition or surroundings are such that the child's welfare is jeopardized."

We are to keep Carley with us while Emily tries to work things out with the tribe. The Camas County Court will hear her petition for custody on Thursday. She told us she would contact the Walls and Kim.

Later, Mara called, screaming accusations of conspiracy. She vowed to get Carley back, and said we were never to set foot on their property again.

Mara's and Buck's hostility is ridiculous, but we're wondering what they'll do next. Maybe they'll do something so outrageous that the courts will see how crazy they are and realize Carley is not safe with them. We don't think we will automatically be given guardianship, but maybe a temporary placement for a long while. I could take a leave-of-absence from work, or Spencer and I could work out a split-shift schedule. We could do it.

Carley is doing much better with her bottles, sleeping and playing easily. I think her digestion problems are gone.

*   *   *

Letter faxed to Tracy Faulkner, 2/23/94:
Dear Mr. Faulkner,

It is very important to the health and welfare of our granddaughter, 5-1/2 month old Carley Wall, for you to talk with us. We have tried reaching you by phone and fax without a return call. Carley's caseworker, Emily Sanchez, has told us you seem to be the one to decide who has custody of Carley. You should know that we do not wish to fight "over" her, but we will fight for her. My point is that I'm not sure you are getting enough accurate information from which to make your judgment.

The complexity is partially due to the involvement of two Multiple-Personality-Disorder patients. Our daughter Kim, the baby's mother, has many emotional problems that cause her to be quite delusional. It is true to say that she cannot take care of herself, let alone a baby. Kim's told us that Mara Wall, the paternal grandmother who is also delusional, has been diagnosed with the same disorder, as bizarre as that sounds.

I won't try to play arm-chair shrink here, but I know from living with Kim, seeing her with Carley, and from dealing with Mara, that being in either's care is not healthy for Carley. The boyfriend and his father have problems on top of that that compound the fantasies in which these people live.

You have been told that my husband and I are "out to take Carley from her mother." That is not our goal. All we ask is that you thoroughly investigate all aspects of the case with Carley's best interest in mind. Emily is very fair and can conduct and report an unbiased investigation.

Please understand that you may have been given an extremely distorted interpretation of reality, and we would like to talk with you about it.

*　　　*　　　*

Journal entry: 2/23/94—Wednesday

Later, I did receive a call from Faulkner. He sounded like a pompous, white Southerner, not Native American. He wouldn't let me talk much, just wanted to respond to my letter with condescending accusations of slander, and told me we were "only adoptive parents of Kim," so we didn't have any rights. Then he said that he loved cases like this, that this is why he got out of court law, he was tired of losing, and in tribal law you never lose. He promised me that he would "win" this one.

*　　　*　　　*

Letter faxed to Tracy Faulkner, 2/26/94:
Dear Mr. Faulkner,

I apologize for not getting back to you on Thursday like I had agreed, and I trust that someone else notified you. The hearing was very short. The court decided to allow CSD to follow through with the background check requested by the tribe. Kim and Dewayne gave their consent.

Carley is very healthy and content with the stability and attention she's gotten from our family. She is regular and not vomiting like she was the first day here. She cries only when she wants something and laughs most of the time. I will mail you a photo for your files, and hope that the tribal council follows her progress.

In return, could you send us some information on the Mukilkis? Our appreciation goes to the tribe for taking an interest in Carley's placement and investigating the situation.

Even though she's only 11/128 Mukilki, I hope you choose to advocate for Carley.

*   *   *

2/26/94—Notes from Spencer's fax to Emily:

"Emily, a few random thoughts:

"Maybe the judge could talk to Faulkner about our rights as adoptive parents; about the best interest of the child even under ICWA; remind him that Oregon has jurisdiction until the tribe makes a motion to transfer it.

"The Mukilki appointed Ms. Keeler from the local Confederated Tribes as their representative in court—how reasonable is she and does she listen to you?

"If Dewayne and Kim make decisions like refusing CSD's help and giving up their child for the carnival, then their decision to turn Carley over to the Walls should be suspect.

"They will probably be evicted, and live in their van parked at Mara's; if they've given up custody, should they still be living essentially at the same address as their child?

"Re: background checks, since Kim says all of Mara's personalities agreed to take care of Carley, then I say they should all be subject to an investigation!

"For all of Faulkner's bluster, I think he is just relying on people's perceptions that ICWA is cast in stone. We want to raise some challenges, as has been done in other states. If we have to, we'll get our lawyer's help, but let's see how the judge handles the State's petition after completion of the background checks."

CHAPTER 12

The order to take Carley back came at eight Tuesday morning. Emily practically cried as she tried to explain why.

Faulkner had told Nina Cowan, that if they didn't release Carley into Mara's custody, he would just disregard their investigative report and CSD wouldn't have any legal ground. Emily said she hadn't given up and would file a petition to keep jurisdiction here. But meanwhile, we had to take Carley to the state office at four o'clock. Mara and Buck would be there at four-thirty; we didn't have to see them.

As I handed Carley over to Emily, I looked through my tears at Carley's sleepy face. Emily gave her a bottle and assured us that she would vouch for Carley's health when she left our care. Spencer and Emily were crying, too, though I'm sure Emily had been through this many times before. For Spencer and me, it was the hardest thing either of us had ever had to do.

Sometime during our drive home, our determination slowly returned. We considered Emily's apprehensions about jurisdiction, and we decided to write a letter to the Circuit Court judge. It was probably not something our lawyer would approve of, but we didn't know what else to do.

Letter to the Honorable Frank Williams, 3/1/94:
Your Honor:

We've come to realize that this case can be dismissed without your knowledge of all pertinent information. Please hear our argument before giving up this Court's jurisdiction.

We have cooperated with the State's Children's Services Division from the beginning, when we felt Carley's welfare was threatened, and CSD has been working hard to help her. Now we're told that the law as we know it doesn't count and bloodlines are the only authority. CSD caseworker Emily Sanchez told us that she has to do what the tribe, as represented by their ICWA Specialist Tracy

Faulkner, demands. He has stated that we have no rights because our daughter, the baby's mother, is adopted.

Today we returned Carley to Ms. Sanchez, who released her to the paternal grandmother, Mara Wall. There are several reasons why we refuse to let this be the end.

The background check on Walter and Mara Wall was limited by Mr. Faulkner. The medical check was a report from one counselor that Mrs. Wall chose, although Mr. Faulkner assured us it would be done by a "psychiatric team." A home check was dropped because the CSD branch director felt it was a waste of time.

In addition to reported histories of police records, divorce proceedings and witnessed accounts of cruelty from their friends, we have seen Mrs. Wall's childish anger, false accusations and name-calling for ourselves. We know Carley was inappropriately fed and medicated by Mrs. Wall and by Kim with Mrs. Wall's encouragement. We've seen the filthy condition of Carley's diaper bag and bassinet when they come from the Wall's house. Mr. and Mrs. Wall have told us to let Carley cry herself to sleep when she stays at our house because that's their method.

Our daughter, Kim, wants to give custody of Carley to the Walls instead of complying with CSD's service agreement. She says she's punishing us because we were talking about adoption and abortion before Carley was born. Mrs. Wall and Mr. Faulkner are accusing us of conspiracy and talk of "winning." Mr. Wall says he must take Carley because she's his "own flesh and blood."

We want what's best for Carley and care about providing her with a stable and loving home. We want the opportunity to submit to any investigation to show we are capable. If there were no tribal interference, we would show the Court the recommendation of CSD, a Camas City family counselor, and a Doolin psychiatrist.

Our attorney has told us that until the tribe officially requests jurisdiction over the state, the Court can rule independently. Please explain this to us at the hearing on Friday.

*   *   *

The hearing didn't happen. On Friday, we sat in the courtroom as Emily's petition came up, but proceedings halted when the judge said he didn't have the case file. Everyone was confused, including the assistant DA who was there to represent the State's case. Judge Williams ordered the case continued until it could be sorted out. We followed the ADA to his office, while Emily went to talk to her manager. We found out the "lost file" was on the Juvenile Court desk waiting for direction from CSD Branch Manager Cowan, on whether they should file. Emily called us later, mad and frustrated, to say that she couldn't get Cowan to let her do her job. She thought Cowan was close to ordering her off the case, which meant we were about to lose CSD's support.

Emily's petition (that didn't make it to Judge Williams' bench) stated:

"The child is within the jurisdiction of the Court by reason of the following facts:

Children's Services Division has been involved with this family since October 1993. The mother, Kim McGhee, has been diagnosed by Mental Health as having Multiple Personality Disorder which needs to be addressed through treatment to insure the mother's ability to care for her daughter, Carley. Kim has described periods of "black-outs" during which she is unaware of her baby. When the baby was barely one month old, Kim described a situation in which she laid down with Carley to take a nap, however when Kim became aware of her surroundings later, she found herself in the kitchen cooking, with the baby face down on the floor. Kim has no idea what transpired or how she came to be in the kitchen. According to family members, as well as Kim, Kim has many periods in which she simply loses touch with what is happening around her. Other concerns include reports from the paternal grandmother, Mara Wall, stating that she is also in treatment for mental problems which have apparently been diagnosed as Multiple Personality Disorder. Mara Wall was selected by Dewayne Wall and Kim McGhee to care for baby Carley while Kim and Dewayne move to California to join the carnival for a minimum of three months. CSD has had several reports of drug use by Dewayne Wall which have not been assessed to date. CSD has held two Family Resource Meetings to assist the parents in providing adequate care to their child. CSD has contacted the Mukilki Tribe regarding protective custody of Carley Wall; the tribe has directed the agency to continue protective custody until a clearance from the paternal grandmother's therapist is obtained and a criminal history check is complete on both Mara and Walter Wall.

Wherefore, your petitioner prays this Court to have an investigation made of the circumstances concerning the above-named child and to make such orders as are appropriate."

*   *   *

It read true and reasonable to us; it surely was a case worthy of the court's attention, if only we could get it there. We decided to try to appeal to Nina Cowan. Spencer wrote and faxed a letter that we hoped would be on her desk when she got to work Monday morning.

We went back to court on Monday without any word from Cowan. The ADA had a petition to dismiss the case, which Judge Williams did. Emily testified that she (the agency) had been directed by Faulkner to release the baby to the paternal grandmother, contingent on a statement from Mara's therapist regarding her ability to care for the child. The county therapist, Judith Edwards, was the only one from whom they requested an evaluation, and she had reported that she had no concerns about Mara. She wrote that "all of Mara's personalities agreed that they could take care of the baby."

The ADA told us that he couldn't believe Cowan's actions, but that there was no further basis for intervention. Emily's face and voice showed how angry she was, and she tried to console us, but there wasn't that much to say. I cried, Spencer cried, and we came home.

CHAPTER 13

The fight Tracy Faulkner wanted with us was on. Our government, in the person of Nina Cowan, had handed him the power. It
was what Emily had been warning us about, but we hadn't imagined
the extent of the impact. After leaving the courthouse, we replayed
the statements and sequence of events aloud to each other to feel
their realness. By the time we got home, our resolve to help Carley
had escalated yet again.

Spencer made some calls and got the name of Faulkner's supervisor. The governing body of the tribe, we discovered, was an elected
council and they gave administrative power to the business manager.
Spencer wrote a letter to her, listing reasons we believed the Walls'
home was not safe. It included everything we could substantiate in
court plus things we couldn't.

*   *   *

Letter to Beth Woodson, Tribal Business Manager, 3/7/94:

Your assistant suggested I write to explain why we believed the
placement of Carley Wall in the home of Mara and Buck Wall was
harmful. We will list some of the reasons, and though each one may
not mean much by itself, added up they show there is something
very wrong about this household. Our sources state that all
statements are true and they would testify so in writing if necessary.

A family that had been close friends to the Walls reports that
Mr. Wall was a heavy marijuana user and is still a heavy drinker; he
was frequently violent and abusive to Mrs. Wall and their children,
and the children were very afraid of him. Mrs. Wall had been treated
for wounds obtained from her husband's abuse. It was common
knowledge in the neighborhood that when Mr. Wall went on hunting
trips, Mrs. Wall would stay home and play around with other men.

This same family often went deer-hunting with Mr. Wall, until he
played a reckless game of chicken while driving on a logging road
and crashed his pickup, killing their boy. Mr. Wall's pickup was
repaired before detectives could examine it, so the case was dropped

55

due to lack of evidence. Mrs. Wall later claimed that she was being harassed by the family's friends and she needed phone taps and police escort to leave her home; police stated that there was no truth to this.

Records show that Mr. and Mrs. Wall were separated and seeking a divorce when Carley was born. A close friend of Mrs. Wall's said Mrs. Wall was receiving daily psychotherapy and collecting public assistance while estranged from Mr. Wall, but staying with him on weekends. She also reports Mr. Wall was being treated for schizophrenia, and that there were many fights in that home. When Dewayne Wall and our daughter, Kim, were staying with the Walls, Mr. Wall had a fight with Dewayne and threw them out.

Children's Services Division acted on a documented case of neglect when they took Carley into protective custody, yet Kim and Dewayne are now staying with her at his parents' house. When Carley stayed with us, it became easier to comfort her the longer she was here, and she cried only when she wanted something. Mrs. Wall told us that she lets Carley cry herself to sleep.

Mrs. Wall told us Carley had the same urinary and digestion problems Dewayne had, for which he needed an operation. She said her family doctor was going to do an upper/lower G.I. investigation. The M.D. told us he never heard that complaint; Carley was constipated and dehydrated from vomiting, probably due to incorrect feeding. Mrs. Wall has ignored the advice of Carley's pediatrician and WIC dieticians since Carley was 3 months old, continuing to feed her solid foods. Kim told us she experiments with formula and reuses plastic bottle liners because she can't afford new ones.

Once when Carley was with us, we discovered Kim had been giving Carley expired antibiotics from Mrs. Wall's prescription. Carley did not have an infection, though she was suffering from a rash over her entire diaper area that was not being treated. Kim was also giving Carley teething pain medication she had gotten from the Walls, though Carley was only 4 months old and not experiencing teething pain. Whenever we picked up Carley from the Wall's, the clothes and bedding stank of cigarette smoke. The diaper bag and bassinet were filthy with moldy dirt, urine and feces.

CSD encouraged Kim and Dewayne to get the help they needed (parenting classes, in-home visits, rides, regular therapy sessions and doctor visits). Mrs. Wall helped them to avoid CSD, telling them that the "Indian Card" would protect them. When Carley was born, she told Kim how long to breast-feed, when to go back to school and when she should get a job. Dewayne made no real plans to do either. Mrs. Wall began stocking a room in her house with baby clothes and furniture. We believe her intentions have always been to raise Carley herself.

Kim recently told us that "Mara is alright as long as she takes her medication." A therapist cannot prescribe medication, yet it is the therapist's report from which it was determined Mrs. Wall is capable of taking care of Carley.

Please check into some of these issues and discuss this with us if you have questions. Even if we are not "real grandparents," as Mr. Faulkner has told us, we have great love and concern for this innocent baby who seems to be slipping through the cracks.

*   *   *

The tribe's business manager wrote back that she had looked into it and, "without getting into confidentiality, I feel the placement is pursuant to the Indian Child Welfare Act and in this case has not been abused."

I wrote to the Children's Services Division Region Manager who was Cowan's direct supervisor. I explained the background, the current situation and why we felt the case was dismissed prematurely. I told him that Cowan had said that "as long as a tribe was involved, there was no way CSD could be involved," and I suggested otherwise. He wrote back a surprisingly thorough account of the actions taken by CSD thus far, which showed that he had done his job. But he, too, did not question the authority of the tribe to place Carley with the Walls "due to her blood ties and that nation's lack of recognition for relationships based on adoption." He told us to continue contact with CSD when concerns for Carley's well-being arose, and that we could go to CSD's ICWA Manager in the Salem office for more answers.

A week of letter-writing and phone calls, and it finally became clear to us that we didn't have anything big enough to break down the barrier the agency had built to protect itself. Child abuse or neglect, at least in a case that involved a tribal nation, had to be substantiated with blood or broken bones. Blood or broken bones. It was a standard we would hear repeatedly.

*   *   *

Our next course of action was to appeal to the doctors.

The agency had given much credence to Faulkner's assurance that an "investigative team" would evaluate Mara's ability to care for a child, not just the one mental health therapist. I wrote to the director of County Mental Health about that. He eventually replied with the usual confidentiality argument, but added an explanation of the limits of their responsibilities. Information supplied by their clinicians would only relate to "psychological difficulties as manifested during treatment" and would not deal with "the physical nature of the home environment, the presence of significant others in the home, etc." We wondered if his clinicians weren't responsible, then who was?

We knew that Kim and Mara had taken Carley to two pediatricians in two separate clinics, apparently diagnosis-shopping. We had talked with both doctors in an effort to understand Carley's condition, and now we followed up with a letter explaining the current circumstances and a plea for help if they saw her again. We realized the improbability of getting a reply; what we wanted was attention. If our words were read by anyone that later saw anything out of the ordinary, it was worth a shot.

*   *   *

Weeks had passed since we'd heard from our daughter, when we got a call one evening and Spencer answered the phone. His voice immediately rose in frustration.

"What are you talking about? ... *That's* what you have to say, nothing about Carley? ... I don't know *who* you are ... You're not my daughter. The only daughter I'm sure about is upstairs in her room."

It ended abruptly and I wasn't sure who had hung up on whom.

"What?" I asked.

"I don't believe this. That was Kim, at least I think it was. She says the property manager said they owe back rent and they'll be evicted if they don't pay by the end of the month. And she was *demanding* that I pay it!"

"Wow. I thought that deal went out the window when she decided she'd quit being a mother. She didn't get that?"

"I guess not," he gave a callous laugh.

"What did she say about going off with the carnival? What happened to that plan?"

"Oh, well. Dewayne's come up with a better thing now. They're getting together with some friend who says they can make more money gathering petition signatures in California."

"Jesus."

58

"But for some reason I didn't understand, they can't go until April and they don't have a place to live because *I* didn't pay their rent. Unbelievable!"

He collapsed on the couch, shaking and breathing hard.

"And Carley?" I asked softly.

"Nothing. Not a word."

I sat across from him, knowing he needed a moment to calm down. We were quiet for a long time. Then I moved to sit next to him because we were both crying.

CHAPTER 14

Without one word in writing and only one phone conversation with Tracy Faulkner in four weeks, we still tried to communicate.

*   *   *

Letter to Tracy Faulkner, 3/21/94 (copies to Emily, to Cowan's boss, and to the Mukilki business committee):

Dear Mr. Faulkner,

Since receiving a letter from your Business Manager, all indications are that no one is taking responsibility for the welfare of Carley. We would like you to respond to that responsibility and assure us that she is safe. Can you explain any of the 17 different concerns we listed for your manager, and alleviate our fears that Carley is living with abuse?

It seems you might have "won" like you told us you would, Mr. Faulkner. But at what cost? Is the heritage of the tribe carried out to the next generation because you place the offspring of Dewayne Wall in the home he was raised in? Is ICWA really about continuing the cycle of mental illness, poverty and alcoholism? One might observe that if Dewayne and his mother exemplify qualities of the Mukilki tribe, the tribe could do better by breaking that cycle.

That's why we are attempting to save Kim's baby, Carley, from suffering the same abuse that Kim suffered due to her biological parents' inability to care for her. She can't cuddle her own baby; she speaks about her like a piece of property, and hands her over to anybody. When we took care of Carley, we comforted and played with her, held her and talked to her, sang and danced with her.

But Kim won't let us help. She and Dewayne could've gone through the steps offered by CSD (and encouraged by us) to become responsible parents. But the only help they have asked for are financial handouts, as advised by Mara. From the day Carley was born, we heard Mara talk about what kind of money would be coming from the tribe.

We're afraid that Mara's immaturity had a direct effect on the raising of her son, and her manipulative skills make easy targets of Kim and Dewayne. There's a pervasive air of paranoia, retribution, extreme defensiveness and hostility in that family. We understand that Kim and Dewayne feel trapped by the situation.

This is not the only choice. We've been informed that there was another baby in this county with ties to your tribe, who was placed in a non-tribal adoptive home. Perhaps this could be considered for Carley. Perhaps an agreement of tribal education could be enforced, whether she be placed in a tribal or non-tribal home, allowing her to get a more tribal influence than she can get from her biological family.

Wouldn't it be better for the people of the Mukilki tribe to know they can take positive steps in turning around the downward spiral of their children? Wouldn't the intent of the Indian Child Welfare Act be better served?

We were told that some Native Americans have a different standard of raising children than we are used to. Can you explain to us how they differ? Maybe that's the issue. It is hard for us to believe that anyone could advocate, after <u>thoroughly</u> reviewing the situation, that Carley is best left with the Walls.

*   *   *

We received no reply.

Throughout the next month, we kept up our efforts to reach the authorities. No one gave us any word on Carley. Our emotions were exhausted, occasionally rallying only when one of us would get an idea of what to try next.

Mary Keeler, the local Indian representative Faulkner had assigned earlier, contacted us to get Carley's bassinet back. The Walls had accused us of stealing it, though they hadn't given us a way of returning it since we weren't allowed on their property. Spencer took the bassinet to the local tribal hall, where Ms. Keeler rebuffed his attempts to communicate.

"She's worthless, nothing more than a whining cow," he fumed when he got home. "She believes everything that Kim, Mara and Faulkner said about us. I asked her very politely whether she could tell me how Carley was doing, and she refused to say anything about her. She would only say that she has no problem with Mara's abilities to care for a child, as long as a county mental health worker had endorsed them."

"Endorsed them? That's what she said?" I asked.

"Yeah, she likes that. She's totally incapable of making any judgments on her own. And get this. I asked her if she was monitoring the Wall household, and she said Faulkner specifically directed her to stay away."

"Huh? Stay away?" I said. "What's he worried about?"

"He probably knows she's a weak link, a loose end. He considers this case over and done with, so therefore there's no need to track what happens to the kid."

*   *   *

By now, many of our friends had heard about our problems and, it being a small town, knew some of the people involved. One covert friend who worked in the courthouse called to tell us that the case against Mara Wall for phone harassment was dismissed. Rumors in town were that Sandra Ryan had quit her job and was leaving the area for good. Another win for Mara.

Our friend also said we might be interested in seeing a recent sheriff's report involving one Kimberly McGhee.

I requested the report at the courthouse and was still trying to understand it when Spencer came home. I told him that it didn't seem as bad as it could've been; Kim hadn't been arrested. Nor had Dewayne. Maybe we wished that they had.

The report listed the suspect in unauthorized use of a vehicle as Jack Horton, the driver of a pickup that had been reported stolen. Dewayne and another girl, also in the pickup, were listed as witnesses. There evidently had been some mix-up about who was driving, but Dewayne, when questioned, denied knowing anything at all although he had been sitting between Horton and the girl.

Our daughter, evidently not in the pickup at the time, had not been questioned. She was listed as "Involved Person—Transient—currently staying in a blue Dodge van located off Transpacific Parkway." Kim, Dewayne and Horton all claimed to be living in the van parked on private forest property, near the place where the pickup had been pulled over.

When Spencer finished reading, he set the report on our kitchen counter. His eyes still on it, he said, "Judging by this, Kim's in worse shape than ever. There's no doubt in my mind that Dewayne's not the only one using drugs. Kim is."

He sank tiredly onto the stool and picked up the report again. "Who's Jack Horton; didn't his name come up somewhere before?"

"From the drug neighborhood," I said. "His mother was the woman Kim kept leaving Carley with, the one CSD said to stay away from. The caseworkers had all kinds of stuff on her for harboring druggies."

"Shit. I can't even think about it," Spencer said, pushing the report away. "It's so pathetic. Kim and these bozos sleeping in an old van, parked at a wide spot in the road, out in the middle of nowhere. The van that Buck gave them, right before he took their baby and kicked them out of his house."

CHAPTER 15

We wrote more letters to Faulkner, questioning the lack of supervision of Carley's placement, and the failure to investigate medical sources regarding Mara's and Buck's stability. We ended every letter by repeating our love for Carley and offering different paths that he might take to place her in good care, while still keeping his ego intact.

We met with our attorney, Jason Norden. He cautioned us that we could petition for guardianship, but might stand a better chance petitioning for visitation. Strong action might compel the tribe to intervene more decidedly against us. So far, there had been no legal action. The recommended first step was his letter on our behalf to Mara Wall, as Carley's custodian, requesting one weekend of visitation per month. He advised us to keep working with Emily. There was a chance she still had some influence on her region manager and could get CSD into the Wall home for an evaluation.

Stress and indecision became constants as Spencer and I went from day to day, waiting for any news, any response from the various factions. Just to be doing something, I tried a written appeal to Kim and sent it Certified to the P.O. box number we had for the Walls.

*   *   *

Letter to Kim, 4/7/94:
Dear Kim,

We're sorry that this is the only way we can possibly get a message to you. We feel that what is important for you to remember is that you can choose. When you get to a point that seems like it just can't get any worse, maybe you'll consider us as an alternative resource. We will offer all we can that will help you. There are choices that can give you back your life, but you have to turn in the right direction. We hope you make it.

There's a lawyer in Camas City that is helping us. He knows the whole story. We're sending him a copy of this letter so that everything is kept straight. We're here for you, if you decide to reach us.

Love, Mom and Dad

*   *   *

After three delivery notices at the P.O. box and one at General Delivery, my letter was returned unclaimed.

Two weeks later, on a weekend, Kim phoned us from Doolin.

"Hi, Dad." I listened on the extension and noticed her voice was friendly, as if we had just talked to her yesterday.

"Kim? What's going on?" Spencer was cautious.

"Nothing much. We're just here doing laundry at Buck and Mara's. They're on a trip. I just thought I'd say hi."

I realized that she was speaking from a different reality, not in the same time and place as Spencer.

"How are you? We wrote you a letter but it didn't get picked up. We've been worried." No reaction from Kim. "It's been a long time since you called. How's Carley?"

"Carley? She's fine. She's with Mara's sister and her husband."

"Oh yeah? Where do they live? There in Doolin?" Spencer asked carefully.

"Just down 10th Street. They've got a girl about two years old, and another girl in high school." Kim kept her chatty tone, but quickly changed the subject.

"Buck got our van tuned up, and I made some curtains so we can sleep in it when we go to California. We're almost ready, and our friends Melissa and Jack are going with us."

I knew Spencer remembered the two names from the police incident, but he didn't mention it. "How long do you think you'll be gone? Will you work with Emily again to get Carley back when you come home?" Silence. "We'll help you, Kim. You're having a rough time, but we know you can do it. You're a smart girl. Think about it."

She changed to a stiff monotone, said she had to go and hung up.

On Monday, we checked with Emily about Mara's sister. She said she knew the family; there had been some trouble with the teenager and there was a confidential case file she couldn't talk about. But, she said, they'd cleaned up their act and she believed Carley was safe there.

Later in the week, we heard from Jason; he'd received mail from Faulkner's local flunky that he said we should see. We read the two

65

letters in his office. From the dates, it wasn't hard to guess what had happened to Kim when Buck and Mara had returned from their trip.

*   *   *

Letter from Mary Keeler, on Confederated Tribes letterhead, to Jason, 4/28:

Dear Mr. Norden:

I am writing at the request of Kimberly McGhee and Dewayne Wall in response to a letter from your office indicating that your clients desired visitation with Carley Wall. Kim brought in a hand written statement, I typed it and they both signed it. That statement is enclosed:

"April 25, 1994

"Dewayne Walter Wall and Kimberly Ann McGhee do not want Spencer and Gail McGhee to have visitation rights with Carley Rebecca Wall. If visitation rights are granted by the court, we feel that all visits should be supervised by the ICWA Specialist.

"We do not want them to have visitation rights because when I (Kimberly) called them about a month ago to tell them of a change in my living situation, they insisted they did not know me, that I was not their daughter and that I was a stranger. Therefore, if I am not their daughter, Carley Rebecca Wall is not their granddaughter, and they are not my parents. Also, when I was pregnant, they wanted me to get an abortion and when it was too late for that, they wanted me to give Carley up for adoption. Also, last time Carley was in their care, they refused to feed her the solids she needs to be off the bottle by one year of age."

Signed by Dewayne Wall and Kimberly McGhee, and witnessed by Mary Keeler, ICWA Specialist.

*   *   *

On May 4th, we told Jason we wanted to go ahead and file for guardianship, since visitation was going to be a fight anyway. He agreed, and sent notifications to all parties, as required under ICWA law.

On May 12th, Emily called us. She said she'd heard from Kim's therapist at County Mental Health that Kim was in the hospital, in the psych ward. I called there and was put through to Kim's bed. She didn't resist talking to me but said she couldn't talk very long. She said she was okay, but "Liz," one of her personalities, had tried to slit her wrists. Dewayne had found her and called her therapist, who put her in the psych ward. When Spencer went to talk to the therapist, she told him that we shouldn't talk to Kim until after they worked on our "relationship issues." He asked her if Kim could be put in a residential care center instead of letting her go back to living on the road, and she said that Kim's "alters" really wanted to keep Dewayne around.

Inexplicably, Kim was released the next day, which was her birthday. Tisha asked us what we should do. At sixteen, she was having an even harder time than we were understanding that her sister had alter personalities that were trying to commit suicide. She couldn't accept that Kim had written us out of her life. So we agreed to send a birthday card General Delivery and we included a stamped envelope addressed to us. The card was later returned unopened.

Like other long-distance members of our family, my mother had been very supportive and had tried to keep up with the turmoil. She wanted to wish Kim a happy birthday, so she tried to reach her at the Wall's phone number. Mara evidently delivered the message because Kim eventually called her grandmother back. All was well, she told Mom; she and Dewayne were working at the carnival, which they would soon be traveling with, and Mara had Carley. The conversation broke Mom's heart and Kim didn't even know it.

PART THREE—JUSTICE

(May—September, 1994)

CHAPTER 16

Journal entry: 6/13/94—Monday

Jason called Spencer at work this morning; Tracy Faulkner had phoned him to say that he, that is, the tribe, now had custody of Carley. Mara had driven to Oklahoma with Carley, and Faulkner immediately petitioned a District Court in Oklahoma for temporary custody because it was an "alleged emergency and necessary for the child's safety," placing her in Mara's and Buck's care. Jason, now alerted to Faulkner's maneuvering, made arrangements to get copies of all proceedings in Oklahoma involving Carley. Today he found out that Faulkner filed a petition seeking to "adjudge" Carley a "deprived child, abandoned by her natural parents," which would give full custody to the tribe. The petition also states that the parents of the child have an adequate means of support and should have to pay child support. Jason is going to intervene so that the Oklahoma courts know about our pending case.

6/23—Wednesday

No word on Carley or Mara, still in Oklahoma, and I can't stand the thought of no one but Mara looking out for that poor baby. Today Jason got a copy of an "Entry of Appearance" notice from Faulkner that was filed in Camas County Circuit Court. It designates Mary Keeler as the Mukilki representative in our case. And it says that "the Tribe objects to placement of a tribal member with non-Indian, non-blood related potential guardians, to-wit: Spencer and Gail McGhee." I am amazed that he actually put our names on it. What did we do to make him hate us so much?

7/16—Saturday

We're still desperately looking for help, some way to get Carley back in a safe home, but there's nothing. It feels like we've tried everything—talked to our legislators, state agencies of all sorts, and the Federal Bureau of Indian Affairs. I even wrote an angry letter to the chief of the Mukilki. Though it wasn't threatening, it was sarcastic and I let him know how disgusted we were about how his tribe was handling things.

Today, I saw Dewayne's van parked at Buck's garage, so I called the Walls' number. Kim answered. I tried to ask her about Faulkner's petition, and the "abandonment" statement. Did she know about the summons for her to appear in the Oklahoma Court, that she could fight to keep Carley? She just answered that she didn't understand why I didn't trust her, and she hung up on me.

7/20—Wednesday

Tisha saw Dewayne in town yesterday and he invited her to come by the Walls' to see Kim. She did. She told us she didn't see Carley but did see Mara peek out nastily at her from a trailer parked in the yard. Kim said she'd been working as a maid at a local motel; Dewayne is not working. Dewayne told Tisha they were all going to Oklahoma soon but she shouldn't tell us. Tisha went back today, but Kim met her at the door and said she couldn't come in because no one else was home. According to Tisha, Kim was "acting real weird" and it scared her.

My friend Cindy at the hair salon told me she cut Buck's hair the other day, and he told her they were going "back east," that they'd sold their house and traded the garage and extra vehicles for a motor home. We talked to Jason, but he said there isn't anything we can do. We're scared, too.

*   *   *

September 16, 1994, Camas County Courthouse

"In the matter of the Guardianship of Carley Wall," Judge Williams tiredly addressed the half-filled courtroom, "I have had an opportunity to read, uh, Mr. Norton's memo and I read the, uh, tribe's motion. So, Mr. Norton, do you want to be heard?" Only then did he look up from the file that evidently had refreshed his memory of our case, the top one of the stack of bulging manila file folders, each bound with a rubber band, that was almost hiding him. He pushed round glasses back on his sharp nose, and I saw again how intently his blue eyes, his only coloring, measured his audience.

I had just witnessed over two hours of Civil Court. The divorce proceedings, restraining orders and minors-in-possession cases came and went, the judge issuing orders with a callous dispatch. By then I was no longer impressed by the interior of the courtroom, the heavy-looking bench and witness stand, or the sturdy railing that separated the old, wooden spectator seats from the front of the room. Spencer, more familiar with courtrooms from his days as a paralegal, told me that was the *bar*. The walls were plain white, and the two, small windows near the white ceiling were covered with dusty blinds. The door had a window, but blinds closed the view there, too. My eyes kept returning to the clock above the door and the slow, synchronized turning of the ceiling fans.

Our attorney arose from our end of the long table that accommodated the two sides in old, wheeled chairs. He appeared even younger and smaller than he had on my first sight of him eight months earlier when we had told him our story. This day, finally, a judge would hear it. Jason explained to us that there would be "the usual blah-blah-blah," before our case came up, and I tried to hide my anxiety about the judge's routine. But, frankly, I was scared that Jason Norden was not up to the task we had given him.

"Yes. It's *Norden,* Your Honor," he said. Though only in his early thirties and less than average height, he handled himself with a dignified professionalism that his good-natured face had hidden. "I would just like to emphasize the point that under the Indian Child Welfare Act you do have the authority to obtain jurisdiction here under the filed motion."

I knew that Jason wanted the record to be clear that our Motion for Guardianship was filed in May, well in advance of Faulkner's Motion to Transfer Jurisdiction and Dismiss, a move that Jason called "forum shopping."

"Did you read Mr. Norton's, uh, Mr. *Norden's* memo, Ms. Keeler?" Williams continued in his nasal voice.

He referred to Jason's memorandum in support of his Objection to Faulkner's motion, which was Faulkner's response to our petition. Jason's memo was a summary of events, with a complete timeline, justifying that jurisdiction be kept in this court.

"Yes, I did," Mary Keeler answered, then stood. She was a chubby, middle-aged woman with bad posture, messy, graying hair, and did look rather cow-like, as Spencer had described her. Her awkwardness revealed what we knew was inexperience.

"Okay," Judge Williams continued, checking the summary. "The petitioners filed their Motion for Guardianship in May. A month later a State Court in Oklahoma granted temporary custody of the child to the Tribe. And then later the Court was informed of our case and then they continued it, uh, until September 23rd, pending jurisdiction issues. And now, my understanding is that the paternal grandparents have left. They aren't here and the petitioners don't know where they are or where the child is."

"That's correct," Keeler said.

"Do you know where they are?"

"They are residing on the reservation in…"

"In Oklahoma?" the judge cut her off.

She stammered, "On the Mukilki reservation, yes."

"Okay. So, what they did was take the child from Oregon to Oklahoma. In what, do you know what month?" He turned to face Jason.

"No, your Honor. We lost contact with them in July."

"It was late July, I think," Keeler said. "They didn't inform me when they left."

"Okay. So basically, there's not much of a disagreement on the facts of this matter?" Williams showed her the memorandum.

Keeler said, "The way they're stated, no. Uh, no but I… I'm not an attorney so I don't know what the procedure is."

"There's an Act called the Uniform Child Custody to Jurisdiction Act, which says the home state of a child is a state where somebody's been for at least six months. They haven't been in Oklahoma, so it would not be the home state. So if this were a State Court proceeding, I would take jurisdiction. I would have a problem with the petitioners for taking the child out of the jurisdiction."

I thought he meant respondents, but he said "petitioners." Spencer and I, sitting at the petitioner's table, the left side facing the judge, exchanged looks. Spencer twirled his ever-present pen nervously. Jason, still standing, said nothing.

Williams went on. "Now the question becomes whether or not those same actions give me good cause to deny transfer. I don't buy your argument," his blue eyes darting to Jason, "that it was filed in an advance stage of the proceeding. I don't think it was, I mean it was, uh, only a month old, as I understand it."

"I believe it was three and a half months after they received notice of this case that they filed their Motion to Transfer. August 29th, your Honor." Jason stayed calm.

While he tried to respectfully straighten the judge out on the dates, I glanced back at the middle row of the theater seats behind us. My mom and sister had driven from Cherry Valley, two hours away, to lend support, which had helped ease the tension of the long morning. They sat with Tisha as all three looked on with the same attentive faces. I looked over at Ms. Keeler as she fidgeted from foot to foot, her face still vacant.

"I just don't find that that's untimely," Williams said, waving his hand at the document impatiently. "What I am concerned about, though, is the fact that this child has been here until she was just taken out of Oregon. Right?"

It appeared he was addressing Keeler and she started to attention. "Right," she said.

There was more back-and-forth while Williams got his facts in order. I felt more confident in Jason's performance now as I watched him tackle what seemed like a very squirrelly court to me.

"Tell you what I'm going to do," the judge said with finality. "I'm gonna go ahead and hear the evidence and then I'll have that down. 'Cause I don't want to make a decision real quickly on the underlying issue of Motion to Transfer without more time to do a little research on the matter.

"In the meantime, people have been waiting for about three months to have this hearing and I can go ahead and take the evidence. If I decide to retain jurisdiction, then I can go ahead and make a decision based on that evidence. If I don't take jurisdiction, then, well, it doesn't hurt anybody to hear the evidence. Okay. You understand the posture of that?"

Keeler didn't answer.

"Okay. Go ahead and call your witness."

"Thank you, your Honor," Jason said. "I'd like to call Emily Sanchez."

CHAPTER 17

It was reassuring to see Emily Sanchez again. We hadn't seen her since we'd handed Carley over to her March 1st when we were all crying. There was not much else to talk about since Children's Services pulled out of the case, but Emily had called once or twice. The rift between her and her manager had been widening and Emily didn't think she could work there anymore.

Calling Emily as a witness, Jason Norden had untied her hands and legitimized her determination to perform her duty as she wanted. I saw courage in her face as she explained to Judge Williams how she had tried to help Kim and Dewayne keep their baby. She walked the Court through the case development and attested to Kim's mental illness, the conditions they lived in and their unwillingness to cooperate with Children's Services.

Jason asked, "If the child was returned to the natural parents, would CSD become involved?"

"Absolutely," she answered.

The judge interrupted, "Just a minute. What were Dewayne Wall's problems, the child's father, if any?"

"He admittedly had a drug problem. He would not become involved with any parenting classes or any services that would help them. Basically, he was just there."

"And both sets of grandparents were involved at this point?"

"The maternal grandparents more consistently. I wouldn't hear from the paternal grandmother until after I'd laid down some guidelines for the parents to address. They would go back and talk to the paternal grandmother and she'd call me and be upset," Emily answered.

The judge turned the questioning back over to Jason, and Emily was allowed to explain how the Mukilki tribe ordered her to take Carley away from us and place her with the paternal grandmother, Mara.

"Do you, as a child protective service worker," Jason asked, "have concerns about the placement with Mara Wall?"

"I have concerns if she's not under a regular treatment schedule with a therapist qualified to treat Multiple Personality Disorder…."

"If who's not under a treatment schedule?" the judge interrupted.

I watched Judge Williams' face as Emily explained that Mara was being treated by County Mental Health therapist Judith Edwards, and had admitted to having nine personalities. Emily told the judge how the tribe was satisfied with the therapist's assessment that all of Mara's personalities could care for the baby, but she was not. I thought Emily's words would have some impact on him, but his grey face showed nothing.

"From conversations I've had with Mara," Emily said, "unless she's taking medication and seeing a therapist on a regular basis, I am not convinced she's in touch with reality."

Jason asked, "Do you see that there's a likelihood that serious emotional or physical harm could come to the child if Mara Wall is caring for the child and not under a treatment schedule?"

"Yes, I think it's possible."

When questioning was turned over to Mary Keeler, she tried to get Emily to admit that ICWA gave the tribe the right to place the child and order CSD to dismiss their case. Keeler's questions were so bumbled that Judge Williams had to restate them. He then got lost when he asked Emily if the child was now in "foster placement" with Mara.

"No," Emily said. "When our petition was dismissed, as directed by the tribe, custody automatically returned to the natural parents. They agreed on their own that the paternal grandmother would be the primary caretaker because the natural parents wanted to join the carnival."

Mary Keeler had no more questions, but Jason did.

"I have some follow up questions, your Honor.

"Ms. Sanchez, would you have dismissed this petition if it had been up to you to decide?"

"No."

"Would you have changed the placement of the child from the custody of Mr. and Mrs. McGhee to Mr. and Mrs. Wall? If it had been up to you?"

"No, no."

The judge questioned Emily again before she was excused. He tried desperately to find something in writing from Mara's therapist or from the tribe that clarified the responsibility of Carley's placement.

"I'm wondering if the Tribal Court itself has entered any orders," he asked Keeler.

"I'm only aware of what's listed by Mr. Norden," Keeler answered.

"Your honor, if I may," Jason said. "I called the Tribal Court yesterday, that is the Court of Indian Offenses. They have no proceedings."

"Darn it." The judge looked down at his bench, set down his pen and stood up. "I need a break. I'm going to take a recess, folks. Come back about one. Break for lunch."

The courtroom clerk struck her gavel, said, "All rise," and the noisy process of moving bodies erupted. I smiled at Emily as she left the courtroom. I wanted her to know that we believed she did all she could. I hoped there would be a time we would get together again, to celebrate.

*　　　*　　　*

When we returned, Jason called Tisha to testify about visiting Kim in Doolin. She was nervous, but she told how she saw Mara shoot her a dirty look from the trailer. It gave Tisha the chance to reveal how she felt being pushed away from her sister and her niece. She left the stand and we smiled at each other. I was proud of her for facing up to it.

Jason then called Mary Keeler to testify, and she confirmed that Mara was "uncomfortable" with our family, but only because we'd harassed them. About Mara's mental capabilities, Keeler would only say that Mara's periodic counseling sessions were because she was a victim of "past abuse."

It took a long time for Jason to question Keeler, without getting any clear answers. Eventually, Judge Williams prompted her. "You dealt with Mr. and Mrs. Wall. What's your summary?"

"They felt people were saying things around town. They felt they were being watched and it was affecting their business. Um, at the encouragement of the tribe, I believe, they moved to Oklahoma to feel more secure."

"Thank you. Do you have anything else to add?"

"Um, I don't know."

The judge gave her a moment while she consulted her notes.

"Uh, it's not mandated, no guidelines or criteria for how the Tribes select a placement preference. The Mukilki made their decision after they got clearance from Ms. Edwards, from Mental Health. After Carley was placed there, I visited the home several times. The child was always happy and well cared for. They sometimes dropped by my office and brought records of their visits to WIC for Well Baby check-ups. I saw no problems of interactions between Carley and the grandparents. The parents would sometimes come to the office, but they never, never had Carley in their care directly. Because they recognized and so does Mr. and Mrs. Wall that they weren't capable of taking care of the child.

"As far as what's happened since they moved, um, I'm not aware of what's gone on. I only have a number for Mr. Faulkner's office."

I thought her vague, wandering testimony was almost worthless. The biggest point she raised, however, was that Tracy Faulkner was running the show. He directed Keeler's movements; the Walls went to Oklahoma because of his encouragement; no one could contact the Walls without going through him.

CHAPTER 18

When Jason put Spencer on the stand, he asked him to explain his concerns. Spencer began by referring to Exhibit 1, the police report about Mara's affair with her friend, Sandra Ryan.

"It states that Mrs. Wall was seeing Dr. William Brown and that she has multiple personalities, and one of them had a sexual relationship with Sandra Ryan. That report, and what people in the Doolin area have expressed, have given me concerns about the relationship between Mr. and Mrs. Wall, and how they raised their children. There's a lot of unanswered questions and it makes me very uneasy that our granddaughter's going to continue in this household."

Jason asked, "Has Mara Wall ever indicated in your presence that she had multiple personalities?"

"Yes, at a family resources meeting at CSD."

"Do you remember what she said?"

"That she had MPD and was seeing Dr. Brown and getting some certain medication to control it. I'm familiar with Kim's multiple personalities and, combined with Mara's, that's just too many multiple personalities floating around for it to be a safe household for Carley." The ridiculous truth of the statement made him smile nervously.

Jason continued, "Do you have any concerns about Walter Wall and his ability to care for Carley?"

"From what I've gathered in the community, he's an abusive alcoholic and becomes violent on occasions."

His testimony went on to confirm that we were denied visitation, by lack of response from the Walls and by letter from Kim and Dewayne.

"Thank you, Mr. McGhee," Jason said. "One thing more. Mr. McGhee, have you been spreading rumors about Mr. and Mrs. Wall in your community?"

"No, I have not."

"Have you been following them around or harassing them in any way?"

"Absolutely not."

"Have you been attempting to contact them?"

"We sent the letter requesting visitation, and we tried to talk to Kim when she called on the phone. Nothing else."

*   *   *

When it was my turn to testify, my mind was a jumble. Even though our attorney had prepared us and I knew what he'd ask, I had trouble getting it out.

Jason asked, "From your contact with Mara Wall, did you notice anything unusual about how she acted?"

"Yes. The beginning was when Kim and Dewayne were first dating, and one of them ran away to get with the other one, and we contacted Mara. We had a family meeting, and Mara was speaking in a baby voice and, yeah, I started suspecting something then."

I didn't know what Jason was after. I waited for his questions.

"Carley Wall is currently placed with Mara Wall. What can you express to the Court about your concerns, if any, about that placement?"

"The day Carley was born, in the hospital Mara was talking about the Indian rights, and that Kim would be nursing for two months and then she would go to school. Mara seemed to have all these plans for how things were going to happen. None of them had something for Dewayne's responsibility. But Mara continued that closeness with Kim and was allowed to keep Carley on several occasions when Kim, for some reason, didn't want Carley in their apartment. So Mara got Carley for weekends. We arranged with CSD so that we could do that also. I mean it was kinda like CSD persuaded Kim to let us have Carley some weekends too, and that would be a good resource for Kim when she felt uptight and needed a break. So when we were allowed, we would pick up Carley from Mara's house." I realized I wasn't getting to the point.

"On those occasions, did you have any concerns?" Jason prompted.

"Yes. Every time we got Carley, there was something weird about the bag we got with her. Everything smelled bad. Cigarette smoke, mold and urine. On all her clothes, her blankets. There was a cigarette in her diaper bag at one time. There were strange medications and foods that a three-month-old baby didn't need to be eating."

He allowed me time to tell more details about that, about Buck's prune treatment and the pediatricians' advice to us. I felt I was finally giving good information. Then he asked, "Has Mara Wall ever expressed in your presence that she has any mental illnesses?"

"Yes. She accused us of playing dirty by bringing that into a CSD meeting, but she had told me that she had multiple personalities and that she was abused as a child."

Jason asked, "When did she tell you that?"

"Um, before Kim had her baby. We went into an agreement with Mr. Wall to rent an apartment for Dewayne and Kim for a three or four month trial so that they would try to get their act together. Mara found the apartment; she lived next door." I was wandering again. "She told me at that time the reason she had been living there and not with her estranged husband was so that she could go to daily therapy at the hospital, where she was being counseled with psychiatric therapy for MPD, multiple personality disorder."

"Do you remember being at a family resource meeting where she expressed that she had MPD?"

For the first time, I referred to notes that I had brought with me to the stand. "Yes. January 31st was the last meeting with CSD, and that's when she said it."

"Have you ever discussed visitation of Carley Wall with Mara?"

"I didn't discuss it, but she discussed it with me. That day that Emily Sanchez advised us to keep Carley, Emily told us that she was going to call Mara and inform her of that. Evidently right afterwards, Mara phoned us and yelled and swore at me, saying that she thought that we were in a conspiracy and that she was going to get Carley back. She called Spencer a lot of names. I finally put the phone away from my ear because I couldn't listen anymore."

"Was it your impression that she intended that you not see Carley again?"

"Yes." I don't know why, but I added, "After you wrote the letter asking for permission, I was wondering how we could set that up if she agreed. I knew that she'd gone to church in Doolin, so I talked to a minister of that church. He agreed we could use his church as a meeting place and he would approach her on that. But we didn't get her permission."

"Mrs. McGhee, were you able to care for Carley Wall?"

"Oh yes."

"That's all the questions I have, your Honor."

"Ms. Keeler?" the judge asked.

Mary Keeler stood, looking at her notepad. "Is, uh, Kim your natural daughter?"

"No, not a biological daughter. She was adopted. She was nine."

"Do you currently feel yourself estranged from your daughter?" Keeler still didn't look at me.

I felt she was trying to put blame on me. I sighed and said, "It's hard to say who my daughter is at this time. I haven't talked to her since July."

"Do you know why she didn't want you and Spencer to have visitation?"

"I kept a journal at that time, and I've gone back and reread it. There were different reasons she gave at different times. Once, she said she'd told us a zillion times to take the plastic tabs off the liners of the baby bottles. She said Dewayne had said that we didn't know how to take care of babies, and that was why they didn't want us to have her."

Keeler looked at me now. "Did you ever suggest to Kim that she should abort the baby?"

"We made choices clear to her when she said she was pregnant."

"Did you ever suggest to her that she put the baby up for adoption?"

"Yes," I said directly.

"And did she ever express that was something that she did not want to do?"

I thought I knew what Keeler was after, but my answer was, "She told me she would think about it. She even went to a crisis pregnancy planning meeting with me. She told me once that she started making the call and Dewayne stopped her."

After a moment, Keeler sat down. "I have no more questions."

Jason's redirect asked, "Do you feel that Kim McGhee and Dewayne Wall are capable of taking care of Carley?"

"No. I don't think Kim is capable of taking care of herself."

CHAPTER 19

With no other witnesses, Judge Williams called for arguments. Jason read from the Indian Child Welfare Act the standard that must be followed.

He faced the bench and continued, "The petitioners have established that the parents are not a viable placement here; I don't think that's an issue. Petitioners have gone on to show, by clear and convincing evidence through the testimony of Emily Sanchez, who can be classified as an expert witness in this matter, and through the evidence of Exhibit 1, the police officer's report, and through their testimony that Mara Wall has a mental illness, or at least expresses that she does have it. Emily Sanchez did testify that based on that mental illness it's likely that serious emotional and physical damage to the child will occur.

"The guardianship should be granted on those grounds, and also on the grounds that Mr. and Mrs. Wall are avoiding this Court and are trying to get this matter taken care of in Oklahoma, first through State Court and now through Tribal Court, so that the witnesses will have difficulty testifying there."

Williams said, "Before you resume, Mr. Norden, let me ask you something. If there is clear and convincing evidence, then I'd have to find not only that the parents weren't proper custodians, but that your clients were. Right?"

"No, your Honor. The actual language," he looked down at his yellow legal pad, "'evidence, including the testimony of qualified expert witnesses that the continued custody of the parent or Indian custodian,' who is Mara Wall, 'is likely to result in serious emotional...'"

"Oh. I understand. Go on." He leaned back, eyes steeled on Jason.

"Additional evidence of serious emotional damage is Mara and Walter Wall's denial of visitation to the maternal grandparents. By taking the child to Oklahoma, essentially, and actually denying visitation to them. It would be in the child's emotional best interest if visitation were allowed, and I believe it is likely to cause emotional harm if the child is denied that visitation.

"That's all I have, your Honor. I believe that guardianship should be granted on those grounds."

As he sat, Jason gave us a quick smile. I thought his explicit words and respectful manner were encouraging. I looked over for my husband's agreement, but his face showed that he was still tense. He wrote something on his notepad and slid it towards Jason, who nodded after reading it.

The judge turned to Mary Keeler. "Do you have anything further you want to say?"

She had several pages in her hands, and flipped through them as she spoke. "Um, yes I do. Um, if the Court chooses to recognize that the Tribe had the right to intervention…"

"What?" Williams asked.

"The right to intervention."

"Oh, okay. I just didn't hear you. Go ahead."

Keeler spoke louder, "If recognized that the Tribe had a right, and made a placement preference and that the child is in care now with extended family, in order to remove that child from care," her voice took on a whining tone, "the placement procedure now, as Mr. Norden indicated, follows the ICWA, and must include clear and convincing evidence including testimony brought by the witnesses. And I don't find that any of the people brought as witnesses today could be considered expert witnesses. So…, so I don't see how he could find that there is clear and convincing evidence to remove… that, uh, that is, that the continued custody of the child was likely to result in serious emotional or physical damage. Hence, this Tribe's wish is to have this matter transferred back to their Courts."

I was lost. Spencer and Jason were looking expectantly at Judge Williams.

The judge said, "All right. The matter of transfer. The Tribe hasn't formally done anything."

"No," Keeler said.

"Have they not formally done anything because they are waiting to see what my decision is, or are they just not going to do anything at all?"

"What do you mean by formal?" Keeler asked stupidly.

"Well, I mean do they require filing of pleadings or do they just say, okay, we have an Indian child, therefore we have jurisdiction?"

"No, they're requesting transfer from this Court."

"Okay. All right. Give me a minute here."

The courtroom was quiet while he read documents on his bench. Spencer reached over and patted my arm. The wait was agonizing, and I began to wonder if we would get a decision today.

Then Williams said, "Okay. I don't think I have to do the research that I was going to do on the question of good cause. Because the problem I have is, I don't think there is clear and convincing evidence for me to say that this child's emotional health is gonna be in danger."

Spencer sagged and slowly put his pen down on his notes. I heard murmuring voices from somewhere in the seats behind me. I didn't move.

"I mean," Williams continued, his glasses off so that his blue eyes penetrated me, "the most I have here is that Mara Wall might have a problem. The only person who has really diagnosed her is Judith Edwards, who said there was no problem as far as she was concerned with Mrs. Wall having care and custody of the child. So people have suspicions about Mrs. Wall having multiple personalities, and the expert, or the one person who's her therapist said she doesn't have a concern about that... Well, I have some question about whether there's expert testimony in this proceeding to prove that. Even if I assume there was some expert testimony, the real expert says there is not concern about the child's placement."

I was unsure what he had said. What about Emily's testimony? Wasn't that expert? One look at Jason's face told me he didn't understand either. Spencer sat back in his chair and stared at the judge.

"If it were a question of the parents taking custody, there's no doubt that it would be easily shown that neither parent could take care of the child. But the Act itself is designed to keep Indian children in extended families. Now, whether or not people see that as fair isn't the question. It happens to be the law."

Each time the judge paused, I felt there must be a clear point coming, something I would understand.

"And I don't find that it's been proven here that the Tribe has made a custodial choice, and I can't do that. So I'm somewhat stuck with the decision that even if I don't transfer jurisdiction, I wouldn't give custody under the guardianship proceeding because I can't make the findings required by the law. And that would then put us in a position of nobody having jurisdiction of this child, and then no one monitors this case. Which, I don't know, maybe that's the way it should be. I don't know what the Tribe would want."

He paused.

"The Tribe's asked to have jurisdiction. But I have some problem with the Walls leaving, even for the reasons they state because that they're *uncomfortable* is not any sort of feeling. And I don't like the fact that they left while this proceeding was pending. It would've been helpful to have them here and participate rather than just to assume that something bad was going to happen to 'em, which was partly... I don't know," he threw his hands up. "Maybe they felt uncomfortable and they said, 'Everybody's against us!' but it certainly makes it a lot harder when people don't stick around." He sounded exasperated.

"In any event, I'm not...," he sighed. "I'm gonna..., I'm gonna just..., I'm gonna dismiss the petition for guardianship and, uh..." He stopped.

"I can't find any good cause. I guess based on... that the only thing I would find after hearing all the testimony I think I can frankly use is that they left the jurisdiction. And I don't like that. I can't. Because, based on my finding, it basically becomes irrelevant that they did that. So, I guess based on that I will transfer jurisdiction to the Tribe, since they've asked for it."

We were rigid. It was starting to get through to me now. The judge didn't know. Somehow, we had not made it clear. We must've left out something important. I felt my eyes begin to water.

He looked at us and continued, "I don't, I mean, I feel bad that you may not see this child again and I don't think that any culture should deny any grandparent visitation, whether it's a Caucasian or a Native American culture. That's not in the benefit of any child at all, and all it does is end up hurting the child. But it happens on a monthly basis when adults get involved and get mad at each other."

I thought he must be trying to get us to understand his position as a judge, that he sees these cases all the time. He didn't know this was different.

"They always end up hurting the child. But I can't do anything about that. That's called human nature."

Jason hadn't given up. "Your Honor, may I make a couple of points?"

"Yes."

"The first is, you indicated that the Act is on key for the child in an extended family placement where there is an Indian custodian. The Act itself makes no distinction between Indian and non-Indian custodian."

"Well, the purpose of the Act itself, I think, is inclined to keep Indian families together. It was designed to take away the abuses of the past, what they thought was a consistent history of placing Indian children with non-Indian families. So…"

I wished Jason would argue this more, but he didn't.

"The second issue I would like to raise is the Motion to Transfer Jurisdiction and Dismiss. I believe the Dismiss part of that is contingent on the transfer of jurisdiction, and for the transfer of jurisdiction to be complete, the Tribal Court has to accept it."

"They've asked for the transfer!" Williams was getting hot.

"The Tribe has, the Tribal Court has not. There's a distinction in the Act. The Tribal Court is a separate Federal Court and…"

"Well, if they don't accept it… uh, if they don't… we'll be left in the same situation that I said might happen anyway… where I denied your clients' petition in any event, and so if the Tribal Court doesn't accept jurisdiction of this…"

"Okay. Thanks, your Honor."

I couldn't tell if Jason got anything out of that exchange or not, but we all could see that pursuing anything at this point would only make Williams hotter. The murmur in the courtroom began as soon as the judge left, and I turned to see the faces of two or three on-lookers that I didn't know. I found my family and they joined us as we walked out.

We formed a group outside on the steps of the courthouse. My sister was agitated.

"How could he not see that Carley's in danger? The state worker made it clear. That part about all of Mara's personalities agreeing they could raise her… Come on! And he's mad that they left the state but what's he do about it? He hands them jurisdiction. His circular logic doesn't make any sense."

I listened numbly as she argued the points with Jason, who agreed with her and seemed grateful for the chance to let off steam. But he finally admitted he didn't have any answers. My poor mother was quiet, with a look of bewilderment on her face.

Tisha, Spencer and I just stood there while meaningless people walked in and out of the door next to us. I waited for Spencer to say something, sure that he understood more than I did. His silence scared me.

Then my mom said, "Well, Jason, the only thing I understand is that you're not mean enough. The mean lawyers on TV always win."

I loved my mother for making us laugh in that moment.

"Somebody tell me what happened in there," I finally said. "Jason, where do we go from here? What do we do next?"

Jason showed some encouragement as he said, "You can still file for visitation. But we have to wait to see what the Oklahoma courts will do, and whether or not the Walls stay there or come back here. You may have to go there to fight it out."

I took a deep breath. Spencer rallied and put his arm around me. "It's not over. We'll do what we have to do."

On the quiet ride home, I asked Spencer, "Should we? Keep fighting, I mean. What if all we're doing is making these paranoid people go even further underground? Putting Carley at even more risk?"

He slowed the car, as if he needed more energy to go towards his words.

"I can't predict how crazy people are going to act. I just know that Kim was our responsibility when she got pregnant, and now we're responsible for Carley. And we love her. As long as she's in their hands, I can't just look the other way and hope for the best. I think if we keep attention on them, someone will see if… if they hurt her." He reached to hold my hand. "We're doing the right thing."

"Yeah, Mom," Tisha agreed from the back seat.

"Okay. Thanks, you guys."

PART FOUR—VISITATION
(September, 1994—November, 1995)

CHAPTER 20

We had last seen our granddaughter March 1, 1994. The last word we'd had from our daughter, Kim, was in May when she had tried to slit her wrists.

Not knowing whether we'd ever see either one of them again, we did what we could to keep our lives going. My job at the Department of Transportation, which I'd had for eleven years, was far from satisfying but it was the steady income for our household. Although Spencer's year-old remodeling business had only sporadic profits, it was a good career. It held promise and gave him direction for his energies towards real accomplishment, a morale boost that helped us both. Besides meeting our household expenses, we managed to pay our legal bills with monthly installments and we tried to save some for the flood we knew was coming.

Tisha was finishing her senior year in high school. Her grades dropped slightly after the semester break but she did better than expected, considering the suppressed anguish she lived with. We took her to counseling with a therapist that no one in our family had seen before, so he was all hers. Since she was no longer under her sister's control, she was beginning to find herself. She was learning to accept anger and appropriate ways to express it. In turn, that helped her learn to love. She helped us just by being there.

After our September hearing, we spent the next few months educating ourselves on ICWA and legal procedure. The dismissal of our case served to shock us out of our naïve belief that justice came to those who followed the rules.

On September 30th, Jason wrote to the Tribal Business Committee and gave them an account of the case as he saw it. He recommended they look into the matter to assure Carley was not in any danger under Mara's care, and that they not expose themselves to "significant liability." He questioned the tribe's sovereign immunity, which, he suggested, might have been waived due to certain procedural steps. The committee members who had previously been somewhat sympathetic now told us they couldn't talk to us anymore. On October 3rd, Spencer sent a binder full of our previous correspondence, court transcripts, police reports and civil cases involving the Walls, and a complete sequence of events for which Tracy Faulkner was responsible. He asked that the binder be reviewed at the Tribe's next committee meeting as a formal complaint against Faulkner.

On the evening of October 5th, we received a fax notifying us of the continuance of the case to declare Carley a Deprived Child in a district court in Oklahoma. We hired an attorney by phone to represent us, and Faulkner, allegedly out of town on the day of the hearing, had his assistant represent the tribe. Kim and the Walls appeared, with Carley, hoping to get the court to transfer legal guardianship to Buck and Mara. Our attorney and, finally, that county's district attorney explained to the judge that jurisdiction belonged in the Tribal Court. Faulkner's assistant testified that there currently *was* no Tribal Court, and hadn't been for months, because they "couldn't get a judge to show up." The hearing ended with dismissal, and Kim and Dewayne were advised that they should file their consent to relinquish custody with the guardianship case, wherever that would be.

Instead, two weeks later the Walls went to a district court in another county. We received a copy of the form, which was signed by Kim and Dewayne, stating that they assigned permanent custody to the paternal grandparents, but were still obligated to support and visit the child. There was no mention of the tribe on the form.

We learned that the Bureau of Indian Affairs can appoint a judge for a Court of Indian Offenses for tribes that don't have tribal courts, and that is what happened. In February, 1995, that court accepted jurisdiction but did not set a hearing date.

We still had no information about Carley's or Kim's welfare. We told our story repeatedly, appealing by phone and letters to BIA directors, the Oklahoma State Bar, the Oklahoma ACLU and child protection agencies. I sent a letter to CBS' *Sixty Minutes* with a faint hope of stirring interest in an investigative report, but it wasn't acknowledged. Spencer wrote eloquent letters, and when he didn't get replies from the addressed officials, he wrote again to their superiors, including our members of Congress and the Secretary of the Interior. (It would be months before we got any responses, and by then the Mukilki Tribe had escaped responsibility.)

In April, we talked again to the Oklahoma attorney we'd used in October. He contacted the tribe and they contended they were no longer involved with the child and they didn't know the whereabouts of the parents or the grandparents. The Court of Indian Offenses had dismissed the case.

Jason Norden advised us to retain his associate in Camas City who had ICWA expertise. When she wrote to the Mukilki Tribe for information regarding Carley's status, she reminded them of their obligation to provide case planning for the welfare of the child. The Tribal Business Committee manager responded that the case had been dismissed because the child no longer lived in the state. Incidentally, it was noted that Tracy Faulkner did not work there anymore.

Our attorney then drafted our Petition for Visitation and Summons notices for Mara and Walter Wall.

We filed in Camas County on April 24th. In mid-May, a friend spotted Mara and Buck's trailer at a park in Doolin. We immediately hired someone to locate them and serve them the summons. Days later, a Doolin lawyer notified Jason that he had been retained as their attorney. At the end of June, on the last allowable day before our petition would be heard and probably granted by default, their attorney filed their response.

*   *   *

I asked Spencer, "How do you think they can afford to pay Richard Hill? Isn't he a big name in Doolin?"

We were having another dinnertime discussion; it was the only time we seemed to have with nothing else going on. Though the case was never far from our minds, we had to wait until we were both focused enough to talk without losing control.

Spencer answered, "Hill's been around a long time. I think Buck knows him from when he had his garage and Hill's clients used Buck as their mechanic. Hill probably doesn't realize yet that he won't be getting paid. They'll skip out on it like they do everything else."

We had found the Walls' bankruptcy case when we researched their legal history. They had several claims against them from local merchants and providers.

"I don't see how they get away with it. Why does everyone find it so easy to feel sorry for them?"

"Hopefully not everyone," Spencer said. "It's just that they've got the victim act down pat. Mara goes into her *oh-poor-me* baby voice, and Buck plays the Southern-hick that's been taken advantage of by over-privileged upper classes like us."

"I wonder if Kim fed them that bullshit. We don't live in an extravagant home, we both have to work, and there's nothing fancy about our lifestyle. How could they think we had money?"

"It doesn't matter. They see only what they want to see. And they get saps like Richard Hill and Nina Cowan and ego-maniacs like Tracy Faulkner to see it too. No one's looking at the facts, the real circumstances that Carley was handed. Then there are chicken-shits like Williams," Spencer said the judge's name with disgust, letting his anger show. "He didn't look at the facts of the case. He saw the word 'Indian' and he fell all over himself handing it to them on a silver platter."

Tisha, who had been listening silently while she ate, spoke abruptly, "It's not fair. You guys can give Carley a better home. It shouldn't matter that she's Indian, for whatever tiny amount she is, anyway. It should've been obvious to the judge."

The irony of her words hit me. When she'd come to us ten years ago, a brown-skinned little girl with a joyous laugh, she didn't know her biological parents and her only family was a sister who tortured her. She'd put her trust in us, and I lived with the doubt of whether we deserved it.

Her graduation was only two weeks away, and she would soon be moving to Camas City where she got a job at a Dairy Queen, the only work she could find. We knew she would need our help, financially and emotionally, for a long while. But we hadn't thought how Kim's departure had completely affected Tisha. Certainly the impact on all of our lives was devastating, but her whole world had been broken apart. She'd lost the one and only relative she'd known since birth.

Spencer calmed himself and said, "I know. But that's the way civil cases are sometimes. No one wins, both sides lose something. No one walks away happy."

"We'll get a better judge this time," I told Tisha.

"We don't know that for sure," Spencer cautioned. "There's four on the circuit and the lawyer said it's still months away so there's no way of knowing who'll we'll get. But she says Williams will more than likely be out of it."

"Months?" I couldn't imagine it.

*   *   *

There would be twenty legal filings before we got to court. What I hadn't known about civil cases was that they get pushed aside for criminal cases. That meant the schedules for available circuit court

96

judges and for attorneys on both sides got juggled. Every changed circumstance meant a new filing. We had consultations and wrote affidavits. We read drafts and signed sworn statements. The ICWA whiz who had been representing us begged off due to her other commitments and we filed a notice of substitution to go back to Jason. Petitions were amended, motions entered; hearings were scheduled and cancelled four times. We had to borrow money to handle the financial costs, but the mental anguish of waiting was the hardest strain.

CHAPTER 21

On Friday, November 3, 1995, we went to court again. We were infuriated that asking for Grandparent Visitation was our only option, but we accepted it. The possibility of living without any contact with Carley at all was a frightening reality.

The sitting judge that day was Circuit Court Judge David Harmon, who, we were told, had a long-standing reputation for being fair and decent in both criminal and civil courts. We felt good about our chances of getting everything we asked for, which was, "reasonable rights of visitation of Carley Wall, and an order directing Mara Wall and Walter "Buck" Wall to provide the location of Carley Wall to allow visitation."

The small courtroom was cold, even though I could hear a humming sound that could've been a heating system. I looked behind me to see that, except for two spectators who I didn't know, all were there to testify in our case. Jason Norden had summoned four of our good friends who were more than happy to testify as witnesses for us. Tisha was with us again, having been given the day off from her new situation with the Job Corps. She sat with George and Lou, close friends of a generation older than us and were grandparental towards Tisha. Front row center was Anna, neighbor and confidant who had been with us from the beginning. Next to her sat Bill, who worked with Spencer and had said he thought we were good people and he wanted to help. I smiled back at everybody; they radiated encouragement.

Kim was there, on the other side of the courtroom, sitting with Dewayne. They looked uncomfortable, twisting hands and hats. Kim bounced her legs continuously, making her head bob. And the Walls, who were the "Respondents," sat at the opposite end from us at the front table. Mara glared at me ineffectively. Buck was looking at some papers with a confused expression.

Ours was the first case of the morning and Judge Harmon entered right on schedule.

"Be seated, please." His voice was solid and loud. I could tell he was much bigger than Judge Williams, despite the black robes. His black-streaked, silver hair had the same boyish cut, but his face had a more outdoorsy color than Williams'.

Jason opened by stating our case simply with a brief history of events. In their attorney's opening remarks, Richard Hill said that since we had ostracized Kim and we were the cause of the disruption in Carley's life, we didn't deserve to have our case heard. He also tried to establish that jurisdiction was still in Oklahoma, and although he wasn't representing the parents, they still needed to be officially notified of the hearing, which they weren't.

There was a moment that I thought Harmon could dismiss the case. After all, nothing much had gone right for us yet. Then the judge asked "Mr. Norton" to call his first witness. It was a slightly comic relief in an otherwise anxious setting. I looked to see Spencer hide his smile, and Jason sighed as he heard his name mispronounced again.

Jason called Kim first. It was strange to see her; she was thin and pale, jutting her clenched jaw out like an indignant child. She had not spoken to us or even looked at us when we had crossed paths outside the courtroom, and now she kept her angry eyes on Jason. He asked her where she'd lived and how long in each place. It was evident that she'd been in constant contact with the Walls, in places impossible for us to reach.

The only other evidence Jason wanted from Kim was her admissions that she wrote the letter saying she did not want us to have visitation, and that she'd relinquished custody of Carley to Mara and Buck.

Kim's testimony under Mr. Hill's cross-examination was more telling. He began by asking her what prompted her to deny us visitation, and she said it started with a phone call.

"I called them and said, 'Hello, Dad, this is Kim,' and he said, 'How did you get this phone number? Who are you?'"

"What did you say?" Hill asked.

"I said, 'This is your daughter,' and he said, 'My daughter's upstairs.' He refused to acknowledge that he knew me."

"Had your parents had contact with you and with Carley up until that phone call?"

"Yes."

He paused before continuing, "So, let me get this straight. Since birth, they'd been having contact with Carley. Where were you living when she was born?"

"In Camas City," Kim replied.

"What was their reaction to the announcement that you were pregnant?"

Jason stood. "Objection, your honor. That's hearsay."

"I'll allow it," Judge Harmon said after a slight hesitation.

Hill said to Kim, "Go ahead."

"They wanted me to get an abortion."

"Did they tell you why?"

"Because I was too young," she said.

"And you didn't want to."

"No, I did not."

"What happened when you told them that?"

"They just kept after me, telling me I should either get an abortion or put the child up for adoption."

I thought back to the discussions we'd had, knowing in my heart that we'd been compassionate with her. As painful as it had been, we told her we'd stand behind her. I remembered her telling me she that wanted to talk about adoption but Dewayne wouldn't let her. My hatred for the Walls swelled to the front of my mind as I listened to Kim's lies.

Hill asked, "How did you subsist when you lived in Camas City?"

"My parents and my boyfriend's parents agreed to share rent and utilities."

"So your parents did contribute?" Hill looked at her. Maybe he was beginning to see beneath the surface.

"Yes, and they took Carley sometimes." Kim hesitated, then added quickly, "But our relationship was shaky, as always."

Hill said, "Tell us what concerns you have now about your parents seeing your daughter."

Kim said, "I'm afraid that, because of the friction with my parents, Carley will think of us as bad people."

"What do you base that on?" Hill asked.

"The fact that I don't think I could sit in a room with them without getting in a fight," she said with more hostility. I knew this attitude. She was starting to pout.

"If you weren't around, though, what would be your concerns?" He seemed to be struggling for patience.

"I know they'd turn me into CSD for any little bruise or scratch if they had her. They'd always be looking for any excuse to turn me in for abuse," she said indignantly.

100

"Don't you think they have a right to look out for a child that might be in neglect?"

"Yes, but not to the point that...," she stopped. "Every child's gonna fall. Every child's gonna have their little accidents. And if I'm having to watch my back because my daughter's falling down, then I'd be so overprotective of Carley it wouldn't be good for her."

"Yeah, but you don't have your daughter right now. Correct?"

"Yeah, correct."

"So-o-o, I have to come back to it again. Is having the child in contact with your parents going to be detrimental in any way?"

She was still in a huff. "They'd do the same thing to Mara and Buck as they did to me."

I wasn't hurt by this presentation, because I'd gotten used to her poorly-acted displays of victimization. It was like watching a pampered first-grader.

Hill asked her, "Have your parents ever said anything to you that could be considered disparaging to Mr. and Mrs. Wall?"

She didn't have a lie ready. "No."

There was a brief pause before Hill asked her, "Why did you relinquish custody of Carley to the Walls?"

"We were thinking of doing it before," Kim said slowly, "before all this started."

"Wait. What do you mean by 'all this'?"

"It all started when CSD took her away."

"But CSD was involved before that. In what way?"

Kim went on to explain how Children's Services had tried to work with her and Dewayne. Kim told this part truthfully, having lost some of the edge to her tone.

"Why were you considering giving custody of your child to your boyfriend's parents at this time?"

"We couldn't give her what we wanted to, and we wanted to go away and get steady jobs so that we could give her what we felt she deserved."

"You were comfortable with the way Mara and Buck were interacting with your child."

"Yes."

"Had you talked with your parents about this idea?"

"Not yet."

Hill moved on to ask, "Why did you come back to Oregon?"

She said she'd tried to get into the Job Corps in Oklahoma but she needed to start the paperwork in Oregon and then transfer. This was news to us, and sounded false, an idea she'd no doubt picked up from Tisha's developments. When she told Hill that she wasn't sure how to reach us for her records, it was obviously phony. Her story was getting wrapped up in itself.

"When Carley was born, were your parents trying to build a better relationship with you?"

"I don't know if they were or not. All I know is they were always bugging me to give the baby up for adoption. I finally told them not to mention it again or they weren't allowed in my house."

"Did they want to adopt your child?"

"They were giving me names of other people that wanted to adopt."

This was so bogus that Spencer and I both reacted with a start. Hill quit at this point, and the judge asked "Mr. Norton" for redirect.

Jason said, "You indicated that you'd enter the Job Corps here?"

"Yes"

"What address?"

"Where I live now, in Doolin. I've been there about two weeks."

"I have nothing further, your Honor."

CHAPTER 22

Dewayne testified next for Jason, again to establish his and Kim's addresses. Under Hill's questioning, he said only that we were negative people, towards him and Kim, and he was afraid that we would "interact" (Hill's word) with Carley the same way. Hill asked him if we'd said anything negative directly to him about his parents, or about him. He said, "No." Before letting him go, Judge Harmon asked Dewayne about what kind of jobs he'd ever had and for how long. Dewayne revealed that the longest period of time he had held a job was three months.

Jason then called Buck, and established that they had been back in Oregon for over nine months, and that Buck had a job. He was working for a trucking outfit in Camas City, but planned on starting his own garage in Doolin. I thought Jason was getting this out to show two things: that the Walls did indeed live in Oregon so there were no jurisdiction issues; and that our visitation was not an impracticality.

"What concerns would you have if my clients were awarded Grandparent Visitation with Carley?" Jason asked him.

Buck had started nervously, but now he gathered strength. "I'm afraid they might take her and try to keep her again, like they did the last time," he said. "They'll try to turn us in to CSD, regardless of any proof."

I thought that sounded like a poor argument, and Hill's cross-examination didn't get anything more. I relaxed. So far, it didn't seem like the judge had heard much against us. Then Mara took the stand, and I expected things to change.

Jason first walked her through the time frames since they'd sold their home and left Doolin. She said they'd lived in a fifth-wheel trailer for eleven months, the three of them, and took their time traveling across the country and visiting in Oklahoma. Mara tried to exhibit her disdain for our attorney, by voice and expression, but his questions seemed so inconsequential that she was soon answering in a chatty tone. When he got around to what her concerns were about

103

us, she said they were the same as what had already been said. She added only that she was afraid we would tell "vicious lies" about her.

"I'm concerned about the rumors, personal stuff, that have been spread about me, about what I experienced as a child. I don't think, at this time, my granddaughter needs to be involved with people that are going to recite them."

Jason said he had no more questions, and Hill didn't want to cross. Mara smiled coyly at the judge as she left the stand.

Then it was our friends' turn to testify, each in their own way, that we were good parents and that we were doting grandparents. They had no concerns about us caring for our granddaughter. Richard Hill asked them about how we had treated Kim, in a failed effort to show that we'd abandoned her. Our oldest friend, Anna, was obviously disgusted with Hill's assertions. She made it clear to him that things were not the way he had presented them.

"They've tried everything to come to some sort of relationship with her and the baby. They advised her as parents of her choices and supported her once she'd made them. And it was Kim that stopped speaking to them, not the other way around," she said defiantly.

Tisha gave Jason much the same testimony, telling him that we were good parents and that Carley seemed real happy when she'd been with us before. He didn't ask her about our relationship with Kim, and Hill didn't have any questions for her.

Judge Harmon again wanted to ask some questions, like he had with Dewayne.

"How old are you?"

"Eighteen."

"You said you were in the Job Corps?" he asked.

"Yes, I just started at the camp near Cherry Valley," Tisha smiled at him. She was not at all nervous and answered clearly and politely.

"How do you like it?"

"It's good. I'm taking the secretary/receptionist course."

"Did you graduate from high school?"

"Yes."

"From where, Doolin?"

"No, in Belleville."

"Oh, that's right. Gold County. Well, thank you. You may step down."

I felt good about their exchange. If Judge Harmon was comparing Tisha's prospects to those of Dewayne's, our girl was miles ahead. She had applied for the Job Corps opportunity when she realized living on her own in Camas City was too much for her. We were proud that she'd taken her first steps toward independence and it seemed to be working.

Testimony continued with Spencer. Jason established that we had had no problems caring for Carley twenty months ago, and we were prepared to care for her again. Then he had Spencer explain how we had worked with CSD to help Kim and her boyfriend to be better parents. Spencer was confident and comfortable in comparison to the whiney and vindictive tone I thought the Walls and Kim had used.

Then Jason said, "Back up to the time when you first found out Kim was pregnant. Did you encourage Kim to have an abortion?"

"Early in the term, we said that would probably be best for Kim," Spencer answered with a straightforward manner. "She was too immature and not ready to be a parent."

"Kim McGhee testified that there was a telephone conversation in which you claimed not to know her. Did that conversation occur?"

"Yes, it did. It came one evening and when I answered the phone, Kim was telling me that they were being kicked out of their apartment and had back rent due. She said I was liable and had to pay their bills. She has a problem with multiple personalities, and I didn't recognize this personality because she was trying to pretend that nothing bad between us and our concerns about Carley had occurred."

"Did you ever contact CSD with your concerns about the way Kim and Dewayne were raising Carley?"

"I sure did."

"In March did you contact CSD?"

"No, not then," Spencer said simply.

"Prior to that time, did you contact CSD about Kim and Dewayne joining the carnival?"

"Yeah. When we'd heard that, and we weren't sure what they were going to do with Carley, I contacted their caseworker, Emily Sanchez."

"What sort of contact had you had with CSD before that?"

"We'd had two or three family meetings, and I'd found out what programs they had set out for them to follow as parents in order to keep custody of our granddaughter."

"Will your attitudes about Kim have any effect on your relationship with Carley?"

"None."

"How about your attitudes toward Mara, Walter and Dewayne Wall?"

"No."

"Are you going to attempt to get custody of Carley?"

Spencer hesitated slightly, "I don't think so. We're here to try to get visitation."

"If Carley's condition where she's living now were to deteriorate, would you attempt to get custody?"

Another hesitation, then he replied, "If custody were offered to us, I would accept it. I would not proactively try to get it."

"If granted visitation, would you return the child at the regular schedule?"

"Absolutely."

Jason ended by establishing that we'd lived at our current residence since 1975 and had no plans to move.

Then it was Hill's turn.

"Mr. McGhee, in trying to fashion an Order of Visitation, you're asking for two weekends a month. Would it have to be weekends?"

The question surprised me. Was he trying to show that, because we worked during the week, we wouldn't be reliable caregivers?

Spencer replied, "No." Good. Right answer, I thought.

"Since that March of 1994, the coming apart of things, have you had any contact with your daughter?"

"A brief phone conversation in April of '94, I think. I doubt she remembers it."

"Have you made any attempt to say 'hello' to her today?"

"No," he said with a certain sadness, "and the converse is true, as well."

"Would you like to say 'hello' to her right now?" Hill asked quickly.

Spencer surprised him with a quicker reply, "Sure. Move your head."

Hill turned around and saw that he was indeed blocking Spencer's view of Kim, and moved aside.

Spencer said brightly, "Hi, Kim."

I didn't hear Kim reply, and I didn't dare turn to look.

Hill then asked, "What would be your suggestion for how the child would be exchanged?"

I caught my breath. This had to mean that Richard Hill felt the Court would decide in our favor, that we would be granted visitation.

"Meet in a neutral place in Doolin," Spencer answered. Jason had told us that was what we should expect.

"What would be reasonable in reestablishing contact?"

"I didn't know there was an intermediate type of visitation." Spencer said evenly.

"Supposing that there is, are you adverse to a break-in period?"

"No."

"What do you think of the Walls' having Carley? Do you have concerns as to Carley's well-being while in their custody?"

"Well, I raised those concerns at last year's guardianship hearing. I have the same concerns: Multiple personalities concerns, responsibility concerns, upbringing concerns. I don't want Carley to turn out like Dewayne."

"Multiple personalities. That's in regard to the Walls?"

"Yes."

"Earlier in your testimony, I thought you referred to multiple personalities in regard to your daughter."

"Her, as well."

Hill was momentarily stunned. He didn't know about Mara's so-called diagnosis. Chalk it up as another thing your clients neglected to divulge, I wanted to tell him.

"You say, 'upbringing'. Does that mean you're not sure that they'll bring Carley up right?"

"I've seen the results, in Dewayne," Spencer said, "and I don't agree with his irresponsible life-style. And they're responsible for how he turned out."

"Does that mean that you're responsible for how Kim turned out?" Hill said dryly.

"Kim was adopted late in life; she was almost ten years old. I think a lot of her problems came from earlier places."

"So, if I'm hearing you right, you haven't changed in your opinion of the Walls. But you don't think that any of that is going to spill over in any of your interactions with Carley during your visitation. Right?"

"Correct."

After a glance at his notes, Hill told the judge he had no more questions. Before he let Spencer step down, Judge Harmon asked what he did for a living. He seemed satisfied when Spencer told him he was a remodeling contractor.

CHAPTER 23

Jason called me next. Guessing that Judge Harmon wanted to know what I also did for a living, Jason had me state my occupation along with my name and address. My voice came out stiffly, a little too curt, as I answered the first few questions. Then Jason asked me if Carley had been happy in our care. The memory of that time made me choke up.

"Yes, I think so. I recently looked at some photos taken then, when we had her for two or three days at a time." I hesitated, remembering one particular baby picture. She was laughing as Spencer kissed her tummy. "I'd like to get to know her again, and for her to get to know us."

He asked me to go back to the situation in March of '94.

I explained how Kim had been working with the CSD case-worker at the time. "I called her one day to see if we could get Carley for the weekend. She told me Carley was at Mara and Buck's, and that she planned on leaving her there. That's when she told me they planned on going out of town with the carnival. When I heard that, I called CSD to ask what to do. Then we got Carley for our weekend, as usual. We didn't know what was happening until Emily Sanchez phoned us and said that she'd gotten custody and would like to place her with us temporarily."

"What's your understanding of why she was then taken from you and placed with the Walls?"

I told about Tracy Faulkner and the Mukilki, and that we were told that CSD was required to do what the tribe asked.

"We took her to the office of Emily Sanchez on February 28th and that was the last time we saw her."

"Have you attempted to make contact in that time?"

"Yes. I did not call the Walls, because Mara Wall had phoned me after receiving that notice from CSD, threatened me and said not to ever step foot on her property. But you sent a letter requesting visitation, and it was denied."

He asked about my attitudes toward the Walls and Kim, whether it would effect the way I interacted with Carley. I said, "Of course not. I don't want a baby to have to figure that stuff out."

"If you noticed any problems with the way Carley was being raised, would you report them?"

"Yes, I would if they were serious. I'd probably call you first, or a doctor."

"If awarded visitation, would you adhere to an ordered schedule for returning Carley?"

"Yes."

Before Jason finished, he asked me to address the court with anything else I wanted to add. I wasn't prepared, but I knew there was more that Judge Harmon needed to hear. I turned to face him, and for the first time I noticed a dark wooden statuette of Blind Justice on the back of the bench between us. I'd never seen one up close, and I appreciated the detail, her delicate, blindfolded head, the dropped sword at her side and the raised balance in her left hand, the one closest to me.

With as much candor as I could, I said, "I'd like the Court to know that Spencer and I worked hard with Kim when she was younger, going to a family therapist, trying to get her to mature. When she was under eighteen and living with us, it was easier. She had some moments, when she blacked out, but she was working on that. When she moved out, which was her choice at eighteen, she didn't allow us to help her. Until she had Carley. Then we were allowed to help her with rent and she agreed with CSD that she'd get therapy with us. I thought that she was trying for a while."

I felt then that I must sound as self-pitying as Mara, so I added only, "I was disappointed."

Jason said he had no more questions, and Judge Harmon said, "Mr. Hill?"

I took a calming breath as Hill stood and walked towards me. I realized that he was at least a head taller than Jason, and his stiff posture and unyielding expression made me think of a heron.

He asked, "How do you envision your interaction with the Walls in regard to discussing Carley's needs? Are you and your husband able to do that?"

I thought a moment before I answered, "I'd like a third party present."

"Why is that?"

"There's a lack of trust, on both ends."

"In addition to your pain, which is very visible, are you hostile toward the Walls?"

"No."

"Has your attitude changed regarding the guardianship."

"No, my attitude hasn't changed."

At this point, Hill asked me to look at a copy of a document, which I recognized as the letter I'd written to Judge Williams the day we handed Carley over to Emily Sanchez, and I said so.

Minutes passed while Jason was given a chance to read the letter, the first he'd seen of it, and the judge received it as evidence.

"In that letter," Hill said to me, "are what I understand are some of the concerns you still have today. Isn't that true?"

"Yes."

"And that means that you're going to have some difficulty with the Walls in discussing Carley Wall's situation. Isn't that true?"

Very slowly, I responded, "It won't affect discussing things like caring, what she eats and how she sleeps, if that is what you mean."

"In part, yes. How will it affect it?"

"I feel like they're going to be looking for our accusations. They said as much. Therefore, to protect myself I want a third party there as a witness to all statements made when making the exchange."

That must not have been the response he was looking for because he hesitated, looking at his notes, before saying, "Do you think it's reasonable, assuming you have visitation, to simply start with a weekend, without a break-in period?"

I was certain then that we'd won, we'd get visitation, and I answered quickly.

"Yes."

"So you expect to go pick her up and take her back to your house and go from there?"

"Yes, with some introductions by somebody she trusts. I expect she'll be afraid of us."

He then went on to remind me that Kim would still get her visits with Carley, and I would have to be able to talk with her. I assured him I could.

Jason's only redirect was to ask whether I'd like a neutral place like the police department or a restaurant for the exchange.

"I guess," I said lightly. "I was kind of hoping the two attorneys would work that out." It felt fine to let it go at that.

CHAPTER 24

Richard Hill's first witness was Mara, and she let out a whimpering sigh as she took the stand again. Her sound seemed to make Hill flinch, but he quickly straightened and asked abruptly, "Before, when the Petitioners had Carley for weekends, how was information concerning her care dealt with?"

Mara said, "That was usually handled by Kim."

Hill said, "Tell us about your feelings towards the McGhees."

Mara spoke as if it hurt to draw breath. "I will not allow myself to be put in a situation where I have to relive pain that I've already worked through. And by them saying the things that they've said to family members, I won't live that again. So I avoid them. I have nothing against them. I won't take that hurt and that anger. And let it eat me up inside."

"So there needs to be something to cut down the animosity."

"I have no animosity."

"The animosity you feel from them. You want that diffused?"

"I would love that."

She went on to tell the court how well-adjusted Carley was, that Carley still knew who her mommy and daddy were and that she and Buck were Grandma and Grandpa. She said Carley was very verbal, but wouldn't grasp what they might tell her about who we were.

Hill asked her, "Do you anticipate problems if Petitioners were to have her overnight, if started right away?"

"Yes, I do"

She agreed with Hill that a mediator should be required before visitation.

In Jason's closing remarks, he pointed out that Grandparent Visitation was meant for exactly these types of situations, where parties don't get along and one family is denied. "There's been adequate testimony that my clients are perfectly capable of conducting themselves on visitation, and the child is happy when in their care. It's in the best interest of the child to have contact with both sets of grandparents.

"Regarding the jurisdictional issue, all parties are here, have been here for nine months, and my memorandum highlights will support that. Mara and Walter Wall are the custodians and they were served.

"We have no objection to having a counselor or mediator to sort out the problems for visitation. The Petitioners are asking for two weekends a month, plus some days at Christmas and extended days in summer."

In Richard Hill's closing remarks, he again said he didn't think we had jumped through the proper hoops to bring our case to this court, and that, as "discombobulated" as the parents were, they still needed representation.

Then he said, "If Petitioners are awarded visitation, there needs to be a mechanism for communication, and since parties can't afford group counseling, the Court has to look beyond just the details, for the best interest of the child. The Court doesn't have that experience, but should get direction from some kind of a study in this particular situation. There's the concern of harassment—and by all means, parties have a right to pursue legal options—there's the case of more than one person with multiple personalities, and there's the strong convictions of the Petitioners. Also, the Court has to consider the long term actions of the parents, who it seems will be staying in Oregon if Kim is pursuing the Job Corps, and the father, regardless of his ineptitude, still has visitation rights. That's all I have, your Honor."

To me, that had sounded like an insult to the judge. I glanced at Jason, who leaned over and cupped his hand to Spencer's ear. Spencer then leaned my way and whispered, "He says Harmon did not like that."

Judge Harmon didn't take long before responding, "Well, the Court is going to accept jurisdiction. The child's been here nine months. I don't have any problem with granting grandparent visitation."

Spencer and I both let out audible breaths. Harmon continued, "I can understand there are some hard feelings in this family. It's almost to the extent, well it is, dysfunctional. Probably each side rationalizes its position and has some basis for it. But the child's the one that's going to be suffering here. A child has a right to know and associate with not only its parents but its grandparents.

"The Court is going to order visitation on the first and third weekend of every month, commencing at 5:00 p.m. on Friday and over at 5:00 p.m. on Sunday. There will be two weeks in July. On alternating Christmases, Petitioners will have two days before

Christmas through Christmas Eve, and Christmas day through two days following.

"I don't think I'm in a position to have the coordinator of this be the police department. Do you gentlemen think you can resolve that between yourselves?"

Hill stood and spoke. "If I may, you Honor. You're asking that we have somebody be there…"

"I don't know… whatever's reasonable." He sounded exasperated. "You know, I think in time these people are going to be reasonable. It's going to become inconvenient to have to get this other party. After a while they're going to have to get along. Out of necessity. If you need something in the meantime to facilitate that, the Court will go along with it."

"If I may, I'm not tying to argue my position, but…"

"Well, I'm telling you that's the visitation."

"I understand, but I'm suggesting, to accommodate that order… where are we now?"

"We're on the first weekend."

"Okay. The order doesn't really go into effect until next weekend," Hill was keeping his cool manner, as if he were negotiating a deal.

Judge Harmon made it clear that there would be no negotiating. "It'll start today."

"I see. So you want the child turned over today?"

"Today," Harmon said. "This child's… what, two years old?"

"Correct," Hill said.

"Any problems they've had in the child not being able to know the Petitioners here have been created by Mr. and Mrs. Wall refusing them the right to even see the child."

"Granted. I'm not going to argue that," Hill said, still arguing. "I'm just trying to figure out how to make this transfer."

"And it's going to be a lot nicer for the child if you people," facing Hill's clients, "would turn to her and say, 'this is such-and-such, you're going to go stay with them for a couple of days.' The child's going to understand. You're going to smooth it out. If you have any *real* interest in the child, you're going to see to that."

Mara replied meekly, "Yes." Suddenly, Kim began sobbing loudly behind us. I wondered if it sounded as overdramatic to the rest of the courtroom as it did to me.

The judge continued, "Now, I'll also say this. And you can put this in the Order, Mr. Norton—you're going to prepare it. Neither grandparent is to say anything derogatory concerning the other

113

grandparent or the mother and father. There'll be no badmouthing anybody here. Because that is just going to harm that child and nobody's gonna gain a thing. I can't change your thinking but I can sure require that you not express those feelings in any way to the child.

"Okay, now what do you want to do about it?" he said to Hill.

Hill, who'd been standing stock-still, lips compressed and hands clasped behind him, spoke quietly, "I'd like to see you in Chambers, if I could, your Honor."

"Sure," Judge Harmon said brightly. He picked up his gavel and adjourned the court. We all rose as he stood and made his way for the door to his Chambers. Richard Hill and Jason followed him, both quickly gathering up their notes and briefcases as they moved.

PART FIVE—CHANGES

(November, 1995—April, 1996)

CHAPTER 25

Judge Harmon was right. We grew to hate the business of making sure there was a witness to our exchanges with the Walls. But we felt certain it was necessary. As spiteful as Buck and Mara were each time they handed Carley over to us, we knew it would be worse if we were left alone with them.

Attorney Richard Hill was wrong, though, despite his post-mandate urging in the judge's chambers. The first meeting with Carley, the day of the visitation hearing, was not distressful. At least not to her. We'd agreed to make the transfer in Hill's office, under the watchful eye of his secretary. Although Kim and Mara went through elaborate antics of voice and gestures to impress Carley with their anxiety, the secretary must've seen that this two-year-old was unfazed.

"Only two days," Kim held up two fingers in front of Carley's compliant, unconcerned face. "Okay? You go with this lady now, and Mommy and Grandma will be here to pick you up in two days."

I watched for signs of apprehension as I knelt to Carley's eye level and smiled at her. Her blue-gray eyes, identical to her mother's, followed my face as I said, "Hi, Carley. I'm your other grandmother. When you want, you can call me Grammy." She quickly reached out her hand to take mine, and that was that.

Hill didn't want us to continue meeting at his office, so we tried other locations, finally settling on a local coffee shop. Mara and Buck even hired a babysitter for a while, to take Carley to meet us at Mac's Cafe on Fridays, and pick her up on Sundays. We liked Diane Logan, and the arrangement was far less stressful for all parties, especially Carley. But the poor woman wouldn't last long because she told us it was a "ridiculous" situation. She would later agree to testify in our behalf at yet another hearing.

Being with our granddaughter again was like nothing we'd known before. We missed knowing our daughters when they were this age, a past I didn't dwell on. Caring for Carley as an infant had been a concentration of touch and sound; we had loved her with the senses we hoped she could remember. Toddler Carley's personality now showed itself with a will. We saw her emerge in postures and facial expression. Every moment fascinated us.

But weekends with Carley were a mixture of joy and despair. Lacking the benefit of decent communication with the baby's parents, like most grandparents have, we had to guess at how to meet her needs and give her comfort. What Mara did tell me made little sense; "Carley throws tantrums and should always be left alone to toss around," and "She *has* to watch 'Barney' at eight thirty," and "She needs nasal spray every morning and cough syrup for her bad cough." We took the nearly empty bottle Mara gave us in the overnight bag that reeked of cigarettes, and noticed that it was five percent alcohol. That explained why it was so hard to wake Carley when we got home each Friday with her.

Mara didn't send any diapers, and had said to take Carley to the potty every half-hour, another direction we ignored. Spencer and I didn't know what Mara did at her house when Carley refused to go to the potty, but we tried to deal calmly with the accidents as they happened. Carley always got angry when she had to leave the action to go with me to the bathroom, and seemed disgusted with her dirty pants. On the first episodes of cleaning her up, Carley turned her backside to me, bent clear over her spread legs and touched her head to the floor. I told her that wasn't necessary, that I could wipe her bottom while she was standing, but I couldn't persuade her. And while giving her a bath, Carley shocked me by gesturing with her fingers that I should wash her genitals.

Carley's peculiar reactions were adding up to a gut-level worry for us. I started keeping a journal again, documenting the little things that bothered us but we hoped were nothing. Once while drying her, I saw marks on her bottom, a healing scratch and a two-inch long welt. I called Spencer in and he had me distract her so that he could take a surreptitious photo. She never minded him helping with her bath or toilet, but one time he accidentally let her see him come out of the bathroom with a bath towel wrapped around him. She ran to hide behind me and cried, "Papa," which we knew was how she referred to her other grandpa.

Changing her clothes for bedtime became more of an ordeal after the first weekend. After too many struggles, we finally learned the best way to handle it was to tell her we would wait in the living room for her to bring us the pajamas. She'd soon come, and one of us would change her while the other read a bedtime story. The routine suited us all.

Since the spare bedrooms of our house were upstairs, we made a bed for Carley in our room downstairs. On the second weekend with us, Spencer woke up to find her standing next to his side with her head on the bed. He asked her if she wanted to get in with us. She did, and then she lay there several minutes staring at the ceiling. We were wondering if we did the right thing when she gave a startled cry, pointed to the other end of the room and said, "Mama." She'd done this in the daytime, too, and we knew that that was what she called Mara. Again I told her there was no Mama here, just her Grammy and Granddaddy, which seemed to satisfy her. Carley cuddled my hand and quickly fell asleep while I assured her that we would always be there for her.

Her toys were kept in the cabinet under the window seat in our room, and on visitation Fridays we noticed that she'd head there as soon as we walked in the door. She wouldn't play with anything right away, she just checked them. Then she hugged Susan the basset hound, then Taffy the cat, and wandered around as if inventorying all things familiar. These small gestures were the moments that gratified us, that showed us we were doing okay. We couldn't control how Mara and Buck were raising her, but if nothing else, we could provide Carley with a sense of stability.

On Sundays, before taking her back to Doolin, she helped us put her new clothes and toys away. When we told her she could wear the new hat that we gave her, she said, "No," and deliberately placed it on the hook by the door, as she'd seen Spencer do with his.

CHAPTER 26

For the time being, we did nothing about the apprehension we felt. At the end of November, Richard Hill called Jason to cancel our third court-ordered weekend. Hill said the Walls had told him that Carley was too sick. Our attorney asked for a doctor's order and added that Carley would be better off at our house where there was no cigarette smoke. We got a faxed note from the doctor's office saying that Carley was being treated for bronchitis and an ear infection, and we had to give up our weekend. As a safeguard against future interruptions, Spencer went to the doctor's office and explained the contentiousness of the situation and gave him a copy of the Visitation Order. The doctor listened to our concerns about the cough syrup they gave her and about the atmosphere of cigarette smoke. He agreed it was harmful but, since we weren't the guardians, we could do nothing.

We continued to make the exchange with the babysitter, Diane, for the next two months without incident. Diane would repeat without conviction the instructions she'd been given by Mara about the various over-the-counter medications that came with the smelly bag. We had relayed the message that the Walls didn't have to send anything, that we had appropriate clothing at our place, but they continued to pack it and Carley toted it, along with the stuffed puppy her mommy had given her, to every visitation.

The prize we got for suffering the Walls' enmity was every precious moment we got to be grandparents, the role we were learning from our fat-cheeked, towheaded tot. We loved introducing Carley to our world, visiting friends, opening presents, going on daytrips and taking a pile of pictures. Everything was a silly game for Spencer and Carley, even doing the chores, and he was a goofy comic for his adoring audience. Like her mother, she matched his sense of humor and they could tease each other endlessly. I couldn't keep up with them, but I never tired of watching.

When Carley started calling Spencer a garbled form of "Daddy," we tried stressing the word "Grand," but "Da-ee" was all she repeated. (Much later, it would evolve into "Gran'daddy" for Spencer and "Gran'mommy" for me.) It appeared that Kim was still in her life, though we had no communication from her, because Carley would say "Ghimm" when we pointed to Kim's picture on the wall. When I asked her if she liked her mommy Kim, she said, "Yes, Ghimm good." I repeated that Kim was her "Mommy," and she said, "Oh." We were relieved when Mara and Buck eventually became "Gramma" and "Grampa" instead of "Mama" and "Papa." Somehow, Carley worked things out.

The visitation terms for this first year gave us the two days before Christmas; we had to deliver Carley to the Walls on Christmas Eve. So our holiday traditions started two days early and we packed everything we could into them. Tisha came home and we proceeded to teach Carley how to celebrate.

The previous visit, we had gone to the U-pick Christmas tree farm and Carley got to help her Gran'daddy saw a six-footer. We gave her an ornament with her name on it and she put it on the tree herself. The night before our Christmas morning, we told her about leaving cookies for Santa and how he'd stuff our stockings after she went to sleep. We stayed up late putting a tricycle together and put it under the tree. In the morning, we explained again about Santa Clause; she caught on and told us, "Sanny Caws is good." She was slow and meticulous about opening presents, loving to help Gran'daddy cut the ribbons with toy scissors, and she tried out each new toy before going on. Friends and family had sent gifts of toys and hand-made clothes, and we got out photo albums to show her who this new family was.

The next day, we managed to get some turkey dinner into her before a long afternoon nap. Then she agreeably put toys away under the window seat and we drove her back to Doolin. We got enthusiastic hugs, promises to see each other in two weeks, then she trooped off with the babysitter.

Our weekends with her became more comfortable. Carley became more affectionate, and would smile and run to us when we met her and Diane at the coffee shop. Her bedtime routine got easier, and if she did wake up in the middle of the night, there wasn't any of the confusion or distress that we'd seen before. Although her potty-training didn't seem to be improving, we found the pull-up disposable diapers were the best compromise.

In late January, we noticed a yellow bruise on the side of her forehead. It was very visible when her hair was wet during her bath.

"Ooo, Sweetie, that's a nasty bruise. How did you get that?" I asked.

She did not respond. Later, while visiting at our friend Lou's house, Lou asked her if she had taken a fall. Carley didn't say anything but put on a serious look. Lou and I began talking again, then Carley said very distinctly, "Mama beat me," and motioned with her hand to her backside.

I asked her plainly, "Did Mama spank you?"

She said, "Mama spank me. Mama hit me."

It startled us because it was so clear, so serious. I told her that she wasn't a bad girl and that no one should hit her ever.

"If that ever happens again, you should tell me. Okay? Do you understand?"

Carley nodded and said, "Okay."

On Monday, Spencer sent a fax to our lawyer and I phoned Children's Services, relating the facts about the bruise and Carley's remarks. The screener asked me a few questions and told me to continue logging notes in my diary. She would staff the case.

CHAPTER 27

Journal entry: 2/3/96—Saturday

Spencer picked Carley up and I got home about a half hour later. Carley was happy and excited, and ran out to greet me with a hug. The evening was lots of fun. We read bedtime stories and she slept well.

She did have a scratch on the front of her forehead that was healing. When I asked her if it hurt, she said, "It hurt." Then I asked if she had fallen, and she said, "I fall down," so I realized she was probably just mimicking me and I quit trying. She seems healthy, except for a redness on her bottom and she let me put Neosporin on it.

2/4—Sunday

The potty-training went much better. She let us take her to the bathroom when we suggested it, and had only one accident all weekend.

We stopped at George and Lou's again before taking Carley back, and Lou was impressed with Carley's ability with puzzles. Also, she thinks Carley's speech is getting better, but sometimes we're still called "Mah-ee" and "Da-ee," and the picture of her mommy on our wall is still "Ghimm."

2/12—Monday

Spencer got a call from someone connected with Children's Services today. He knew who it was, but she'd told him she needed to stay anonymous. She had a tip that allegations of sexual abuse had been reported by a doctor treating Carley, and they'd started an investigation. Spencer said his first reaction was to demand to know whether Carley was safely away from the Walls. The woman told him, "I heard it was you that is being accused." He said, "That's bullshit! We didn't even have Carley this weekend. We haven't seen

123

her in over a week." He couldn't get any more information. We have to wait till tomorrow to get hold of someone at CSD.

2/13—Tuesday

A call to our attorney's office told us he was on vacation. Both Spencer and I called CSD at different times during the day, but were told that we'd have to wait for Irma Pierce, the assigned caseworker, and she was at the Wall's to see Carley today.

Spencer is trying hard to keep calm. There isn't anything else we can do.

2/14—Wednesday

Spencer finally got to talk to Irma Pierce, and followed up with a faxed letter. He told me he tried to be respectful on the phone, but she didn't respond. He told her that we were scared for Carley's safety with the Walls, considering their history, and that we requested that she be placed in protective custody. Also, he wanted clarification regarding our visitation for this weekend. We have an appointment to see Irma tomorrow.

2/15—Thursday

Irma is a middle-aged woman with a weak voice, has trouble looking you in the eye and says, "Uhh," a lot. She didn't ask us anything, wouldn't answer our questions, so we tried to give her as much information as we could in thirty minutes. We said we would cooperate every step of the way and we wanted CSD to get to the bottom of whatever happened to Carley. We tried to get her to see that there was something terribly wrong, and couldn't they get Carley some help? She said she could tell from her visit that Carley had a "bond" with Mara and Buck and wasn't in any danger from them. It was clear that Irma believed Spencer to be the abuser.

She handed us a hand-written note stating that our visitation for the weekend was suspended.

*   *   *

Letter to Nina Cowan, Director, Camas Co. CSD, 2/17/96:
Ms. Cowan:

For the second time, we ask you to give your attention to our granddaughter's welfare. Irma Pierce is the caseworker, and by the time you get this letter the case will be over a week old.

124

The situation is this: an investigation of sexual abuse has been initiated on the reference of a medical doctor. The family that has physical custody of Carley since placed there by your agency in February, 1994, has accused us. We have accused them.

We encourage a full investigation of all parties with urgency. Our cooperation with the investigating officer is assured. We've talked on the phone and in a meeting with Ms. Pierce and offered as much information as we could. Yet our pleas for the agency to place Carley in protective custody were ignored.

From an impartial perspective, consider the possibility that we are innocent. That would mean you have left Carley with people that have physically hurt her and taught her to say that her granddaddy did it.

Your agency has failed to help this child since we first alerted you to her situation two years ago. Her parents, when faced with the care-program CSD presented to them, could not be prevented from handing her off to her paternal grandparents. One man's voice chose that home for her and CSD followed his order, solely because he had the job title of ICWA Specialist.

More than a year and a half later, we had the first opportunity to request court-ordered visitation, and it was granted. Our responsibility to our daughter's daughter is stronger than ever. The responsibility of your agency to serve the welfare of the child is ineffective. Please don't let her down again. Place her immediately with a protective family that will allow her to feel safe from confusion and manipulation.

*   *   *

Journal entry: 2/19/94—Monday

We were told that Detective Brady in Gold County was assigned to investigate. Spencer called the sheriff's office and requested he meet with us and our attorney. I called the Women's Crisis Center and told them my fears for Carley and that the Walls might just take off. The screener phoned me back later and said all she could do was leave a message on Irma's voicemail. Spencer went to see the Doolin Police chief, and was told that no one in their department had been notified, which is not how things are supposed to go.

2/21—Wednesday

Jason got back from vacation and we told him everything we'd tried, all the communications we'd had. He advised us to not provide any information, written or verbal, to anyone from the State Office, the sheriff's office or anyone else without talking to him first.

He did say it was all right to call the Doolin Police and ask for a welfare check on Carley because we were so worried about her. The officer there agreed. She called us back and said Carley wasn't there, that she'd been removed from the home by Children's Services.

2/27—Tuesday

In his office, Jason swore with frustration at Cowan's handling of the case and her delay in getting Carley away from Mara. He has no doubts that Mara devised the whole thing, noting that the doctor's visit came less than two weeks after we'd given them our July visitation plans. It helped to hear him get as mad as we were, but he did caution us that we'd have to go easy because he didn't trust Cowan. The agency could take serious actions against Spencer. We left with his assurance that he'd keep following up with all parties and let us know.

There's not much to feel good about.

CHAPTER 28

We sat facing each other at the myrtlewood bar that separated
the kitchen and living room, our usual after-work arrangement.

"God, I'm tired," I said. My eyes were fixed on my beer glass but
I didn't reach for it.

"Yeah. Me too." Spencer sounded mad. I looked up just as he
stood. He went to the refrigerator and got out a Pepsi, drank and
stayed standing.

Finally, he said, "I talked to Jason today. He said the only thing
we can do is file for contempt of court against the Walls for denying
our visitations."

"We have to go to court again? How long will that take?"

"He doesn't know. Depends on how backed up things are;
family court cases get bumped for criminal cases. He said it could be
a few months."

"Jesus Christ! What are we supposed to do meanwhile? Just sit
tight and wait? What about what they've done to her? Somebody in
that household's hurt her, and all we can do is..."

"Don't yell at me about it," Spencer snapped back.

I remained sitting, watching as he turned away from me and
stared out the kitchen window. He took another drink, set the can on
the counter and turned. Quietly he said, "It's just the way it is."

"I know. I'm sorry." I stood and went to hug him. We stayed
holding each other for a moment, then sat again.

Spencer said, "Jason said the best course of action is to send the
Walls a letter requesting they communicate with him or he will bring
contempt proceedings against them. He's also going to send a letter
to Detective Brady to try to find out where the investigation of
sexual abuse is going, and to urge him to get the State Police
involved so that they can schedule a medical exam with the
pediatrician that works these cases."

"Who's that?" I asked.

"A specialized doctor in Camas City. Evidently there's only one
and she has to be directed by the State Police to examine a suspected

127

victim. We don't know if Carley's been sexually molested, because whatever that doctor in Doolin said, he's no expert. If there's any physical sign of abuse, we'll go after the Walls and try to show that Carley was in their care when it happened."

My head ached, and I realized that I had been clenching my jaws. I took a drink of beer.

"Shit!" My voice was loud again. "No one cares that it's still abuse even if there isn't any physical molestation? That Mara is teaching Carley what it is? What words to say?" I put my head in my hands, looking down at the bar.

Spencer sat across from me and said softly, "We can't know what they've done if we can't see her. And we can't see her unless we get them to court. Let Jason do it the legal way. We haven't done anything wrong and an investigation will show that, and maybe show those idiot authorities that the Walls shouldn't have had custody in the first place."

I started to cry. Spencer pulled my hands down and held them lovingly. "It's just going to take time, and we have to hang on."

"I know," I said. I was starting to cry hard, but first managed to say clearly, "I hate them so much."

"Yeah. Me too."

*   *   *

Spencer kept up the communication with our lawyer, which slightly eased our feelings of helplessness. His faxed notes explained how we wanted to demand that the Sheriff's investigation focus on the Walls. Then, Spencer directed, he wanted Jason to go after the agency. A sense of relief that Carley was safely away from Mara and Buck gave us energy to take the offensive. We wondered if we could mount a civil case against Cowan for mishandling things. We wanted the Doolin doctor to be held accountable. And most of all, we wanted Mara and Buck in jail.

But our fears resurfaced. What if CSD botched the investigation? They were working with agency offices from two counties, under-qualified caseworkers and budget restraints. The one person who knew the most about all of us, Emily Sanchez, was barred from this case by Cowan, who had a grudge against Spencer for accusing her of kowtowing to the tribe two years ago. If Cowan didn't get evidence to put the blame on him, would she do anything at all to help Carley?

Understanding the seriousness and complications of sexual abuse of a child this young became clearer after talking to our

128

nephew, a pediatrician. He told us that the initial report from a general practitioner had little bearing. Even he, a practicing pediatrician, might not be able to determine whether a two-year-old girl had been sexually abused. It had already been three weeks and Carley had not been seen by a qualified doctor, nor had she received any specialized counseling. We implored Jason to force CSD to get it done. We hadn't forgotten that a similar, inconclusive case of sexual abuse had been recorded about her mother as a young child. Kim hadn't received any early intervention therapy either.

For days, we heard nothing. Then we got another call from our confidential insider. Carley had been placed with relatives of Mara's, a family that had previously lost custody of a child through CSD's intercession, and had an adult daughter with a drug problem living there. Mara had volunteered this arrangement, and Irma Pierce agreed with it to keep her from making more trouble. It wasn't protective custody; Mara was still calling the shots and the agency had just ducked the issue. This family, our informer said, was complaining about the unlimited, unannounced visits by the Walls, especially Mara. They said that Carley got very upset after her visits and cried for hours.

The other alarming news was that CSD had interviewed Carley and tried to video-tape it, but something had gone wrong and so the interview was conducted again.

"Jason was absolutely livid when I repeated that bit of information," Spencer told me when I got home. Since I couldn't make these kinds of phone calls from my office, he did most of the communicating. Some days, there was nothing to tell. This day, Spencer was anxious to talk.

"He said he hasn't gotten one word from Detective Brady, who must've been the one doing the interview," Spencer said angrily.

"What did she say in the interview?" I asked.

"We don't get to know. At least not unless I'm officially charged and I get to face my accusers."

We went silent. By now I was used to the moods changing abruptly during our evening conversations.

Spencer picked it up. "The Walls hired Richard Hill again. They must've paid him something for the last hearing, surprisingly. And we got notice in the mail today. A hearing was scheduled by Judge Williams for May 6th."

"Almost two more months," I sighed. "Of this. And then what? If we win, we go back to what we had before, not knowing what they did to her?"

Spencer was energetic again. "I want to sue CSD. I want them to know how they screwed up Carley's chances to make it through life unscathed, emotionally and now physically."

"I don't know," I said. "That might just make them build up their defenses. They're a bureaucracy. Don't you think they have the legal resources to insulate themselves? Then people like Cowan get even more isolated from the kids they're supposed to be helping."

"Do you think she's going to do anything good without a kick in the ass?"

"I don't know. Maybe we should try to work with her a little more."

Spencer made a noise of exasperation.

"Did you ask Jason about me getting a supervised visit with Carley? Will CSD allow it?" I asked.

"He'll contact them. He doesn't want us to talk to them directly, but he doesn't think they'll object. As long as I don't see her."

Again, we were silent.

CHAPTER 29

I'm going to read this before Spencer gets home. I need to get through it. When Jason told us he'd send it, I thought it'd be good to finally get some information; now I'm not so sure.

Transcription from tape recorded Deposition in the Matter of Visitation of Carley Wall, a minor:

MR. NORDEN: This is time set for deposition of Walter Wall and Mara Wall in Circuit Court Case No. 95CN1512. Today's date is April 26, 1996.

In preliminary discussions with Mr. Hill, the Wall's attorney, we have agreed to waive the formalities and to reserve all objections for the time of the trial. Do you have any preliminary matters you want to put on the tape?

God, I hate this. I'm repulsed. My guts hurt, and I can't unclench my jaw. I picture the conference room in Jason's office, the recorder and microphone, and file folders on the table. I can see them sitting there, three against one.

MR. HILL: No.

MR. NORDEN: Then I will proceed with my questioning. Do you have a preference as to which one goes first? It doesn't matter to me.

Can't he be more aggressive? Don't be polite to these people! They don't deserve any courtesies.

MR. HILL: It doesn't make any difference to me.

MR. NORDEN: Okay. I'll start with Mara. Could you please state your name for the record?

MS. WALL: Mara Rose Wall.

MR. NORDEN: And what is your age?

MS. WALL: My age is 42—43, excuse me.

MR. HILL: Don't you want to swear her in?

Oh no, Jason, what are you doing? You can't be nervous?! This arrogant son of a bitch is making you look bungling. Oh please, don't let that be what's happening.

MR. NORDEN: Oh, okay. Yes. To back up, you're going to be giving sworn testimony here. I am a notary and I will swear you in.

Do you, Mara Rose Wall, solemnly swear that today's testimony is the truth, the whole truth and…

I envision her sanctimonious face, staring into Jason's with what she imagines are innocent eyes, so angelic, so full of crap. I wonder if there was a Bible.

Q. Ms. Wall, are you currently employed?

A. No, I'm not.

Q. How long have you been unemployed?

A. It's been four years.

Q. How long have you had Carley Rebecca Wall?

A. Since the age of either four or five months.

Q. And how old is she now?

A. She's two and a half.

Q. So you've had her about two years—a little over two years? And Carley Wall is your granddaughter, is that correct?

A. That's correct.

Q. Do you have any court orders granting you legal custody of Carley Wall?

A. Yes, I do. From the Court of Oklahoma.

Q. Can you tell me where you've lived during the time you've had Carley?

A. When Carley was first brought to us, we lived in Doolin. Then I took her back to Oklahoma to visit, then to live there for a while, to help get custody through the tribe, which we did proceed to do.

Q. When did you leave Oklahoma?

A. Uh, February, of 1995.

Q. And where did you travel to?

A. The upper United States for about a month, and then back to Doolin.

Q. What addresses in Doolin?

A. At first, at an RV park. Then I stayed with an elderly lady from our church, the Pentecostal, because she needed someone to keep an eye on her, make sure she was eating, taking her medicines.

This is news to me. Must've been a freebie until they found a house. I don't see anything relevant here, except that she, Carley and Buck were living there in a dinky fifth-wheel trailer for seven months. In addition to the year of living in it before that. Sounds real healthy. Then here she says Dewayne lived on the same property, in another trailer, at the same time. No mention of Kim. And here it goes on to say Dewayne stayed with them sometimes after they bought their house. Nothing else, until here…

Q. Who has been responsible for taking care of Carley?

132

A. I'm her primary caretaker.

Q. Is there anybody else that feeds her, bathes her or changes her clothes?

A. Um, Mr. Wall would feed her if I'm not there. But all the other, basically, I do.

Q. Does Mr. Wall ever bathe the child, or change the child's clothes?

A. He has in the past, but she's pretty much to the point where she can do it herself.

That's wrong. Of course she needs help; she's only two and a half.

Q. Is there anybody else that you can think of that has bathed, fed or changed her clothes?

A. Yes. My sister, Christine Lane.

Q. And what has she done specifically with Carley?

A. Took care of Carley for me, for almost a month and a half, following your clients' accusations.

Q. Which accusations are you talking about?

A. That the molestation took place in our home, not in theirs.

Q. You said that Carley has been attending Diane's Day Care on weekdays. Has that been fairly consistent?

A. There was a period when Christine had her that she didn't want to go there. Diane said Carley wasn't doing well at day care.

Q. What did Diane say about that?

A. That Carley didn't really want to participate in activities, and she seemed real emotional. She started wetting her pants and messing in them.

Q. Was this before you became aware of sexual molestation of Carley?

A. No, this is after, when Christine had her.

Q. Did Carley exhibit any of these behaviors prior to the time she went to live with Christine?

A. Um, maybe a few times after your clients' visitation.

Mara, you're such a phony. Nail her, Jason. You've got to get somewhere with this.

Q. Aside from what we've already discussed, has Carley exhibited any unusual behavior within the last six months?

A. Yes, she has.

I wonder what tone of voice Mara says this in. I picture her sitting straight up, jutting her breasts out like she does. When she's trying to look smart, she tosses her wavy, brown hair back and turns her pug face upward. Her plan is in motion.

Q. What sort of behaviors, and when did she exhibit them?

133

A. After, uh, the first of February when Carley came home from visitation. She had never been frightened of taking baths or having her clothes taken off of her. And this time she was very fearful.

Q. What specific changes in behavior have you seen within the last six months?

A. She has a great need right now to be assured that she is loved. She expresses that over and over…

Here we go. The rehearsed speech.

…and we're just now getting her to realize that she wasn't naughty or bad. She tells us all the time that she is a bad girl. She has difficulty sleeping. Only in the last two weeks, I'd say, have we finally got her to go back to her bed. She has nightmares.

So, Carley is back with them, not at the relative's place. Spencer said he thought he saw Kim and Dewayne buying diapers at Safeway. Which means Carley's potty-training is still screwed up. What she must be going through, with all of them there.

Q. Does the child act strange around anyone, as far as you've observed?

A. She is frightened of men when we take her out—men that look somewhat like your client.

Q. You indicated she's been having nightmares for the last six months. Has she told you what any of these nightmares were about?

A. I'm not sure we're speaking of six months. I believe we're speaking of approximately the first of February.

Q. Okay.

A. No. She doesn't really put a lot of things in words. You can gather a lot from her crying in her sleep—screaming out, "Don't hurt me. Don't hurt me. That hurts. Stop."

Sure. And you can gather a lot from watching this shit on soap operas, Mara.

Q. Okay. Has Carley discussed with you any specific incidents of sexual contact?

A. On the first weekend of February, speaking of a man hurting her.

Q. Is that as specific as she was?

A. At that time, yes.

Q. And this was how long after the visitation with Mr. McGhee?

A. She basically tried to tell me Sunday night, but I wasn't sure exactly what she was saying. She specifically told me a man hurt her, Tuesday morning.

Q. Tuesday morning—

A. Excuse me, Monday morning. Correction.

134

Mara's tripping herself up. And she says, "a man." She doesn't know that Carley calls Spencer "Da-ee."

Q. Monday morning, immediately following the visitation?

A. Yes, when I was trying to put her into her bath. She was crying and very upset, didn't want me to take off her nightclothes.

Q. Did you discuss this any further with Carley at that time?

A. Yes. I asked her what man hurt her.

Q. What was Carley's response?

A. "The man." And at that time I asked her, did her papa hurt her? And she said, "No." I said, "Did your daddy hurt you?" "No." "Did your Uncle Tim hurt you?" "No." I said, "Carley, what man?" And I was just—And then she told me where he hurt her.

Q. Was that the same day?

A. Yes. She said the man hurt her "popo."

Q. What did she mean by her "popo?"

A. Training Carley to use the toilet, I give her body organs names so that I could tell her and teach her to wipe herself. Her popo is her, um, vagina—that area. Then she started crying and grabbing between her legs and showing me.

Q. And what did you do at that time?

A. I told her Grandma needed to look to see if she had on "owie" down there.

Q. And did you inspect her vagina?

A. It took me about fifteen minutes for her to permit me to take her pajamas off.

Q. Okay. Go on.

A. At that time, I laid her down and looked to see if she had a rash or any indication of a problem down there.

Q. And did you see any indication of any problems?

A. She was very red around the vagina area.

Q. Was there any rash, or bruising?

A. Not that I could detect.

Q. Was there any bleeding?

A. Not at that time.

Q. Have you discussed this matter with the child any further?

A. No. I was really set back by what she told me. I just didn't know what to do or how to deal with it. I didn't know how to tell her mommy and her daddy and her papa. I needed to find out what man. That was my need at that time.

Q. I just need to clarify this. This incident, where you discussed this with Carley and inspected her, occurred on the Monday immediately following visitation in early February?

135

A. Yes.

Q. Have there been any other incidents that Carley has brought to your attention, or you've been made aware of in any way, involving sexual abuse of Carley?

A. No.

Q. Did you take the child to a doctor specifically relating to this incident?

A. Yes. Doctor Smith, in Doolin.

Q. When was that?

A. I believe it was on Wednesday.

Q. Did you discuss this with anybody between the time of the incident and the following Wednesday when you took her to the doctor?

A. After she had told her mommy and daddy, and her papa. I just said I didn't know what to do, and asked for their suggestion.

Q. So the child actually told her parents and Mr. Wall about the incident?

A. She has a picture book. Pardon me, a photo album. And basically what I did is give her the picture book, and she went and told them and pointed out the person that hurt her popo.

Q. And who did she point out?

A. Spencer McGhee.

Q. And who asked her the question? What was this in response to?

A. Carley loves for people to sit and look through her album with her. There was nothing—I just gave her the album and asked her to show her mommy and daddy. And she did, and when she came to his picture, she indicated in the same way that she did for me—by grabbing her crotch—that that was the man who hurt her popo. Not once, but several times throughout the pictures.

What pictures? This is incredible. Carley has never taken home any photographs of us. Where did Mara get these?

Q. Whose photographs are in the album?

A. There's her papa, some of me, there's some of her mommy and daddy, her cousin, her aunt, her uncle, and Mr. and Mrs. McGhee and some of their family members. Carley's mother had given pictures to her.

I get it now. What a con job, Mara. I only wonder if Kim is in on it. How else could she let this happen? How could she possibly hate us this much?

CHAPTER 30

(RECESS)

Mr. Norden: We're back on the record after a five minute break. I would like to remind the witnesses that they are still sworn, and I'll continue my questioning of Mara Wall.

If they can have a recess, I guess I can too. Only I needed more than five minutes. I wish Spencer was home. No. He'll need his own time to read this. It's going to hurt him more than anything. But we'll help each other. Right now I just have to get through it.

Q. You said you took the child, Carley Wall, to Dr. Smith on Wednesday. Did he give you an indication of what he found during that examination?

A. Yes, I was right there. He said that she'd been ruptured. There were all the indications of sexual abuse.

So it's not just a story. She physically did something to Carley, to make it look like...something. And then, what, force her to repeat the lines, the playacting? This woman's insane. To do this to a baby.

Q. Did the child make any statements to the doctor.

A. Yes. At that time Carley had her book and she also indicated in the same manner, pointing out the man and grabbing her crotch as she had indicated to us.

Q. Does Carley know Mr. McGhee's name?

A. I do not know what she calls him.

Q. So you're not aware of any specific name or reference that Carley uses to refer to Mr. McGhee?

A. No.

Q. What is the reason that you're denying visitation between Carley Wall and Mr. and Mrs. McGhee?

A. I am not denying that.

Q. Carley is in your physical custody. If Mr. McGhee were to ask you for visitation this weekend, would you allow it?

A. I would ask him to ask Irma Pierce.

Q. That is apparently the caseworker at CSD?

A. Yes, she is.

Q. CSD does not have any legal custody or placement of Carley. Is that your understanding?

A. I don't know that I'm following what you are saying.

Q. Has CSD, or Irma Pierce or any workers there, removed Carley from your physical custody?

A. Yes, they have. About the middle of February. To Christine Lane's home.

Q. Was that a voluntary removal on your part?

A. Yes, it was.

Q. To the best of your knowledge, there's no court order giving CSD jurisdiction over the child?

A. I'm not sure.

Q. Is there any particular reason why Spencer McGhee should not have visitation at this time?

A. Are you asking my opinion?

Q. Yes.

A. Yes, there is.

Q. Is that related to allegations of sexual abuse?

A. Yes, it is.

Q. Is there any reason that Mrs. McGhee should not have visitation with Carley at this time?

A. Yes, there is.

Q. And what's that reason?

A. Because I'm not sure that she didn't take part in it.

Q. Has Irma Pierce or anybody else from CSD given you direction to not allow visitation?

A. At the last time I spoke to her, Irma Pierce said that visitation should be going through her office.

Q. Did she indicate that they would step in and remove the child from your custody if you allowed a visitation?

A. No, they haven't.

Q. But it's your understanding that you are supposed to coordinate all visits between Mr. and Mrs. McGhee and Carley with CSD?

A. Yes.

Q. And not allow any visits without their approval?

A. Yes.

Q. What's CSD's current involvement in the case?

A. I'm not really sure. I know they're still active because of the allegations, and until the investigation is finished they will still be active in her case.

Q. And what worker specifically told you not to allow visitations?

A. None specifically told me.

Q. Okay. How did you come to the realization that CSD did not want these visitations to occur?

A. Um, I think it was through—Detective Brady said at this time there should not be any.

Q. The Gold County Sheriff's Deputy?

A. Yes.

My god, Jason must be pulling his hair out. What a mess. I can't tell if he's pinned her down or not. Mara's managed to blur the edges of all blame.

Q. Is the child currently in counseling?

A. Irma Pierce has set up counseling for her. She has not gone yet. We haven't been given any date.

Q. Has the child been examined by any other physician other than Dr. Smith?

A. Yes, the woman pediatrician in Camas City, Dr. Little.

Q. Did the child make any statements to Dr. Little concerning the sexual abuse?

A. I'm trying to think. She did tell her that the man hurt her popo, and Dr. Little told me that she needed to see. Carley told the doctor, "Don't hurt me. Don't hurt me," and, "No man." That was because the doctor's male associate was in the room with us. Afterward, she took Carley out of the examining room briefly.

Q. What discussion took place while you were there?

A. Basically that she had a tendency to believe what Carley was saying was true, because for a two and a half year old to lie about something this drastic would be nearly impossible. She also told me not to be upset if her examination—because it was a long time since the incident first happened—it could vary from Dr. Smith's report.

Q. You've indicated that the child has, on two or three occasions in your presence, said that the man hurt her. Has she ever given any other explanations other than those that you have explained to me?

A. Are you speaking about to other people? I'm not sure what you're asking.

Q. It's hard for me to think with these long questions. I'll start over, and I'll try to keep my questions short.

Great, Jason. I hope you're faking this just to put her off guard.

Q. Were there any other incidences, while you were present, that the child explained what happened?

A. One that I can recall was when Dr. Smith determined that Carley had been sexually abused, he sent us into the office of the woman who does the billing. Carley told her the same thing. The only other thing she indicated to her that was different was that there was a floor down here and a floor up there.

Q. I'm sorry. Where was that?

A. In the doctor's office.

I think I see what Mara's setting up here, but Jason doesn't understand. He doesn't know that our house has two floors and the doctor's office doesn't. Mara's coached Carley to say something happened upstairs.

Q. I'm going to go into some stuff here that is personal to you. It's stuff that we discussed at the last hearing. If you want to take a break or anything, that's fine. I'm not trying to prod you. I just want to get some answers. To be blunt, do you have multiple personalities?

A. I've been diagnosed with them, yes.

Q. How many personalities are you aware of?

A. Possibly seven.

Q. Do they have distinct names?

A. I've been told that, yes.

Q. Do you know the names of those personalities?

A. Um, not offhand, no.

Q. Are you aware of what each of those personalities is doing when your body is controlled by that personality?

A. Uh, basically, yes.

Q. Do you have periods where you don't recall? Blackout periods?

A. I used to. At counseling.

Q. Counseling would actually cause you to shift into a different personality?

A. Yes.

Q. Are you currently in counseling?

A. No, I'm not.

Q. Are there any situations aside from counseling that triggers a switch from one personality to another?

A. Um, not that I can tell, no.

Q. Do you know when the last time was that you shifted from one personality to another?

A. It's been three years.

Q. Are all of your different personalities female?

A. There's one male.

Q. One male?

A. Yes, there is.

Q. Are any of your other personalities violent?

A. No. I wouldn't say they were violent.

Q. Are any of your distinct personalities capable of sexual abuse of a child?

A. No.

I don't know what else you expected her to say, Jason. I guess you had to ask the question. But I wish you had tripped her up on her phony MPD diagnosis.

Mr. Norden: I believe that's all the questions that I have.

*   *   *

Mr. Hill: I have a couple.

Q. I think you've made it clear, Mara. All of Carley's behavior changes have happened after the February abuse incident. Is that right?

A. Yes.

Q. The denial of visitation, did you agree to that for what you thought was best for Carley? Is that really what motivated you?

A. Yes, it is.

Q. The discussions that Carley has had with you, you condensed some of the incidences in your answers today, didn't you? Wasn't it more drawn out than just an all-of-a-sudden conversation?

A. Yes, it was. It took approximately three days.

Three days of intensive brainwashing. Poor Carley, you sweet baby.

Q. During that three days, you observed some of these behavior changes, but you were uncertain as to what they meant?

A. That's correct.

Q. Might there have been some other people she talked to in your presence that you don't remember today?

A. Yes. There was Irma Pierce, too.

Q. Did Detective Brady talk to her?

A. He did talk to her, but not about this issue in my presence.

Mr. Hill: That's all.

*   *   *

Mr. Norden: Okay. I'd like to ask a couple more questions, to clarify.

Q. When Carley talked with Irma Pierce, was there anything in her relaying that story that was different from how she told it before or after?

A. Somewhat, maybe a little bit because she was not familiar with Irma. The other thing was that Irma had drawn a picture of a little girl, and was interested in knowing if Carley could point out the body part, to clarify what she meant by popo.

141

Q. But the substance of what she was saying was consistent with what she had said before?

A. Yes.

Mr. Norden: I have no further questions.

*   *   *

Mr. Hill: I need to talk to her for a minute.

What now? This is maddening. So they go off-record again and Jason leaves the room, assumingly so that Hill can prompt Mara with the proper answers to his next questions...

Q. The last thing I want to ask you, Mara, is when did your counseling end?

A. It was in June of 1993.

Q. Have you needed counseling since then?

A. No, I haven't.

What did he expect her say, yes I needed it but I didn't get it?

Q. You have had no incidences of multiple-type personalities since then?

A. No.

Q. And why are you not back in counseling?

A. Because my personalities have integrated. There is not any need for them anymore. I dealt with it. I realize that I was a victim then. I am not a victim now.

Q. Okay. Were you a victim of sexual abuse?

A. Yes, I was.

Mr. Hill: I have nothing further.

*   *   *

Mr. Norden: I have nothing more. I'd like to proceed with the deposition of Mr. Wall if he is prepared.

Mr. Hill: He is.

Prepared. Nice word these lawyers use. I can only hope that when we go to court, the judge can see through all this preparation.

Q. Could you state your name?

A. Walter Buck Wall. I go by Buck.

Q. And what's your age and occupation?

A. Fifty-one. Mechanic.

Q. Do you work outside the home?

A. No. I have a shop at home, now.

Q. How much time do you spend with Carley, Mr. Wall?

A. I no more than step in the door and she's got me.

142

I can see his stupid, grinning face as Jason must have seen it—just a corn-fed country boy, innocent as a calf and as proud of this child as if he'd given her birth himself.

Q. Do you take care of providing for Carley's basic needs?

A. On occasionally. Like this morning, I got her breakfast.

Q. Do you change Carley's clothes?

A. I help with it, once in a while. She wants me to help her with the bathroom. Just help. Anything major, "Gramma, hurry."

He thinks he's funny, this is just a chat about his cute family.

Q. Do you ever bathe Carley?

A. No.

Q. When you spend time alone with Carley, what kinds of things do you do?

A. Oh, I take her down to Mac's for coffee. We go down and walk on the beach or walk to the park. I take her to the grocery store. I spoil her.

Q. You were present during the deposition of your wife. Other than the incidences she has described, are you aware of any others that involved Carley discussing an incidence of sexual abuse?

A. Yes.

Q. Okay. Can you describe that?

A. Well, when she told me, she showed me the picture album, and I was befuddled. I didn't know what to do. So, I took Carley and her book and went down to Hill's office. He wasn't there, so I just give the book to Hill's secretary and said, "Look at the album with her." She did, and then Carley was pointing out who this was and who that was. When she comes to Spencer's picture, same thing: "Man. Hurt my popo, bad." Every time she would come to Spencer's picture it was the same thing.

Well, I've been thinking. I didn't say anything. I just told them to look at the album with her. I stayed in the hallway. When Mr. Hill got there, he took Carley to his office, and she done exactly the same thing for him. I asked him, "What do I do?" He said, "Take her to the doctor." So that's what I done.

Q. Have you ever heard Carley give a different explanation of what happened?

A. No. It's been the same every time. It's almost carbon copy.

Much like a practiced nursery rhyme.

Q. Have you ever heard anyone coaching Carley about what to say about this incident?

A. No, I haven't.

Q. Have you dealt at all with Mr. and Mrs. McGhee regarding visitation?

A. No.

Q. Have you dealt at all with Diane Logan?

A. The day-care lady? Yes. I was paying her to be the advocate. I didn't want any part of the McGhees, so I had an advocate to do it for me.

Q. After the last visitation that the McGhees had with Carley, did you have any conversations with her at all?

A. No, I didn't.

Well, we're sure going to. Diane was the first person Carley saw after this horrible thing was supposed to have happened.

Q. Have you had any conversations with Irma Pierce or anyone else at CSD regarding visitations?

A. Yes, with Irma. I said, "It's just about time for their visitation. What do we do? If this did occur, we can't allow it to happen again." And she said there would not be any visitation. She told me that visitations were cancelled until the investigation is over.

Just like that.

PART SIX—RECOVERY

(May—December, 1996)

CHAPTER 31

It was another four months before we got to court. The original hearing date of May 6th was changed to August 12th, pending results, the judge said, of the open investigation. There would be two more continuances before the closing hearing, and the judge's findings, much later. Until then, we had to keep our frustrations in check.

We both had lost the privilege of being with Carley, but Spencer had the added, unimaginable anguish of being accused of molesting her. I knew he was seething, still he somehow maintained his control over the pain and anger he felt. Spencer had a natural acumen for grasping the bigger picture. His experience with legal work helped him focus his need for action on communicating. He wrote letters. He made phone calls to every level of every branch of the system that kept our granddaughter in danger. When polite talk failed to get responses, he yanked chains. The director of the Camas Branch of Children's Services, Nina Cowan, made herself a particularly hostile antagonist.

Cowan protected her throne by ardently defending the actions of her caseworker, Irma Pierce, meanwhile instructing Pierce to rescind the hastily written directive that had disallowed our visitation. Evidently, when we went over Cowan's head to Region Manager Jim Foster, someone checked their legal standing. They had none, which only made them pull their heads in further. Overall, Foster didn't do much besides getting his people to return our phone calls, which was an improvement, but there was no substance to their words. Nina Cowan explained to me by phone that she'd received legal advice that CSD was "not in a position to take protective custody of Carley, because that would again involve the tribe," an involvement Cowan saw as insurmountable. In response to questions, she said that Carley's original caseworker, Emily Sanchez, hadn't been taken off the case, just reassigned, and that their findings of sexual molestation were justified by Carley's consistent statements, medical exams and Gold County's video-taped interview. I was told that the attorneys should work things out.

147

Our attorney was indeed working. His first letter to Irma Pierce, immediately following the accusation, countered that it was the Walls that imposed a threat to Carley. It included the history of the Walls' manipulations and copies of their police incidents. For several months, he continued to hound the agency, the Walls' attorney, and Gold County's investigative team in an attempt to nail down the blame for the violation of our visitation rights.

My energies were first directed towards trying to get to see Carley. I was told by Irma Pierce that my request for a supervised visit was "not consistent with normal procedures." This was in the same conversation that she admitted that the Lanes, Carley's temporary placement family, had complained about Mara bothering them with unannounced visits. But, she told me, she "took care of that," which explained how Carley ended up back in Mara's home.

After many attempts to schedule an arrangement for Carley and me, all thwarted by the Walls, I finally persuaded Jim Foster to intervene. On May 23rd, he allowed me, "only as a favor," an hour with her and an agency worker in a room at their office. I knew in advance that there was a one-way mirror in the room and I could bring a friend with a video camera. Buck and Mara Wall had to wait in the lobby. My friend, Anna, was on the other side of that mirror taping our playtime.

Carley was at first timid, nervously watching the young woman who had escorted her into the room. I was nervous, too, wanting so much to let Carley know how we still loved her, but afraid of her reactions. After all, it had been almost four months since she'd seen us. That was why I wanted the videotape, so there could be no accusations later.

I was so happy to see her that I cooed like I was talking to a baby, and soon she returned my smiles. I had brought with me a toy I hoped would be familiar, a "nest" of farm animals that we'd given her for Christmas. We shook the big plastic cow so that the smaller animals inside rattled. Carley kept looking over her shoulder at the CSD worker, as if we were breaking a rule making all that racket, and beamed at me when I shook it even harder. I'd also brought a photo album, an idea of Spencer's. Carley sat on my lap as we turned the pages. I was careful to keep the tone happy and watched for any sign of distress when she saw his picture. She was fine. The talking was mostly mine, but I managed to get some comprehensible, playful words out of her. One word she said clearly as she pointed to a photo of herself and Spencer in our front yard: "Home."

Then it was over. What did it accomplish? She knew we were still there. I made her laugh. I got a hug. It had to do.

*   *   *

Spencer and I kept trying, kept searching for ways to get the truth out. With the help of small-town connections, we tracked down Diane Logan, the intermediary to whom we had given Carley at the end of our last visitation. We found out that Diane had just moved to eastern Oregon, but we finally reached her by phone. She said she didn't think she'd be able to help us, but was surprised that she hadn't been questioned at all by the authorities. Mara had called her the Monday or Tuesday after that last weekend. Mara wanted her to come over and "see signs of abuse on Carley," but she refused, suggesting a doctor instead. Diane told us she didn't believe at the time that the abuser could've been Spencer, because of the way Carley always looked forward to going with us. In fact, Carley had been "stand-offish" towards Diane on that particular occasion, not wanting to say good-bye to Spencer. Diane said we could give her name and number to our lawyer, that he could get her testimony if it would help.

It was easy to keep an eye on the activity at the Wall house because it was on the main road I used on my way to work. Only once did I spot Carley, standing at the window looking out. Buck was moving vehicles around in the driveway. At one time they had a sedan, a pick-up, a boat and a small RV. I started worrying when the vehicles began to disappear. At first, I saw Buck working on them in the garage, then they were gone. We knew Buck had worked with a local car dealer before, in his capacity as a mechanic, and it occurred to us that Mara and Buck could be collecting ready cash. Now, flight risk was a new concern.

On May 31st, we got the only good news we'd had in four months. Our attorney told Spencer to stop by his office on the way home from work; Jason had gotten a message from the Gold County District Attorney. With no information of what actually occurred, Spencer was now told that they were no longer investigating him for the sexual abuse of his granddaughter.

CHAPTER 32

Letter to Jim Foster, Region Manager, CSD, 6/2/96:

Mr. Foster:

It has been four months since our court-awarded visitation with our granddaughter was denied, and we have nothing in writing that justifies it. CSD is seemingly able to walk away claiming no responsibility.

Since February 14th, we have, or our lawyer has, contacted the agency at least fifteen separate times. The first returned call from the caseworker was May 3rd, in which she said to send her our list of unanswered questions. I've enclosed the list of those still unanswered questions, dated May 16th.

My supervised visit with Carley took place on May 23rd. The CSD worker present witnessed Carley and me looking at photos taken of her weekends with us, including shots with Spencer, who she calls "Da-ee." I'd be interested in seeing that worker's report because it was clear that we had fun together and that Carley misses us.

We've been told that Gold County is not pursuing the investigation. What now? We were told in April that there was a pending investigation, and therefore we were forced to ask for a continuance of our May 6th contempt hearing. Now we have to wait till August to have a judge hear the issues of our denied rights.

Meanwhile, what is happening to Carley? Enough time has passed for the system to do whatever it is supposed to do to protect her. We feel now more than ever that Carley is not safe from abuse in the Walls' house.

Enc.: questions to Irma Pierce from Jason Norden

1. Why was Carley Wall not taken into protective custody?

2. What are the dates that Carley was placed out of the Walls' home?

3. Has the child been involved in therapy? If not, why not?

4. What is the nature and extent of CSD's involvement with the child? With the investigation?

5. Has anyone from CSD spoken with Diane Logan or with other references given to you by the McGhees? If not, why not?

*   *   *

Journal entry: 6/11/96–Tuesday

We got a fax from Irma today, addressing the questions Jason sent to her. The call Spencer made to the boss in Salem probably helped to push buttons. The fax just said that she thought she'd answered the questions on the phone, and I should send them again. She noted that they don't conduct investigations; their "job is to assess the safety of the child."

Last week Spencer wrote a good letter to Jim Foster, CSD Region Manager, reminding him of the sequence of events and our reaction. Spencer gave him the main points of the research he'd done on child sexual abuse:

* Studies show a child can believe a new "reality" if so trained through repetition.

* A child who doesn't yet have the ability to express themselves understands only that repetition of a story is pleasing.

* Theorizing about how a "normal child" behaves doesn't apply to Carley because of her abnormal childhood, as asserted and backed up by Emily Sanchez's files.

* The recurring point in all studies is that sexual abusers have been abused themselves; not an issue in our lives, but is in Mara's and probably in Dewayne's.

* The motivation is usually gratification. Our marriage is strong and healthy, Mara and Buck were seeking divorce when Kim got pregnant.

He reminded Foster that the workings of the system have rewarded the Walls with exactly what they wanted—cessation of our contact with Carley. He pointed out that Nina Cowan and Irma react with personal prejudices that keep them from looking at real issues and from accepting information from other caseworkers. And Cowan's threat of tribal ICWA involvement is unlikely because, 1)Tracy Faulkner was terminated, and 2)a recent ICWA case in California supported our case for guardianship.

6/13—Thursday

Foster called today. I told him I was concerned about Carley's mental health (due to the agency's actions and the delay in getting her counseling). He admitted the cyclical nature of sociopathic

151

behavior, and he must be nervous because he promised he'd look further into the assessment.

I wrote to Irma, sending her the phone number of Diane Logan, and George and Lou, the people we'd given as references because they saw Carley with Spencer right before he returned her on February 4th. None of them have been questioned yet. I asked Irma when was the last time anyone saw Carley and how did she know Carley "continued to thrive," as she put in her fax. I asked her to quit "advising" the Walls to deny our visits, and that we'd be disputing her actions in court.

6/21—Friday

I decided today to just go to Mara's front door at five and ask to have Carley for the weekend visitation. At the door, I saw that Kim and Dewayne were there; Mara wouldn't let me see Carley. As I was leaving, a police car was approaching so I went back and talked to the officer. He asked me to wait, then went inside for 20 minutes. He saw Carley sleeping and said she was fine. He told me what his report would say. Mara had called him because I was trespassing. I told him my version, that Mara was refusing our legal right of visitation. Mara had showed him the court order, as well as her guardianship papers. She told him about the abuse investigation and showed him doctors' letters (one stating damage to Carley's hymen and the other stating no abnormalities). She said CSD advised to deny visitation, then showed him the letter rescinding that recommendation.

He said it appeared to him that I had a legal right, but no crime had been committed because Mara was not refusing visitation "long term." She had said that she wanted arrangements for supervision during the investigation. I told him I would welcome supervised visitations, but their lawyer hasn't cooperated. He did say he would give his report to the chief and to the district attorney.

8/1—Thursday

The last few weeks, Jason has sent us copies of everything, including court filings, subpoenas, and letters to and from Richard Hill. Hill's responses angered me the most, not only by ignoring Jason's demands for visitations, but he actually accused us of cruelty. He wrote that Jason's motions were out of line. Attorneys being what they are, Jason told me, Hill was all right, just doing his job for his clients.

8/8—Thursday

Cowan finally put something in writing, but there's so much bureaucrat*ese* in her letter that it's hard to find the point. Basically she said that, at her request, assessment was continued after an initial disposition was founded. Whatever that means.

The good part is, "As a result of more comprehensive review of this case, I have agreed that the disposition shall be changed from valid to unable to determine."

Then she states that although it's apparent Carley was sexually victimized, they are unable to determine how or by whom. The only hint of responsibility was, "This agency supports Carley's participation in continued counseling and we encourage both sets of grandparents to work together on their granddaughter's behalf."

CHAPTER 33

Jason called us into the conference room of his office where the video camera was set up.

"This may be hard for you to watch, because it's definitely strange, but I don't want the courtroom to be the first place you see it. Let's just, well, watch it and then we'll go over my notes and you can give me anything else you want to add."

Spencer and I positioned ourselves to face the television, note-paper and pen on the table in front of us.

Jason talked as he inserted the videotape. "This is the only tape the D.A. sent me, but I understand there were two. As you know, something went wrong with the first one—the audio wasn't working, apparently—so they did it twice, about a week apart."

Spencer let out a sharp laugh. "Yeah, that's terrific."

Jason brushed a hand through his surfer hair-do and shook his head. "I know, these guys are incredible. Detective Brady and the CSD director in Gold County," he looked at his notes, "uh, Eva Dillon, interviewed Carley March 4th. Then they discovered that the audio hadn't been turned on, so they interviewed her again, same questions I'm told, on March 11th."

"Oh, sure, just in case Carley didn't get her lines right the first time," Spencer said with the sarcasm he and Jason had in common.

With only days before our hearing, we were anxious and upbeat. We felt prepared for anything from the opposition. Jason assured us we had a good case, but he was pissed off about the state's slimy way of getting around normal legal procedures. We'd hoped to show how Emily Sanchez's assertions about the Walls had been overridden by Cowan, but Jason's motions to subpoena Nina Cowan, Emily and their records were quashed. Our case would have to be made by Diane Logan's phoned-in testimony in defense of Spencer, our own testimony, and the evidence of this slanted interview.

We saw Carley on the screen, looking tired and irritable, sitting at an office table with Brady, who we knew from newspaper photos, and a middle-aged woman with graying, unkempt hair.

154

"I guess that's Eva Dillon. She's the same rank as Nina Cowan, but it's a smaller office in Gold County and she does more case work than Cowan. Either that or she just wanted in on this because she hates Spencer, too," Jason glanced at Spencer to make sure he knew it was a joke.

"Doesn't everybody?" Spencer said. I was glad they were laughing, because it helped to view the tape from the perspective of its absurdity.

Brady had on a suit but there was no mistaking his clean-cut cop demeanor. Carley eyed him with a grim look, while Ms. Dillon talked in an awkward tone, obviously having difficulty making a two-year-old comfortable.

"She's as bad as Irma. Where do they get these people?" I asked. "These are professionals? Supposedly work with children everyday, and they act like they never talk to kids."

"Maybe it's her first time in front of a camera," Jason said, "but it gets worse. Watch."

The two adults took turns asking Carley questions, having her identify the people in the photo album in front of them, which we couldn't make out. Carley's undeveloped speech must have made it hard for Dillon to understand her, because she kept leaning towards Carley and trying to repeat what she heard. I understood the words, "other daddy," and "mommy too." Carley got more agitated and clambered up on the table on hands and knees, pointing at different pages of the book. Brady occasionally reached in and marked something with his pen. At one point, Carley softly mumbled something as she tucked her head and looked down.

Dillon asked Brady, "What was that last word?"

Brady said, "She said, 'popo, that man hurt my popo.'"

Seeing Carley's anguish made me cringe, and I looked over at Spencer to see how he was taking it. He sat motionless, then quietly said, "That's shame. She's ashamed of herself for lying."

"Yep," Jason said.

They were right. The language Carley's little body put across—the drawn in shoulders and tucked chin, the furtive glances at her questioners—this was the posture of a child who thought she was doing something wrong.

Carley had grown quiet and rubbed her dark-rimmed eyes. Dillon tried to make light of the moment and handed Carley a little stuffed bear. She took it and glanced up at Dillon without expression.

"Carley looks disgusted with these idiots, doesn't she?" Spencer remarked.

"Poor baby. She's so worn out," I said.

"This is the second time she's been through it with them," Jason said, "not to mention all the other times she's had to give the same speech. Dillon wrote in her report that they used anatomically correct male and female pictures when they did the first interview, had her point to the right body parts. They didn't bother with them this time because Carley's obviously tired of it all."

The tape ended and both of us blew our breaths out. Spencer put his hand on my back as we looked at the blank notepaper on the table.

Jason sat down across from us. "I wouldn't worry about this. I think this is, in fact, a great piece of evidence for us to show as a whole screwed up mess. It shows exactly what we've been saying all along... Mara contrived the whole thing, and CSD blew it."

*   *   *

On August 12th, we went to court. The worst thing about the hearing was the waiting. Out in the hallway, while we waited for our case to come up, both sides had to coexist. It was getting easier to ignore Mara and Buck but Kim and Dewayne were also there. Kim glared at us and I tried not to look back. I had to pretend she was someone else, not our daughter. I saw that their witnesses included Dr. Smith, Detective Brady and the CSD people, Irma Pierce and Eva Dillon.

I whispered to Spencer, "I can't get over that they took these guys from their jobs for a contempt of court hearing."

"That's because they all think I did it, but they don't have decent evidence. This is exciting for them because if the judge believes I'm guilty and we don't get our visitation back, they could justify re-opening the investigation."

"That's ridiculous. Why would we be the ones to file for contempt if we were the abusers? That doesn't make sense."

"Since when did sense have anything to do with anything?" he said with some humor, so at least he wasn't nervous.

I asked, "Who do you think is taking care of Carley?"

"Whoever it is, it's probably a good break from these people. I'm just glad that Hill told them not to bring her to the courtroom."

Once inside, the first thing Jason did was request that Judge David Harmon exclude witnesses from the courtroom until called. Everybody but Mara and Buck had to endure the hard chairs and the boredom out in the hall even longer. In deference to his age and his practice, Dr. Smith was allowed to testify first so that he could leave.

Although he was called by the opposition, I liked the doctor. He was using a cane and we had heard that he would be retiring soon, which was sad because he was the best doctor in town. On the witness stand, he read from his notes and told the court what we knew already about Mara bringing Carley into his office.

Then he added, "I suggested to Mrs. Wall that Carley should be examined by a pediatrician." No one had mentioned that before. I wanted someone to make Mara explain why she ignored his advice.

Under Jason's questioning about what Carley had said in his examining room, Dr. Smith said, "I don't have that in my notes. It's not usually what I consider relevant. If you get the confidence of a child, you can get the child to say whatever she thinks you want her to say." I felt like kissing his bald head for that.

Then Jason questioned Diane Logan on speaker-phone, a consideration given because she now lived in eastern Oregon. She said Carley hugged Spencer good-bye on that last day and didn't want to leave him. She added her opinion that she thought Carley was doing well with our influence, that her speech was much better since beginning visitations with us.

I almost felt sorry for the opposing witnesses out in the hallway when we were then adjourned for lunch. Spencer and I went to a nearby café with Jason, hoping none of them would go to the same place.

"If the Walls or the state guys come in, just be cool. They gotta eat and there's not that many places, so it's likely," Jason warned us.

"It's hard to see Kim, looking like she does, isn't it?" I said to Spencer.

"I think they both look stoned out of their heads," Spencer said.

"Did you notice, they disappeared for a while before our case came up?" Jason asked. "And they were wiping their noses a lot when they came back? I see that a lot in some of the criminal cases I do. The tension gets to them and they can't wait, so they go out to their cars to snort something."

"You're kidding," I said.

"It doesn't surprise me, about Kim and Dewayne," Spencer said. "Except how they afford it. Stealing, or dealing?"

I thought about this without comment, and considered how things might be better for Kim if she was caught.

*   *   *

157

The hearing continued with the playback of the taped interview. I watched Judge Harmon's face, a frown that gave the appearance of disapproval, but I couldn't say of what. Spencer and I both testified to the sequence of events on the last day we had Carley, and our efforts to push the investigation along.

On my turn, I tried to tell the judge how frustrated we had been when we were shut out.

"We wanted to get everything out, to find out what had happened to her. We went immediately to Irma Pierce and begged her to question us, to watch Carley interact with Spencer, to contact people that had seen them together on that last day. We tried to contact Detective Brady and have him investigate us. We said we'd take polygraphs. We wanted them to get to the bottom of it."

Judge Harmon stopped me. "Wait a minute. Did you say you and Mr. McGhee volunteered to take polygraph tests?"

"Yes." I looked straight at him.

"You volunteered this to the CSD workers, and no one took you up on it?"

"No, they didn't."

Harmon had a distinct look of incredulity on his face and, for the first time, I felt I knew what he was thinking.

There were few surprises from Richard Hill's witnesses. The two interviewers gave their credentials and how the taping of the interview came about. Neither had talked to Carley before the interview, and they both stuck to their belief that a child's consistent statement was contraindicative of coaching. Eva Dillon stated that a child that young cannot grasp such a complex scenario.

When the issue of the photo album came up, Jason asked Dillon, "What about adding pictures to a child's album, pictures that weren't there before, can that cause a strange reaction?"

Dillon answered, "It depends on the circumstances."

"What did you see in Carley's reaction?"

"Her body language was less than effervescent," Dillon said.

Jason said, "When Carley pointed out Mr. McGhee's photo, she looked down. Isn't that consistent with a child repeating something she knows is untrue?"

"I suppose that's possible."

Irma Pierce's testimony was a weakly given account of her "investigation." She looked even more timid when Jason's questioning revealed that she'd not seen the taped interview of Carley. Funny thing—the new caseworker who reassessed the determination of abuse to "unable to determine," had seen it. Jason asked her about the instruction she'd given the Walls to deny our visitations. He then got her to admit to canceling that direction, so he could put the blame back on Mara and Buck.

But when Mara was on the stand, she gave her performance of a naïve, small-town girl who didn't mean any harm.

"I never denied them their visitation rights, and I'm still not. I just said I'd do what CSD said I should, to protect Carley."

Spencer and I have never understood how she gets people to believe her act, but it happens time and time again. One of Hill's witnesses was a therapist who had just started seeing Carley, and she stated that she believed what Mara told her, and was very uncomfortable about us having unsupervised visits. No one seemed uncomfortable with the testimony that Carley's therapy session included Mara.

Most of Mara's and Buck's story matched their depositions, and Jason didn't make an issue of the small incongruities. I assumed he thought there was enough to make our case already. And Hill must have realized the risk of putting Kim and Dewayne on the stand because they weren't called. I remembered what Jason told us about judges not liking to be "beat over the head with evidence." Both closing statements were short.

Judge Harmon was quick with his decision. "I have trouble understanding, when Mr. and Mrs. McGhee volunteered to submit to polygraph tests in order to facilitate the investigation, why that wasn't done. Well, I will order it done. For Mr. McGhee and for Mara Wall. You both will take polygraphs and have those results sent to this Court within three weeks.

"I'm suspicious in cases like this. You've got motivation by the Walls. In my experience, kids can go over a picture book with repetition and mimic whatever you say. You can teach a kid to look at pictures and say different things. Let's see what the polygraphs indicate.

"And I see no reason that the petitioners shouldn't get to see their granddaughter. I will continue this case until the polygraph results are done, and until then I order interim visitation for the petitioners on Saturdays, from 8:00 a.m. to 5:00 p.m., beginning this Saturday."

CHAPTER 34

Journal entry: 8/31/96—Saturday

We picked Carley up at Mac's. She was delivered by Kim and Dewayne, who glared at us but at least they didn't appear to be high. Carley was wide-eyed and ready to go. Once we got her talking, she jabbered cheerfully as she hugged Susan in the back seat. We went to the beach. Letting Carley romp with *her* bassett hound was a good way to show her everything was back to normal. At home, we didn't let up for a moment. It was non-stop playing and when we took Carley back to Doolin, she was exhausted. I worried then that we had overdone it, because the Walls would bother her with questions instead of letting her sleep.

Tomorrow I'll make phone calls, telling all the family how things went, and what to expect next.

9/5—Thursday

Spencer took his polygraph today with a private investigator in Camas City. He said he thinks he did okay, but isn't sure because he doesn't know how these things usually go. I could tell that the stress wore him out; he went to bed early.

9/7—Saturday

We were at Mac's at nine this morning and no one came. So we went to the Walls' house, knocked on the door and told Mara we were there for Carley. Mara went crazy, shaking her head and saying, "No, no," over and over. Carley was on the couch staring at the TV, and didn't turn her head. Mara finally spit out that "the judge said every *other* Saturday," and we calmly told her she was wrong. She was incoherent as she shut the door on us, and I waved at Carley through the window before Mara sat on the couch to block my view. Carley hadn't moved her eyes from the TV. Since no one else appeared to be home, we were worried about Mara's mental state. We called Mara's daughter, who we knew worked at Safeway, and explained the situation, asking her to please check on Carley for us. We got a non-committal, "thanks." That's all we could do. We'll talk to Jason Monday.

9/9—Monday

We got a copy of the polygraph exam, which stated clearly that Spencer answered the questions truthfully (creepy ones about touching Carley sexually). Jason sent a copy to Hill, along with clarification regarding our Saturday visitation. He sent a copy to Judge Harmon too.

9/13—Friday

Jason told us today that Judge Harmon is on vacation, so the order that spells out our visitation won't be signed until next week. Nothing from Hill about Mara's examination yet.

*   *   *

Spencer and I tried to make the most of our Saturdays with Carley, but Mara and Buck, even their lawyer, did everything they could to break us down. Richard Hill didn't return Jason's phone calls, and his replies to letters were delayed and obnoxious. Because of the judge's two-week vacation in September, Hill said he didn't have to force Mara to give us visitations every Saturday; we didn't have it in writing. When we asked for special consideration for a weekend with Carley so that she could attend my mother's 75th birthday, Hill rejected it.

Meeting Mara and Buck at Mac's to make what we called "the exchange," became more and more traumatic. They always sat in a booth having breakfast with extended family members (never Kim and Dewayne) as if it were a party. We had to sit at the counter and wait for Carley to finish her sausage and pancakes while she sneaked smiles at us. Then there was a big show of kissing Gramma and Grampa good-bye and taking her by the hand to us, where Buck lectured us about the return time. Patrons and staff must've thought we were the evil step-family. At the end of the day, Carley became withdrawn when we told her we were heading back. She'd give us hugs outside the door of the restaurant, then rush to Buck's open arms and half-toothless grin when we went in.

Progress with the case dragged on for months. Every time we'd think there was a defining moment that no one could fail to recognize, another incredible failure of justice slapped us in the face.

Mara's first attempt to take a polygraph test failed because she had taken pain medicine for an injury she got from falling off her kitchen counter. That was September 24th. Since it had been longer than Judge Harmon's three-week deadline, Jason drafted a motion, *pendente lite*, for an order to resume our regular visitation schedule. This was something that, if Hill's clients agreed, would facilitate the judge's final determination at our next hearing. They didn't agree.

On October 8th, Jason called with the results of Mara's second polygraph attempt.

"The investigator said she was a strange person to run a test on," Jason told us. "The notable points were: she has had seven different personalities, one was a boy; her fingers quivered during the exam, and when asked why, she said the questions made her angry; there was a lot of movement during testing and he couldn't get a decent chart; the results are inconclusive. He said she is not a 'testable person.' Harmon will see this as confirmation that she's lying. I have no doubts."

Then Nina Cowan resurfaced to dampen our spirits. Jason received a copy of a letter she wrote to the judge, reporting a referral that alleged a new disclosure of sexual abuse. The report was from Carley's therapist, and this time both maternal grandparents were being accused. The therapist stated that because Carley wet her pants while playing with a therapy doll, she was exhibiting symptomatic behavior. Cowan's letter said that repetition of the same "popo" phrase clinched it for the therapist. The interesting part, Jason's digging later discovered, was that Mara was there when the "disclosure" was made.

Spencer immediately went to the county mental health office and demanded the director explain why Mara was allowed to control the counseling.

When he told me about it later, Spencer said, "That asshole is just another spineless wimp. He wouldn't respond. So I got about six inches from his face and told him, 'You and the idiot therapist treating Carley have both been played like cheap violins,' and I walked out."

Jason Norden also took the offense and fired off a three-page letter to Cowan, suggesting that she talk to the polygraph examiner. Maybe then she could see that "this is another blatant and obvious attempt by Mara Wall to prevent visitation between my clients and Carley." He told her it was inconceivable that Wall was allowed to be present during counseling sessions.

"It is our position that this child is clearly in danger being in the custody of Mara Wall. Ms. Wall has not passed a polygraph examination to determine whether she in fact sexually abused the child or whether she encouraged the child to falsely identify my client. The fact that Mr. McGhee has been excluded as a potential perpetrator should provide sufficient grounds for your agency to become involved in the protection of Carley from Mara Wall or those parties who Mara is failing to protect the child from. When you add Ms. Wall's admitted psychological problems, the contact of the child with the biological parents, the potential for manipulation of the child by Mara Wall, as evidenced by her presence during most of the investigation and counseling sessions, the fact that there is a contentious custody/visitation dispute occurring, and the fact that Ms. Wall is uncooperative with the court's orders, it is patently obvious that she is manipulating the child.

"The child should be removed from the current placement and taken into protective custody. There is adequate evidence to indicate that the child is not safe there. Mara Wall should not have custody until, at a minimum, she submits to a psychological test and that test is evaluated.

"It's time that the investigation point in the appropriate direction and that Carley be given the protection she deserves."

Copies went to Detective Brady and to Eva Dillon. To ensure that no one in the departmental team was left out, Spencer and I wrote to Cowan's boss, Jim Foster. He replied that he and Cowan weren't aware that Mara had been in the sessions with Carley but would now request that be discontinued. Secondly, he would request that the counseling increase to two or three times per week. And thirdly, he would have a CSD regional consultant review the case as an outside expert. He closed with the reminder that the agency did not have a legal basis to put Carley into protective custody.

Spencer got angrier with each communiqué. The natural flow of our complimentary emotions worked as they did when raising our problematic children; we took turns freaking out. Whenever one of us reacted strongly, with either anger or depression, the other remained calm. During this time, I tried to analyze the directions of the agency, to understand the binding laws and procedures. Spencer wrote the letters, and I edited with a more diplomatic touch. In this way, we drove home the point that we would not let the agency back out of their culpability in hurting Carley.

"Either the therapist is not reporting fully about what has been going on, or Ms. Cowan has not been supervising this case as closely as she should, or both," our letter read.

"And please explain to us, what does it take for a case to rise to the level where CSD can and will take legal action? How badly does our granddaughter have to be hurt before your agency 'protects' her?"

*   *   *

On November 20th, we returned to Judge Harmon's courtroom. It had taken three months for Mara and her attorney to attempt to satisfy Harmon's order to take a polygraph. Now the reports were on his bench.

"I've heard the testimony and received evidence, and I am ready to give my decision today regarding the petitioners' restricted visitation with the child. Mr. McGhee has taken and passed a polygraph examination indicating that he did not sexually abuse the child; Mrs. Wall has deliberately failed to comply with the order to complete an examination. I order visitation to resume as set forth in the grandparent visitation order entered on November 22, 1995, and the first visitation shall begin on November 22, 1996."

I looked over at Mara to see that she was shaking her head and rolling her eyes in disbelief.

"I also order the respondents to keep the child in counseling to deal with any traumas associated with any allegations of sexual abuse. None of the parties shall encourage the child or direct the child to say anything or to not say anything to the child's counselor.

"Mr. Norden, you will submit the order. You and Mr. Hill will submit further arguments regarding the contempt and payment of attorney fees. I'll review and find on those issues when we have a new hearing date."

*   *   *

The ensuing negotiations during the next few weeks were more than I could understand. In between our precious weekends with Carley, Spencer and Jason debated about how to proceed, assuming we'd win the contempt of court determination. Spencer wanted to ask for a continuous block of nine months of visitation to make up for the time we missed with Carley; Jason said no, we would come off as the spiteful people the Walls said we were. Spencer wanted to state our intention to seek supportive counseling, during any lengthy visitation, with a new counselor because of the poisoned atmosphere with the current one; Jason said it was more customary to ask for monetary damages.

In the end, our Requested Orders were that the respondents shall: pay attorney fees; be placed on conditional probation including the direction not to manipulate Carley to make false statements and a written apology from Mara; concede make-up visitation time equivalent to the number of days we'd lost; pay fines to defray court and agency costs. In addition, we asked for four extra hours of visitation per week to attend family counseling with Carley. Finally, Jason included the request for an order that Mara undergo psychological evaluation geared toward multiple personality disorder and toward sex offenders.

Jason's argument was a concise summary of the legal hoops we'd jumped through in the last year, and the obstacles placed in front of us by CSD and the Walls. He didn't hold back his own opinions that Mara, in particular, "intentionally, and without valid reason, withheld visitation," and had "given every indication that this contentiousness will continue. The horrifying thing is that there is physical evidence that the child was sexually abused. This could have only happened while the child was in the care of Mara Wall. Either she sexually abused the child or someone in her life was able to do so with or without her knowledge."

We believed we had made our case.

CHAPTER 35

"Hello?" I said into the receiver as I switched on the desk lamp.

"Hello." There was a long pause while I waited silently. She always said "hello" the same way, as if I should've expected her call. As if she hadn't been telling people she wished we weren't her parents. As if she hadn't said she never wanted us to see Carley again.

"It's me. Kim. Uh, is Dad there?"

"Well, yes, he's here but he's in bed. We were both asleep. It's after ten." I kept my voice neutral and mouthed her name to Spencer. He raised his eyebrows and sat up in bed.

"I wanted to ask him a legal question."

"What question?"

She went on in her maddeningly slow way, "Would you ask him if he... knows if... if the paper Dewayne and I signed in Oklahoma, giving guardianship to Mara and Buck, would be a...a major roadblock to me getting Carley back?"

"Okay, I'll ask him in the morning, but I'm pretty sure it's something that has to be argued in court. The paper you signed is one thing, but you stated to a judge that you agreed to relinquish custody. It was a legal proceeding, so to try to get her back you'd have to go to court." I looked at Spencer for a sign that he understood. He nodded, more in resignation than anything else, and got up to bring me my robe. Since he didn't go to the extension in the kitchen, I assumed he was okay with me continuing on my own.

"If you want, I'll ask our lawyer and get back to you," I told Kim, hoping she'd give us a way to keep in contact with her.

"The reason I'm worried is because of a recent conversation I had with Mara. I just don't know what to think. She's now telling me I can't have Carley back. She said something like, 'After all I've done for this child, you think I'm going to give her up?' It just really shocked me."

I heard Kim's words and felt like I was in a scene from a bizarre comedy, complete with laugh-track playing over my look of astonishment. "Well, Kim, that's what Mara had in mind all along. She wanted a baby of her own. I'm sorry." I wondered if she knew how much I meant that.

Kim said, more softly, "I just want Carley back. I'm worried about her being with them." I couldn't tell if she was crying, but I thought not.

"I know, Kim. But they have her and you can't just ask for her back. The biggest problem I think you'll have is your own ability to be a mother. You would have to prove that your lifestyle has changed, that you're stable and healthy."

"I am." Now her voice changed to a lighter, upbeat tone. "I have a good, supportive network of friends here. I've been working since September for this book-binding company and my boss and her husband are really nice to me," she said. "She told me that if I have to go get Carley, I should just go and they'd hold my job for me."

"Where? What town are you in?"

"Salt Lake City."

"Salt Lake City? How'd you end up there?" I glanced at Spencer. He looked back from the bed, still following the conversation.

"I came here with a girlfriend a few months ago. Dewayne and I weren't getting along, so he stayed in Doolin and I left. I get a week off in February and I want to take a bus back to see Carley. But my boss assures me that if I need to go before that, to get Carley back, my job will be saved for me."

Her stubborn determination was familiar to me. The ineffectiveness of it made me flash between anger and compassion.

"It's going to take time, Kim. Keep working and getting better. I'm glad you have people that want to help. Meanwhile, we're still battling to help Carley. We've got every other weekend with her and we can keep a closer check on any mistreatment by Mara."

"I'm worried about Buck, too," Kim said. "Last September when Dewayne and I were staying with Buck and Mara, we were fighting one night and I went down to the bar to calm down. I was playing pool with some friends and Buck came in and said Dewayne sent him to get me. On the way back to the house, Buck actually hit on me!"

"Buck did? He propositioned you while taking you back to Dewayne?"

"Yes. I told him he was disgusting and told him to fuck off."

"That's something that would be important for CSD to know. Are you willing to tell that in court?"

167

No answer. In a few seconds, I realized Kim's sense of reality would be a problem in any courtroom anyway.

"Kim, I'm sorry that happened. You probably have a lot of bad things like that in your head and they need to come out. Do you have a therapy group, or a counselor?" I was thinking she probably had a church group but didn't want to tell us. At least it would be better than nothing.

"No. I have a guy friend that's going through custody problems with his ex-wife, and he's been advising me."

"Okay, but please try to find someone to talk to, someone professional that knows how to help you. You can look in the yellow pages for counselors or legal aid for people with no money." I was choosing my words carefully, hesitant to push too hard for the therapy.

"How long does it take to stop adoption proceedings?" she asked, as if she hadn't heard what I'd said.

"I don't know. Why?" I rolled my eyes for Spencer's benefit. He nodded in comprehension. He knew she'd ignored my words.

"The Walls might be working on adopting, not just custody of Carley."

"Did they say something about adopting her?"

"No. I don't know. Before I left, Dewayne signed something that said they could adopt her."

She was faltering again. I waited a moment, then asked, "Did you sign something?"

"I might have. I don't remember now."

"Well, if you're not sure, why don't you write a letter now, saying you oppose adoption."

Spencer spoke up, "Get it notarized and send it to both lawyers."

"Spencer's awake. He says to get it notarized and send copies to Jason Norden and to Richard Hill." I gave her Jason's address.

"I already have Hill's," she said. "I wrote him and asked him for help."

"But his clients are the Walls. He won't do anything for you. But if he knows you're opposing their adopting Carley, he might not want to represent them."

I was drained. The room was cold and I wanted to get back in bed. This was hopeless anyway.

"Mom, I realize now that I made a lot of mistakes in the past two, three years. Starting with leaving you and Dad. I'm sorry."

"I know, sweetie. It's okay."

168

"I want to come talk to you."

"We'll talk in February. There's no hurry in coming to Oregon now. You just do what you have to do to show everyone that you're stable." I still didn't know if I was getting through to her. "We need to see who you are."

"Yeah. I understand. But I can prove I've changed. Since leaving the Walls and coming here, things seem clearer to me. I feel better. I even haven't had a cigarette in six days!"

"That's good. Keep it up, Kim." I wanted to mention therapy again, but knew I had to drop it.

"Well, I better go," she said slowly. "But one thing. Don't tell Mara that I'm talking to you again. I don't want her to know yet that I'm against her."

Poor Kim, still thinking she can out-manipulate Mara.

"Sure. I won't say anything. Can we phone you?"

"I'm using a friend's phone that I promised I'd pay back. I can't afford a phone yet."

"You could write us, and give me an address where I can write you?"

"I'm making good money now, though, and saving some," she continued, again like I hadn't said anything. "No matter what it takes, I'll pay it to get Carley back."

*   *   *

The decision from Judge Harmon came in the mail December 18th. Addressed to Jason Norden and to Richard Hill, it simply said, "Gentlemen, The Court has reviewed the arguments submitted in the above referenced matter.

"The Court has strong suspicions that the Respondents interfered with the Court ordered visitation, however, the Court cannot make a finding of contempt based on the facts submitted.

"No attorney fees are awarded to either party. Mr. Hill will submit the Order."

After Spencer showed it to me I asked, "What does that mean? He knows they interfered but they aren't responsible? I don't get it."

Spencer responded loudly, "He didn't want to go out on a limb, to say these poor, stupid bastards should be held accountable for their actions." He huffed a breath, calming himself. "I don't know. All it says is that we didn't make our case. Maybe I should've listened to Jason and not asked for everything." He was sitting and staring out the window at the dark yard.

"Are you all right?" I sat on the arm of the chair and put my arm around him.

"Yeah." Then he shook his head. "I don't know what to do. Where'd we go wrong?" He made fists with his hands and put them in his lap.

"We didn't. It didn't hurt anything to make the argument for more time with Carley, or any of the other things we asked for. Harmon knows we got screwed. He saw us in court and he saw the Walls. He's got to know our interest is in caring for Carley, not getting back at them."

I looked at the letter again. "I bet it's because of the interference from the state. CSD messed this thing up and the blame goes partly on them, not just the Walls. That's why Harmon won't agree with the contempt charge."

"So what now? Go after CSD?" Spencer asked.

"Yeah. I want to. Don't you?"

"It's going to cost a lot. We're already into Jason for I don't know how many thousand, and no money's coming from the Walls."

"I wonder how they pay Hill," I said, not for the first time.

"They don't. He'll figure it out soon." Spencer's mood was improving. He stood and went to the counter in the kitchen, where he got a pen and pad and began making notes.

"I'll tell Jason tomorrow to withdraw as our attorney so that we're not billed for any more hours. He was probably going to do that anyway. He'll recommend someone for the case against CSD, but he's already told me it's not his area."

"What about the Christmas visitation? Was that worked out yet?" I asked as I joined him at the bar.

"Not yet. Hill is still screwing around with the wording because the Walls say we can't get Carley on Christmas Eve at five *because* the order says 'Christmas Day and two days following' on even years."

"AUUGH!" I howled. "What is the matter with these people! What do they want to do, exchange Carley at midnight?"

"Yeah, it really shows how much they're regarding the welfare of the child, doesn't it?" Spencer said. "Jason said Hill says they will only agree to nine Christmas morning."

"And we have to do everything the way they want it, even if it ruins Carley's Christmas morning."

Spencer hugged me as we stood together.

"We'll be there to pick her up Tuesday at five, and if they're not there we'll be there again the next morning. What else can we do? The 25th is Wednesday; we can have our Christmas morning

Thursday. That still gives us Thursday and Friday till five to play with her toys with her."

I started crying. "They are such cheaters. And they always get away with it."

"Yep. They do. We just gotta keep going, and hope someday things will turn around."

"How old will Carley be when that happens?" There was no answer.

CHAPTER 36

Journal entry: 12/20-22/96—Weekend before Christmas

I'm glad that our every-other-weekend visitation came this close to Christmas because we got to do holiday stuff. Friday, after I picked Carley up, the two of us shopped for a gift for Spencer (a birdfeeder!) and she got to help wrap it.

It was a fun weekend, except for two things. Saturday afternoon while Carley was playing with Fuzzy and her other stuffed animals, we watched her spank Fuzzy and tell him to go to bed because he pooped his pants. Spencer asked her if that ever happened to her and she said yes and looked ashamed. We told her Fuzzy didn't have to go to bed, he just had an accident and he was still a good puppy. On Sunday, when it was time to go, she cried and said she didn't want to, that her Grampa and Gramma had said she could stay with us for two days. When we explained that it had been two days, she let us dress her but kept sobbing and saying she didn't want to go. When she woke up in the car at the restaurant, she cried for a moment, then put on a blank look. She hugged us outside the door, then went in to Buck and hugged him, but continued the blank look. Buck said he would see us Christmas morning at nine; we said, no Tuesday at five. He just repeated himself, so we said we'd talk to the judge. Carley didn't look at anybody.

12/23—Monday

I called a screener at CSD and reported about Carley's spanking. She asked for more background, and when I told her that Buck had testified that he made Carley confess to him whenever Mara sent Carley to bed for pooping her pants, the screener was surprised that the judge hadn't remarked on that. However, she said this was not enough to "go out" on but that I should continue to report.

Jason sent us a copy of a letter from Richard Hill stating that we had threatened his client. We told Jason it was completely bogus and that we were writing to Judge Harmon. Jason didn't need to help.

172

My letter to Judge David Harmon, December 24,1996:
Your Honor,

I'm asking, *pro se*, for clarification of a point of contention regarding the court's order for visitation, dated 11/22/95. This letter may also help to show how Buck and Mara Wall have been treating us.

Respective attorneys, Mr. Hill and Mr. Norden, have been corresponding since 12/6/96 about the time and day our Christmas visitation starts. We contend it starts Christmas Eve at 5:00 p.m., exactly as it was last year. Your ruling expressed the intent to give Carley alternate Christmas days with her grandparents, and it's our turn to have Christmas morning with her.

When Mr. Wall argued with us in front of Carley and some café regulars at Mac's last Sunday evening, we were shocked. Rather than add to Carley's trauma, we chose to get help. I believed we could prevent a scene by asking the Doolin police chief to explain the order to the Walls before the event. We were told that law enforcement can only help after the Walls violate the order and a Writ of Assistance is issued.

One obvious problem is with Mr. Hill's naïve belief in the self-serving lies his clients tell. In a letter to our attorney, Mr. Hill has described, in his usual over-played theatrical style, how we've terrorized these poor victims with "threats of kicking the doors in" with our "gang of thugs."

I have been to the Walls' house twice for Carley, as described in my notes (attached). Both times I was within my rights as I knew them, and I left when Mara asked me to. No one else was involved. No one was victimized.

Contrarily, we've lost visitations on 12/1/95 due to Carley's smoker's cough, 9-1/2 months of weekends between 2/26/96 and 11/22/96, and two weeks of planned summer vacation with her great-grandmother. When we asked in October to have Carley with us to attend her great-grandmother's 75th birthday, we were ignored.

So how does anyone expect us to sympathize with the Walls' family get-together? It is cruel of them to interrupt Carley's Christmas morning to make her get dressed and leave, while putting the blame on us.

Post script from Spencer:

Mr. Hill is twisting the facts to fit the situation. I did not threaten, "in effect" or otherwise. The Walls have not been

173

"following the Order," but instead have been pushing the limits of the Court's tolerance to their personal benefit, to the detriment of Carley. They are not "allowing visitation," but are involuntarily obeying the Court's Order. No neighbor had to run my wife off.

We will be keeping very specific documentation about future violations by the Walls. We will also notify CSD with notes and photos of any and all physical abuse we notice on Carley. We won't hesitate to notify the Doolin P. D. of same.

*   *   *

Journal entry: 12/24/96—Tuesday

We talked to Doolin's police chief about the latest goings-on with Mara and Buck. He said he could pursue an investigation through the multi-disciplinary task force set up for "these kinds of things," but without any physical evidence (obvious signs of beating) that's all he could do. He called us later to say that Buck had requested the police station for the meeting place because the café would be closed tomorrow at 9:00 a.m. Did we agree? We told him we didn't seem to have a choice.

12/25—Wednesday

Buck drove up behind us at City Hall at 8:50 a.m.. The police station was closed. We got out and stood under the eaves of the building out of the rain. Carley could see us and gave us a big smile. Buck held her and talked to her in the cab of his pickup for about ten minutes while we waited. Finally, he walked to us and held out a bottle of medicine. He said, "When she got back from your house she had a cold, so…" I said, "No, she actually left our house healthier than she arrived. She was getting better." He shook his head and continued to tell us she needed this cough medicine, "prescribed earlier by the doctor," and children's Tylenol for her cough, fever and congestion. We said okay; he said we could buy the cough syrup at a drug store, as he pocketed the bottle.

He went back to Carley and stood between her and the open door so that he could say something to her without us seeing her face. I said, "Hi Carley! It's good to see your smile because I thought you might be mad at having to get up so early." She got out of the pickup and went with Spencer to our car, not looking at anybody. Buck said, "I'll be here on Friday at five." I said, "Wait a minute. If 'Christmas and two days' start at 9:00 a.m. then they end at Saturday at 9:00 a.m." He just repeated, "Friday, five." I tried to talk some

174

more, but he said, "Kidnapping is a serious charge," and shut the door.

I sat in the back seat with Carley, but she was quiet and looked out the window. I said, "What happened to your smile I saw a few minutes ago?" She shrugged a little. "Did your Grampa say something to you that made your smile go away?" She gave a little nod, and kept staring. A couple of minutes later I said, "I bet I know what your Grampa said. Maybe he said we were bad." Carley nodded twice. I said, "He was just kidding. We aren't bad. We will always be good for you and never, ever hurt you." After a few more quiet minutes she turned towards me and said, "We're almost getting there!" which was our usual, playful routine.

At one o'clock, we were surprised to see Buck's pickup at the top of our driveway. It stayed there for five or ten minutes, then drove off. Some time after that, we received a phone call with no one there. Just before four, a Gold County deputy called, as requested by "a Mrs. Mara Wall," to see if Carley was getting her medicine. I told him that she had the sniffles but no cough or fever. "We're giving her plenty of fluids and rest, feeding her right, and we're not medicating her because she doesn't need any. She just had a bowl of soup and is feeling fine." I told him about the pickup on the driveway and the phone call, and that we were starting to feel harassed. He said, "If they call again, say that you are noting the time for a police inquiry, and hang up. Mrs. Wall wants me to drive up to do a welfare check, but I don't need to. I'll call her back."

CHAPTER 37

Despite all the hassles from the Walls, we managed to have a memorable Christmas. Tisha was home on holiday leave from the Job Corps, so for three days we had a family.

Tisha had learned to love Carley and had also been hurt by losing her. Because we were having such a hard time, we hadn't noticed the toll it was taking on Tisha. Sometime during the ordeal, she had stopped talking to or about Kim. The big sister that had ruled her life, rewarding and punishing her since before we entered the picture, had taken her niece away from her. We had worried whether she'd finish high school, but she did. Tisha barely had enough strength to make it to adulthood. It would take more time than that to forgive her sister.

As a young adult, Tisha could never get into the spirit of giving; it was hard to get her to have fun at anything, in fact. Since adolescence, she hadn't shown joy or said "thank you" when opening gifts. When she was downstairs with us, there was always a feeling that she was waiting for us to do something. It was tiring and depressing. Her unease usually made it hard for us to relax, but Carley's presence added the right magic. That Christmas our focus was Carley, which seemed to suit Tisha.

The first day, we had the usual break-in period to get through the transition. The exchange with Buck had caused such anxiety, but Spencer was great at playing the goofy Gran'daddy, so it didn't take long before Carley was over her shyness and laughing and running. We put the futon mattress in our bedroom and made up a bed for her, telling her all the while how things worked when she was here, how she slept here, we slept there. It was repetition of the previous visits, but we knew she needed the reassurance she got from our consistency. She quickly grasped the idea of celebration, the Christmas tree lights, wrapped gifts and decorations, and having Aunt Tisha here, only Carley sometimes referred to her as "your friend Tisha."

The game that day was Put-Gran'daddy-under-the-Futon-and-Beat-him-with-Stuffed-Animals.

"Where's your Bear? Oh, there it is! Ah - ha!" Gran'daddy's long arm reached out, grabbed the stuffed bear and pulled it under the mattress edge. Carley toddled up and down the length of the wobbly, tilting mattress, trying to keep the weapons to herself. The penguin and Fuzzy were safely tucked in her arms. Spencer, lying on his back with only his head and one arm sticking out from the edge, teased her by putting the bear back on top and wiggling it.

"Oh no! The bear is going to escape!" he cried in a high-pitched voice.

Tisha and I were the audience, sitting at each end of the two-foot high futon, serving as fall protection. Tisha was in the desk chair and I was in the window seat, both of us with our arms available in case Carley took a header. We admired Carley's show as she tromped back and forth in her new red jumper and white socks. We laughed and made appropriate cheers, but we lacked the childish spirit that the performers had. Tisha's plump body moved stiffly and her laughter seemed forced. I was just plain tired.

Carley set her armload down on one end of the mattress and made a lunge for the bear. But it was quickly pulled away, and then knocked down out of reach. Carley plopped on to her seat and slid off the edge of the mattress in one motion.

"Whoa!" she pretended surprise and laughed as we all made moves to catch her.

She faked us out. She ran to pick up the bear, handed it to Gran'daddy and climbed back up.

Spencer said, "Oh, are you giving him to me? How nice!" but tossed the bear right back at her in a quick counterattack.

"Ha-ha, you missed me," she sang.

Spencer got the bear in his hand again and used it to hunt for Carley in blind swats. "Where's that Carley?" he said in his deep, monster voice.

Then Carley let her body drop flat, face down on the mattress, which caused Spencer to let out a lung full of air and a groan. She sneaked a look over the edge and yelled, "Boo!"

As Spencer screamed in mock terror and we laughed, Carley bounced up again and jumped over to Tisha for a huge hug. As she merrily trotted back across the mattress to give me a hug, too, her feet tangled and she fell over. But she landed safely and laughed as we all breathed a loud sigh of relief.

177

Carley's treasured stuffed pet, Fuzzy, caught her attention from the pile of animals on the futon. She grabbed him up by the arm, we thought to signal the end of the activity. Fuzzy was her security-blanket buddy, the ever-present consolation in times of stress. Evidently he also served as her partner in crime, because she swung him by the arm and began hitting Gran'daddy over the head with him.

"Hey-hey-hey! That's not fair!" Spencer cried as he tried to protect himself with his one free arm.

Carley jumped down to the floor and climbed on top of his chest, pummeling him with first Fuzzy then all the animals she could get her hands on. When the supply was exhausted and we were all teary with laughter, she stood up and slapped her hands together in a grand finish.

Our Christmas had begun.

In the morning, we had stockings filled with a zoo of little plastic animals and other goodies, but the biggie was the beribboned easel sitting under the tree with "To Carley from Santa" painted on the first sheet of art paper. Carley and Gran'daddy were struck by the muse and had to paint something right away.

While I helped Spencer open the paints, I saw that Tisha hadn't moved from the recliner and looked bored. I told her, "You know this is going to be a Christmas morning like no other, so we're going to have to go with the flow here. As you can see, it might take a while to get to the rest of the presents."

Tisha smiled, then gave a nervous laugh and said, "Okay you guys, one picture. But then can we see what's in all these presents?"

She got up and went to the tree. Reaching for a red foil box-shaped package, one of the biggest in the front, she said, "Let's see, this one says, 'To Tisha,' so I might as well open it."

"No, no, you have to wait for me to help you," Carley piped up.

"Well, you'd better hurry. I'm getting anxious," Tisha teased.

Carley handed her brush to Spencer. "Good idea, Carley. We'll paint some more later," he said as he moved the easel aside, and Carley ran to help Tisha unwrap her present.

"Whadizit? Whadizit?" Carley's expressed anticipation made Tisha laugh as they fought with the huge box on Tisha's lap. Together, they eventually revealed the purple and black parka inside.

I said, "I hope it fits, so that you can wear it right away. Do you like it?"

"Yeah, it's nice," Tisha answered with little enthusiasm.

Carley, who didn't need any encouragement, picked up the jacket and held it up, the soft, puffy material nearly engulfing her.

"Put on. Stand up and put on, Tisha."

Rising and heaving a good-humored sigh of surrender, Tisha did as ordered.

Carley's energy and excitement level lasted through the whole morning. There were moments of pure enchantment, when we just sat with huge grins on our faces and watched her. She delighted in every gift, trotting back and forth to make sure she didn't miss a thing. When the gift was for her, which was often, she'd take it to Spencer and plead earnestly, "Help me get it out, Gran'daddy." He let her use scissors to cut the ribbon, and she did this with great deliberation.

I tried to get the festivities tape-recorded, but Carley jumped up and down in front of the camera to get my attention. "Hey Gran'mommy, where's your eyes?"

I realized the plight of the photographer is to be left out, so I put it away and received a hug and a kiss in exchange. "Thank you, sweetie. Now, how about a cinnamon roll and some hot chocolate?" Yays from everyone.

During a break in the action, I watched Carley and Spencer play an elaborate game of peek-a-boo with the knitted cap that my mom had made for her. I was in awe of how she observed and learned, quickly adapting actions and reactions to information that the adult mind missed. While we had been satisfied with the joke of being invisible because her eyes were hidden under the cap, she improved on it. Spencer said, "Where's Carley? I hear something, but where is she?" Carley pushed back the hat and Spencer said, "Oh, here's Carley!" To which Carley had a quick reply, "No, I is Santee Claus."

She surprised us again when she later settled in for a pre-nap storybook with Gran'daddy. Her new book was about jungle animals, and Spencer was pointing them out with appropriate adoration. To our dismay, instead of getting sleepy Carley hopped out of his lap and went for her stocking on the hearth. She dumped the entire contents out on the floor, searching for something in particular. Finding and grabbing a small item, she proclaimed, "Oh, here he is!" She then climbed back up and showed Gran'daddy a little plastic gorilla that matched the one pictured in the book perfectly.

*　　*　　*

Journal entry: 12/26/96—Thursday

There was another phone call today. Tisha answered, but hung up when she didn't hear anyone there. We'd had an exhausting day, and at bed time, Carley began crying softly. I comforted her and asked if she was afraid of anything or of us. She said, "No, Gran'mommy. I love you and I love Gran'daddy." Then, in tears again, "But I want my Grampa and Gramma." I told her we would take her to them tomorrow. She said, "My Grampa said you guys would not take me back to them." I was having a hard time understanding her; she repeated something about us going to their place or them coming to our place and somebody throwing somebody out. I told her, "There isn't going to be any fighting. They won't come here, and we won't go there. We'll take you to Mac's just like always. Your Grampa and Gramma are just mad because they didn't want us to see you, but we get to see you because it's a rule. When they get mad, they sometimes say things that scare you, like your Gran'mommy and Gran'daddy are bad, or that we do bad things to you. But none of that is true. The truth is that we will always do what is good for you and never hurt you." She said, "You never hurt me, Gran'mommy." I told her I loved her and she said she loved me too, and everything was okay. Then we talked about her "two beds, in two houses," because she said she wanted her bed at her other house. I said, "When you're bigger, you can sleep upstairs here, with your toys, and your clothes all there in your own bedroom." She was interested in that, and agreed to think about it. But for now, she said, "This bed is okay."

12/27—Friday

Before we took Carley into Mac's, Spencer and I went in alone, while Tisha kept Carley company in the car. Spencer stood directly in front of Buck, looking down at him sitting at the counter, and said quietly, "We won't tolerate any more harassment, Buck. When we have Carley, we don't want to see you parking on our driveway. If we get any more harassing phone calls, the police will know about it. Your bad-mouthing us to Carley is only causing her confusion and scaring her. And your potty-training by spanking is being reported to CSD. I'll go get Carley now." I looked around the café to see all customers pointedly minding their own business.

PART SEVEN—DEALING

(January, 1997—April, 1998)

CHAPTER 38

Spencer and I started the new year with optimistic courage. Together we recounted the tragedies of 1996, dubbed the worst year ever, as if we were checking them off a list we'd completed and could now toss. Besides the emotional pounding the Walls had put us through, the other blows we'd survived made us marvel at our own strength.

Our car had been stolen in June. It was taken from a parking lot in Portland, along with my purse, our suitcases, sleeping bags and bicycles. It was found two months later, trashed but not totaled. We had to deal with the police and the criminal courts, the towing company, the insurance and rental agencies, banks, credit card companies, the DMV, as well as the personal impact of loss and violation.

In late fall, Susan, the basset hound we'd loved for three years, was killed by a car as she chased a deer across the highway. In our years together, Spencer and I had to bear the death of six dogs, and each time we cried and felt the heartbreak for months. This time too.

My job with the highway department went through changes all year. My work as a materials inspector was modified to include more office work, which helped to relieve back pain but was more demanding and less satisfying. New directions for office administrators had a lot of bugs to be worked out, so personalities clashed. I hated going to work every day.

Spencer finished building his first spec house in May. He had done a great job and he felt good about it. But the market was poor when it finally sold so he didn't make as much as he'd hoped. He went back to remodeling, which meant he had to constantly hustle to find jobs and that was his least favorite thing about building.

There was a proud moment when we learned that Tisha was going to graduate soon from the Job Corps. With some start-up cash and a new outlook, she would try to find a receptionist job in Cherry Valley. A two-hour drive away was close enough for us to give her help if she needed it, and far enough to give her space.

Late in November, I finally had to admit that I needed back surgery. Worn out lumbar disks could be removed, my surgeon said, without too much trouble. It was a three-day hospital stay and a six-week leave of absence from work, and, as promised, I was up and about by Christmas. I chalked it up to shitty-year-phenomena, and Spencer helped me get through it.

We were still happily in love, and clung to each other with hope.

There was more work to do. We set up a payment plan with Jason Norden to get out of debt with one lawyer before hiring another. The problem was finding one willing to go against the State Children's Services Division. We heard the same story from each lawyer we talked to. Nina Cowan's influence often reached into their legal avenues, and if they ever wanted to work with her agency again, they had better not cross her.

Our frustrations grew, and we reached out to friends, and friends of friends, for contacts, anyone who might help. My hairdresser told me about another Doolin guy we knew slightly, Wade, who worked in the county Victim's Assistance Department, part of the District Attorney's office.

Spencer went by to see him, explained our problems, and in the evening was still riding a wave of enthusiasm.

"Remember that multidisciplinary task force the police chief told us about?" he asked me. "Wade is the social worker representing the DA's office. He says they discuss cases referred by anyone on the team, cases that have fallen through the cracks, for one reason or another, and if someone like Wade sees a red flag somewhere, he brings it to their attention."

I asked, "Who else is on it?"

"A sheriff's deputy, someone from the juvenile section, Cowan's got somebody on it—Wade couldn't give me the name, they're supposed to be confidential—I can't remember who else. Someone from the State Police, I think."

"And Wade thinks these guys will really listen?"

"He says there's a good chance. He knows all the particulars of our problems with Cowan and CSD, how the court dumped on us. I didn't have to report everything because he had seen some of the files already. He works closely with the juvenile part of the courthouse, and Carley's case was reviewed there. He also know the Walls and has dealt with them before, so he's really interested in helping us."

I was starting to feel some of Spencer's hopefulness. "What happens now?"

"They meet next week, and Wade will make the case to have the team open an investigation of sexual abuse based on what we've reported to CSD."

I exhaled tiredly. "Okay. God, I hope we can trust these people."

"Well, all we can do is try. I have faith in Wade. For one thing, he quietly told me that he can't stand Nina Cowan. I'll give him copies of the letters we sent to her recounting our calls to the screeners."

*   *   *

Letter to Nina Cowan, January 8, 1997:

The following is an account of our continuing reports by phone call to CSD screeners:

December 9:

• When Carley came to our home on December 6th, she had a bruise on her forehead. When we asked how she got her "owee," she would not answer. This was repeated when we tried again later.

• In the bathroom, Carley spread her legs and bent over completely, with her head on the floor, to have her bottom wiped. The screener said this was not strange potty-behavior. In the bath, Carley spread her legs wide and wanted her "popo" washed. The screener agreed this was strange behavior.

January 6:

• When we tried to change Carley into pajamas after she had fallen asleep on the couch, she held her legs together tightly and put her hands protectively against her crotch and cried. She was very upset and we just held her until she was comforted. She said she was mad at Gran'mommy but not at Gran'daddy, at first, but then said she loved us both and was not afraid.

• Carley told us, "Gramma spanks me a lot," and, "You can't keep me because my "Gramma and Grampa need me."

• When we picked her up on Friday, she had been very listless and non-attentive. She had a glazed look and wouldn't move. This was unusual behavior compared to all other times. Mr. Wall said she had just come from therapy.

We also have witnesses who say that while the Walls are waiting for us in the restaurant with Carley, they tell people within earshot untrue and offensive stories about us.

We're very disturbed about these indications of child abuse at home. We will continue to report details to your staff so that it is all documented.

*   *   *

Wade met us for coffee at Mac's in mid-January.

"The task force is going to reopen the case. You know Emily Sanchez?"

"Yeah," Spencer said, "She told us she was leaving CSD. Couldn't take it anymore."

"Right," Wade nodded sympathetically. "But she now works for the Youth Authority, another state office. Don't repeat this, but she's also on the task force, so there's a good chance we'll get somewhere. I don't want to worry you any more than you already are, but I know Buck and Mara. They're scum. I've dealt with them before, with agency issues and seeing them around town. I've seen them interact with Carley, and there's no doubt in my mind they're harming her."

That hit me with a sickening dread, and at the same time a relief that someone with some authority was believing us.

Wade continued, "They always go right up against the limits of the law, but not far enough for us to do anything about it. I can't tell you everything I know, but… well, let's just say that I have little faith in Nina Cowan's agency when it comes to protecting children."

But Cowan wielded more power than we could imagine. A few weeks later, the channel we'd finally found dead-ended. Wade called to tell us that Cowan had convinced the D.A. that she had everything under control.

"I'm sorry," Wade said. "But unless there's physical evidence of abuse, like broken bones or marks of beatings, the case will remain closed."

CHAPTER 39

In February, Richard Hill sent us a copy of a Motion to Adopt—Petitioners, Walter "Buck" Wall and Mara Wall—Child, Carley Rebecca Wall. The hearing was scheduled for June 23rd. We continued our letter-campaign to everyone we could think of. Sometimes we tried a polite and reasonable tone with Nina Cowan, giving her updates on Carley's unusual behaviors:

"…She is having great difficulty with potty training. She avoids going to the bathroom and will lie when she has dirtied her pants, even though we have told her we will not spank her or get angry. She stops talking and puts on a face that you'd expect on a much older, defiant street kid. This show of defensiveness is surprising; I believe a child of three is usually more self-conscious about messing themselves. Check your sources, but we think this is cause for alarm that there is something wrong.

"We would like to know if Carley is attending therapy sessions, as ordered by Judge Harmon. In CSD sessions last September, your social worker alerted you to what she felt were signs that Carley was traumatized (i.e. playacting mama rescuing the baby). It's noteworthy that Carley still plays those games.

"I think I understand the predicament you're in, because of your perception that it is too late to correct certain procedural omissions in the sexual abuse investigation. But we know there are some in the law enforcement system who would like to investigate further. All they need is a call from you. What could it hurt? The cost of allowing a closer look can't be that great. Surely someone can afford the professional embarrassment for the chance to prevent harm to this child."

Sometimes our anger couldn't be held in check and our letters were more aggressive, especially when we went over Cowan's head to her manager, with copies to the division director:

"…The obvious deception and misinformation from your Camas City office is a strong indication that the original investigation was one-sided and blind to the truth. The fact remains that Carley

187

was hurt and because of Ms. Pierce's initial misfeasance in the case, we may never be able to bring the culpable party out in the open."

It was incredible to us that this agency ran in such an irresponsible manner, giving one woman such power to make poor decisions and then allowing her to tidy up with procedural rhetoric months later. We wrote to our representatives in the state and in Congress, all of whom replied with heartfelt sympathies but no recourse. We found a Children's Ombudsman Office in the capital and began efforts to reach them, but we didn't get a reply. One state senator alerted us to pending sub-committee hearings on oversights for government agencies, and we made sure we stayed on his mailing list for updates.

As futile as it was, we wrote to Judge Harmon again. Besides recounting the latest problems with the Walls (cheating us out of occasional weekends, bad-mouthing us to Carley) we informed him that Cowan hadn't yet arranged for Carley's therapy sessions. That prompted a response from Cowan, stating that Carley had been "discharged" from counseling days earlier, and that the therapist described her as happy and adjusted and that "her trauma appears to have been resolved."

Spencer was not quiet as he read Cowan's long, three-bulleted letter, then skimmed the four page, fifteen-bulleted attachment. He swore, laughed in disbelief and blurted, "What?" often as he flipped the pages.

"I read it," I told him, "but I don't quite get what it's about."

"Oh, this is a perfect example of cover-your-ass bullshit, and she's a pro at it," he yelled.

"Okay, one thing at a time." I picked up the letter and laid it on the dining table. "The first point is the change in disposition in the sexual abuse investigation to 'unable to determine.' She refers to the attachment, a letter Foster wrote us in November."

Cowan had written, "I've taken the liberty of highlighting the language I'm referencing. I've had an opportunity to compile information that I believe may be of interest to you."

Spencer said, "The only thing highlighted in Foster's letter is this, 'The new caseworker, Don Baines, was asked by Ms. Cowan to interview your references and to review the case when she concluded that there was a need to do so based on additional information you provided her.' What crap! We referred *her* to the babysitter and to George and Lou right away, none of whom ever got a call. We told Pierce to talk to them in February, and when did Cowan say *she* requested this? At least six months later!"

I drew his attention back to Cowan's letter. "There's this part about counseling, begun on June 19th, 1996. You know, when I saw that date I looked in my journal. That was right after we wrote a long nasty letter to Jim Foster about the mess his agency was in. One question we raised was why Carley hadn't been given any therapy."

"Well, I guess our letters achieve something sometime." Spencer picked up Cowan's document and turned to the second page. "So this counseling service finds Carley 'developmentally normal,' and they addressed her behavioral problems and her sadness when 'her mother left her.' Left her? You mean when the Walls sent her packing. But what I want to know is, how many sessions were there? We don't even know when they started the visits *without* Mara, like the judge ordered."

"Well, since the state was paying for them, it probably wasn't enough." I pointed to the third bullet in the letter. "I really don't understand this next part."

"It's just so much slimy bureaucratese to obscure facts. The only clear point is, 'Closure of our case terminates our work with that family.' The Walls, she means. The ending is cute. She reminds us, and informs the judge, that she's still looking for a mediator, and that 'it is this agency's hope that an outcome will be agreement between members of Carley's extended family to mutually nurture, love and support her.' She's so full of shit," Spencer said as he threw the stapled papers across the table.

My head hurt and I knew I had to get dinner started. We were quiet as we both got up and went about other business. Spencer finished sorting the mail and cleared the table. I got out the leftovers and salad material. When he came in to help, I asked the inevitable question.

"Where do we go from here?"

"Cowan thinks she's done with this. We'll go to the facilitated meetings with the Walls and everything will be rosy. She doesn't give a shit about Carley. She doesn't have any idea how messed up Buck and Mara are. If and when we ever get to these meetings, they won't stand for reasonable solutions and we'll be right back where we started."

He blew out a long breath and added, "Meanwhile, we keep writing letters, I guess."

CHAPTER 40

Since our visitations were still being granted (not counting the all too frequent cancellations due to "colds") we had Carley for Easter, and I had a buddy to dye Easter eggs with, something that I'd been missing for several years. Unfortunately, Spencer had to be away, visiting his mother back in Maryland. So I promised to capture all of the festivities with the video camera.

"When he gonna get back?" Carley asked me, looking suspiciously into the camera as I focused on the table. It was covered with newspaper and the collected materials I'd put out for our project: a carton of twelve hard-boiled eggs, two paint brushes, the six little jars of tempura paints and the plastic palette that came with her easel, and a roll of paper towels. Carley sat in her high chair, bedecked in her trusty smock and her sleeves rolled up, her stringy blond hair kept off of her face with clips *and* a scrunchy.

"He'll be back next time you come here, and then you can watch this tape with him. Wouldn't that be funny, to watch yourself coloring these eggs? It will be just like he was here doing it with us."

I had decided to forego the usual cardboard boxed egg-dyeing stuff that requires monotonous dipping and examining for the right color that never seems to appear, a procedure that tries *my* patience, though I did sort of miss the traditional smell of the vinegar mixture. Since this was all new ground for Carley, she seemed ready to tackle the project as laid out.

I left the running camcorder on the tripod and moved to the opposite side of the table from her. Our new dog, Rosie, another rescued basset hound, kept a watchful eye on our activity in case it involved something she wanted to eat.

"Show me how you paint eggs. What color do you want to start with?"

"That stuff," Carley pointed to the red dab in the palette with her brush in her left hand, apparently satisfied that the camera was no longer a threat.

"Good choice! I think I'll start with green." Picking up my brush and egg, I talked as I moved, allowing her to follow my actions instead of giving her instructions. She was a very good student.

"I gotta paint *dis* egg." She picked out an egg from the middle of the carton and carefully painted until every last bit of white was gone.

As we slowly painted away, I told Carley again about how the Easter bunny liked it that children decorated the Easter eggs, like her mommy and Tisha did when they were little, and the Easter bunny would expect to find them left out in the carton the next morning while we were sleeping.

"Then he'll hide them outside—not too hard, though—because he's a rascally bunny, and he'll leave an Easter basket on the table instead of the carton for you to use to collect them. And, as a present, there'll be candy goodies in the basket. Maybe a chocolate rabbit, or jelly beans, or something he thinks you'd like."

Carley's eyes lit up, and she nodded her head in full agreement before continuing with the purple stripes on her blue egg. When she finished it, she added it carefully to the row of drying, dripping eggs on the towels and waxed paper in the middle of the table.

She admired our work so far. Because I had been kept busy as the attendant to the artist, I hadn't managed to paint that many. But, since I didn't want the project to last past dinner time, I stepped up my pace.

"Deez are yours, and deez are mine! Take a picture of all both of dem," she directed as I was checking the running time on the video tape.

"Yes, ma'am! I got it," I assured her from behind the camera. "I'm very impressed with our work, especially yours. You're very good at this Easter egg business."

Then Carley slowly picked up the second to last egg, and gave me a thoughtful look, as if to say, "Now let me see if I got this right."

What she did say was, "When we finish painting all deez eggs and den we go to sleep and the angel plays with dem and he hides dem outside for us."

"Right!" I didn't think it necessary to clarify the confusion with the angel business. Actually, it was a fair comparison. "And he leaves a pretty new basket with some goodies for you in it, and you get to use the basket to go hunt for all the hidden eggs."

I let it go with that, and we continued our work, chatting about artistry. As the last egg was set up to dry, Carley gave a pleasant sigh.

191

I started cleaning up, and she began to explain the deal to me in a kindergarten teacher's voice. "We'll keep the eggs inside, the Easter Bunny will find dem. Afterwards we go outside and find dem, and I will be happy about the Easter Guy!"

"I will, too, be happy about the Easter Guy," I told her, barely able to keep the lump out of my throat.

"So the Easter Bunny is good," Carley said in what sounded like defiance. I guessed that it was directed at her Gramma and Grampa. Who knows what they had told her? Was I giving Carley more trouble, introducing the sin of false idol-worshipping? I had wondered about it when she seemed unfamiliar with Santa Claus.

I decided that here was one smart cookie who could, and should, learn all there was in the world, and she would make up her own mind.

"He's always been one of *my* best friends," I divulged enthusiastically.

Carley smiled and nodded her sweet face. "Him one of my best friends, too."

CHAPTER 41

Our persistent letter-writing paid off with the award of an in-home visit in April from Jim Foster, the Children's Services Department Region Manager himself. He made a big deal of the offer to meet with us, and we agreed. Not because we thought it would solve all the problems, but because he was coming with Nina Cowan and we thought confronting both of them face-to-face would save time. The recurring misinterpretations, whether intentional or not, could be dispensed with quickly.

We didn't do much to prepare for their visit. We both took off from work, cleaned up the living room a little, and made coffee. It occurred to me that we had several photos of our family, including Carley, in plain sight. The dusty frames attested to their long-standing placement—a small point, but I hoped they'd notice.

Foster was what guys I worked with called "a suit," all smiles and handshakes. Though I hadn't met Cowan before, I was not surprised that her appearance fit her phone voice perfectly. Her pale, long face with a tight mouth tried to smile and look sincere when she spoke, but Foster did most of the talking. He opened by quoting the law and procedures regarding tribal children, custodial matters, and the limits of the agency's involvement. He ended his speech by reminding us of the local branch's caseload.

Then we took our turn, listing all the reasons to suspect the Walls of child abuse, and the inept responses Nina had provided: from removing Emily Sanchez from the case, to Irma Pierce's mishandling of the sexual abuse investigation, to Nina's turning away the task force's request to reopen the case. Whenever Spencer paused to remember something else, I took over, and vice versa. We watched their faces turn pale as the impact of our words pushed them back in their chairs.

Then Spencer calmly asked, "Are we mistaken in thinking that the main goal of Children's Services is to protect children? Maybe your agency wouldn't be so overloaded with work if more energy was spent on actual follow-ups by experienced, qualified caseworkers than on covering your tracks."

The emphasis shifted to convincing us that they were listening. We learned there was something called a Household Review, whereby an independent social worker visits the home of prospective adopting parents in families with case history. Though unprecedented in grandparental adoptions, tribal ones at that, Foster said he would authorize it.

We received Nina Cowan's letter days later thanking us for the constructive session, acknowledging that they had left with a better understanding about the issues we posed. She said they now had a very clear sense of our love for Carley. I wanted to believe it, but I wondered how she had missed that realization before.

As one of the actions promised at the meeting, Don Baines was assigned as Carley's regular caseworker. We knew his name as the one who re-evaluated the sexual assault investigation, stipulating that too much time had passed to come to a reliable determination. Not much to go on, but Spencer and I held out hope that there might be someone in that office, maybe Baines, who was as good as Emily Sanchez had been. Cowan assured us that we would have on-going contact with him regarding any assessments of referrals, regardless of the source.

We didn't hear anything for six weeks, and the Walls' adoption hearing was approaching. The Household Review, as well as an evaluation of Carley from Educational Services, was supposed to be completed in time for the hearing. We questioned the progress in a letter to Cowan, and shortly thereafter received notification that the adoption hearing was continued to August 1st. She also said she'd located a mediator to facilitate our meetings with Buck and Mara, and schedules would be worked out soon.

We made the most out of our weekends with Carley, making every effort to just have fun with her and give her a relaxed, consistent place with us. She continued her disturbing behaviors and remarks, but nothing we hadn't already reported. She repeated often that Grampa said we might take her and not give her back to them. She wasn't even supposed to say "Belleville," our town, because they told her it was a bad word.

I called CSD only once, to report to Don Baines Carley's story of a bath she'd had at her Grandma's house. Mara and Buck had another granddaughter, Mara's daughter's child. She was the same age as Carley and sometimes stayed with them. Carley had told me, "She's in trouble with Gramma because she touched my popo when

194

we were in the bathtub. She does it a lot, but I don't do it anymore." It was the denial and the fearful look on her face that concerned me the most.

Don followed up with a phone call to me later, saying that he had looked into it.

"I'm helping the Walls with teaching Carley and her cousin about inappropriate touching. I also told Mara she needed to supervise more, and there shouldn't be shared baths anymore."

He didn't tell us of any other referrals, from daycare workers or others. But we suspected that there wasn't anyone else who saw much of Carley. The Walls kept her with them constantly.

We spent our two-week visitation in July camping and visiting relatives, probably more exposure to other people than she'd had in months. Carley was happy, having all the fun a kid usually has in summer. We didn't want to see it end.

"I wish I could stay here forever," she'd say whenever she found a dandelion or a star to wish on. Then, after a hesitation, she always added, "And I wish I stay with Gramma and Grampa, too."

In August, Don came to our house for a consultation. He was a nice enough guy, if not quite as assertive as I'd hoped. When he told us "a little bit about" himself, it included a childhood of abuse, a painful divorce and his years as a recovering alcoholic. I didn't know how any of that was supposed to help us; maybe he was trying to tell us that he could relate.

"The good news is Nina is trying to line up someone from another CSD branch office to do a Household Review, and meanwhile the adoption hearing is postponed. The bad news is I have to conclude my casework.

"There just isn't enough to go on," he told us repeatedly. "I thought there'd be more referrals."

"Who else would report anything besides us?" I asked him. "She doesn't go to daycare or Sunday school."

"They said they tried to get her into daycare, but she's not eligible because she's not potty-trained," Don said, throwing his hands out in defeat.

"My point is, she's not going to confide in anyone but us."

"And that's a problem," Don leaned into us as Spencer and I faced him at our dining table. Don had been working hard for almost three hours to explain things with extreme care. "Carley is being asked too many questions, and she answers with what she thinks you want to hear."

"Don't you think we know that, Don?" Spencer said.

I argued, "We aren't asking her any questions, other than, 'How did that owee get there?' or something like that."

"I don't necessarily mean you. But Mara and Buck... I tell you. After every visit here Carley's being questioned right and left," Don stopped himself.

"I'm just trying to caution you," he spoke more slowly, "to not make any referral phone calls that the agency might regard as trivial. Most of the things Carley tells you might be things that someone encouraged."

He sat back and nodded reassuringly. "In time, true revelations will come from unprompted conversations."

CHAPTER 42

One weekend, a couple of days before her fourth birthday, we took Carley camping. It had been a favorite place of our daughters when they were young; it had a swimming hole on a scenic, little river, tent sites in the open areas under the myrtle trees, and it wasn't ever crowded. To surprise Carley, we brought the makings for a birthday party and kept them hidden until Saturday afternoon.

After lunch, we told her to go into the tent and change into her swimsuit. When she came out, we sang "Happy Birthday" as Spencer carried a pile of wrapped presents to the picnic table, and I lit four candles on the iced cake.

Carley asked "You brought this for *me*?"

"Well, it's your birthday, isn't it?" Spencer said. "Oh wait, maybe it's my birthday."

I pointed to the cake. "No, Gran'daddy, it says, 'Happy Birthday Carley' right here."

"But Gramma and Grampa said it's not my birthday for three days." There was confusion in her voice, but her eyes were wide as they swept over the cake and the presents.

Spencer said, "I think it's close enough. Now, you'd better blow out these candles before we start a forest fire."

"Make a wish!"

She gave me a sly smile and then blew a full breath, extinguishing the candles. We laughed as she picked them out and licked the frosting off.

"I know what you wished for. You wished you could eat all the frosting all by yourself," Spencer teased as he nabbed the last candle.

"No, Gran'daddy. I wished for doing this all the time."

She slept in the backseat of our pickup with Rosie on the way home Sunday. We were all tired, slightly sunburned and smelling of campfire smoke.

"Too bad we couldn't have had other kids with us, to make it a real party," I said.

"There'll be other chances. Don't worry; she had a blast."

197

"Do you think she should have a bath before we take her back to them?"

"Nah. Knowing them, they probably give her a bath when she comes back from our house anyway, to wash away our poison." I knew he was only half joking.

"So what if they know we took her camping?" he continued. "On our weekends, we can do what we want."

"I know. I'm just worried they'll think we didn't take care of her."

"Who cares what they think?"

"I know."

As he drove down the mountain road, my tired thoughts floated back and forth between the memory of our fun campout and the dread of taking her back.

"I just hope she doesn't get in trouble for having a good time with us."

Spencer reached for my hand and kissed it, as he sometimes did when we were in the car—he says because he just likes to.

"Buck and Mara will bombard her with questions like Don said they do, and she'll tell them what she wants to tell them. There's nothing we can do about it, so ignore it."

After a while I said, "If the tables were turned, if we had custody and they had visitation, could we do it? Could we take care of her for permanent?"

"Without a doubt. Our lives would be different; we'd have to figure out our work schedules, for one thing. But we'd do it. Let's see what the so-called Household Review turns up. If it shows what we want it to, maybe she'll be placed with us in protective custody while they sort things out."

My spirits picked up a bit. "Wouldn't that be nice?"

*   *   *

Our faith in the system was incorrect again. We read our copy of the Household Review, and it struck us as a colossal work of fiction, written by yet another starry-eyed, under-educated civil servant. We were repulsed by her flowery prose from page one. She painted a touching profile of a "straightforward and guileless working-class family" who "believes money and material wealth do not necessarily provide happiness." She noted that the Walls are perceived as "the poor relations" in their current circumstances (meaning us). She quoted Buck describing himself as "a straight-talking guy," adding that "he is rather direct, which can put some people off, but is refreshingly unpretentious."

About Mara, she wrote, "I sensed that Mara has a fragile aspect just under the surface, a quality some might miss at first blush. She holds a certain weariness to her demeanor at times, without actually looking tired or aged by it. And yet, one can make out an intestinal fortitude there, a clear, strong character that takes over the subliminal lassitude and shows off her mettle."

This investigator walked away with several other delusions.

Mara, reportedly diagnosed with Disassociative Personality Disorder, integrated nine personalities and her "core" is currently handling her life well (the counselor who wrote that report could not be contacted, but the statements were corroborated by Buck).

According to Buck and Mara, they very infrequently swat Carley; their usual choice of discipline is to give her choices and explanations. Mara deals with "how she was naughty" directly, and doesn't believe in sending Carley to her room to wait until Buck comes home.

Carley is able, Mara avowed, to verbalize that they are taking care of her because they are family and they love her. They "intend" to utilize the Early Intervention Program's in-home speech and language services for Carley, as well as Head Start enrollment "soon."

While separated from Buck and getting psychiatric therapy, Mara said her friend (the one we'd read about in the police report) had made trouble for them by loaning Mara money and trying to create a wedge in their lives. She had tried to buy Mara's affection, but Buck's filing for divorce was enough to "galvanize Mara and give her the strength to thwart the woman's attempts."

Buck said his auto repair business cannot generate enough business because he isn't allowed to advertise on his property. This is due to his failure to get permits before building his shop (he claimed we were the ones who reported him), and his lack of finances to build it to specifications.

The summary glorified Buck's and Mara's exceptional efforts to work through adversity and come out with their uncommon familial love intact. Their involvement with their grown children's lives and in their tribal heritage was said to be "inspiring." Throughout the document, the writer described them as resourceful, candid, comfortable, proud and capable.

The recommendation: "Innately, family connectiveness is important and should be given priority; children should have the opportunity to be raised by the birth family." She cited "their years of parenting, their obvious attachment, and the family's connection with a strong cultural recognition of Carley's heritage" as her reasons for recommending Buck and Mara as the adoptive parents.

*   *   *

"It makes me sick," I cried to Spencer. "How naïve can this woman be!"

Spencer groaned in disgust. "I don't know why I even let us build our hopes up."

"Is it us? If we're the only ones that see these people as hateful, abusive creeps, maybe we're ..."

"No! We're not the only ones. Emily, Wade, the local cops and almost anybody you talk to in Doolin. Hell, even Don Baines knows what they're like; he's just too spineless to do anything about it. Judge Harmon didn't like them, Jason hates them. It's not us. They *are* creeps."

As I listened, I let my anger return. Spencer was getting more fired up.

"But of course CSD sees them as the perfect, down-home folks. CSD protects themselves, because they need to justify their existence, show how they're keeping families together. They assign a *review* to an employee in another office and call it 'independent.' Of course they're going to back up the initial office's call. This caseworker just kisses the ass of another manager—what the hell does she know? She's a lowly worker hoping to look good."

"What she wrote about Mara's depression and working through her childhood abuse, did you get the impression this woman comes from an abusive childhood, too?"

"I think it's a prerequisite for the job. Caseworkers don't need to take courses on child psychology or counseling. They just need to be victims."

CHAPTER 43

With the agency's glowing recommendation, Richard Hill represented Buck and Mara at the adoption hearing. Judge Harmon allowed us to give statements and we tried our best, but without an attorney present we stumbled in our presentation. No decision was made, but we felt we knew how it would go. The Walls had tribal approval, and the approval of Oregon's child protection agency. Legal adoption of Carley wouldn't make that much difference to how she was being treated anyway. At least the judge emphatically stated that our visitation rights would still stand.

Less than a week after the hearing, Don Baines called Spencer and asked him to meet for coffee and a chat. When Spencer phoned me at work afterwards and told me what Don had to say, I was stunned.

There was another allegation of sexual abuse.

Since it was Friday, the day we were to get Carley, Don had asked Spencer to voluntarily give up our visitation. He said that would take the pressure off of the agency to act right away, allowing more time to do a better job than the last time. Don said he wouldn't let this get screwed up like Irma Pierce did. He wasn't allowed to divulge the particulars, but said Carley would need to be interviewed.

"Not by the same idiots as last time, I hope," I told Spencer.

"No. This time in Camas City, but only because of convenience. It was obvious that the fingers are pointing at me. If we push them, demand visitation today, they might charge me."

"Oh god. Arrest you?"

"I don't know how long it would take, but they wouldn't let us have Carley anyway. They'd just leave her with the Walls. Then I'd have to prove I didn't do it."

"Prove the negative," I said, staring down at my desk. "And your name would be in the paper."

"Yeah. So Don asked me to take a poly as soon as possible, and I said I would but I wanted the others to take one also. And I told him I wanted Harmon to be informed as soon as possible."

"Good," I said. I wanted to say something encouraging, but I was still reeling. "Why on earth did they do this shit again?"

"That's what Don asked. He's sure that they'll be granted the adoption and this is just going to hurt them. I told him I think they're pissed that we still get visitation and they want to drive a wedge between me and Carley."

"I can't stand that they're doing this to her." I wanted to scream, cry, pace circles around my desk, but I forced myself back to my work-mentality. "Okay. Here's what we can do. It's closed now, but Monday morning I'll go to the D.A.'s office and see about getting Carley some protection. We have witnesses that nothing happened to Carley the last time we had her. So if she's saying stuff, it's because they're manipulating her."

"That's right! Your mom was here that weekend," Spencer said. "I forgot to tell Don that. Shit. It's too late to reach him now—I'll have to wait till Monday."

"I'll call Mom and tell her we're giving her name and number to CSD."

"When I reach Don, I'm telling him he's got two weeks to get this investigation wrapped up. We're not giving up another visitation."

*   *   *

The District Attorney's receptionist sent me to Victim's Assistance, where I met Pam. She told me she already knew something about this case because she worked with Wade, the guy who'd tried to help before.

"I'm sorry, but with this in CSD's hands, all I can do is bring it up at the MD task force meeting," she said, referring to the multidisciplinary team with whom Wade had already struck out. "If I handle it carefully, though, initially with Don Baines, I might not get shushed up by Nina Cowan."

I stared at her. "What?"

"Wade and I would try to talk about this case before, and Cowan would shush us. She told me she was waiting for Carley to get old enough to tell her own story."

"That's ridiculous!"

"Oh yeah. Kids lie to protect themselves, whatever they see as safe at any given moment. It blows my mind that Nina Cowan doesn't get that, but she's the one pulling the strings. If you ask me, she's got way too much power for one person."

I agreed.

202

"But put your trust in Don Baines. He'll do what's right."

*   *   *

Our pleas to Don to get the investigation going went nowhere. He was taking the same slow, procedural steps that frustrated us the last time; he was just nicer than Pierce. Carley was interviewed, then examined by the county pediatrics expert. All inconclusive. Don called me to convince me that if we gave up another weekend, if we waited till Spencer passed the polygraph, the investigation would have to be directed elsewhere.

"Carley had contact with Mara, Buck and Kim in the same time period," Don said.

"So Kim's with them again. I'm glad she's getting to see her daughter. And I don't believe any sexual abuse came from her."

"Everybody Carley saw will be looked at," he said. But his voice lost it's conviction when he added, "I don't understand them, though—a bad-faith disclosure from the Walls at this point, when the adoption was a sure thing. In fact, Buck is angry at Mara for making the disclosure and screwing things up. It doesn't make sense."

I was sure he wasn't supposed to reveal who made the disclosure, but his frustration told me something more significant.

I said, "You expect her to make sense. You don't see that she's psychotic? That she would do this out of hatred for us?" I didn't wait for an answer. "Don, we'll agree not to demand our visitation again this weekend, but only to help the investigation. And it is the last time."

Waiting for the polygraph results was hell for Spencer. In the first place, Jason advised against it, saying that he thought CSD was giving him false encouragement so that he'd incriminate himself. Secondly, Spencer worried about the futility of proving a negative. At the last moment, he decided to cooperate, but entered the interview with a statement for the record, reserving the right to review and possibly decline questions. When it was over, Spencer was exhausted and insecure about the interviewer's vague response.

Eight days passed before Don Baines called us into his office.

"Sit down. I'm glad you could come in; it makes it easier to discuss this kind of thing."

We sat stiffly, neither of us taking our eyes off Don's face.

"Buck finally got his polygraph done. They're all over, but it didn't work out the way I'd hoped."

Spencer placed his hands on the arms of his chair, shoulders hunched. We waited for Don to go on.

He looked from Spencer to me, and back to Spencer. "I'm afraid I have to close the investigation, with 'Unable to Determine' as the finding."

Spencer sprang to his feet. Don shrank back in his chair, maybe expecting Spencer to lunge across the desk. But Spencer stood rigid, hands at his sides. I watched him from my chair, understanding that he deserved to handle this the way he wanted to.

"You and your agency have pushed us for four years, not achieving one thing to benefit this child. We tried to work with the system, but it's a ridiculous waste of time." He kept his voice strong but not loud, every sentence coming faster and with more heat than the one before.

"I have absolutely no faith in your polygraphs nor your investigation. You can tell Nina Cowan and Jim Foster that the next time they want our help, they can kiss my ass. We volunteer nothing from this point on. If we don't get our visitation, we'll go back to the courtroom. We're telling anybody and everybody what a joke you people are. I think *The Oregonian* might be interested in hearing about your tactics, like that phony Household Review and your biased investigations."

Don straightened, cleared his throat and said, "The Household Review is confidential. I have to advise you of the illegality of sending that to a newspaper."

Spencer was heading for the door with me when he stopped. Turning back to Don, he said, "Thanks for the warning. But just how does that affect Carley's welfare?"

We left without an answer.

CHAPTER 44

I waited at the counter at Mac's, nursing a cup of coffee and occasionally glancing across the restaurant at Carley, who was in a booth with Mara and her cousin. She sneaked impish peeks at me, too, while dangling a French fry above her mouth like a bird with a worm. Mara made no attempt to acknowledge me. When the wall clock read exactly five, I put my money for the coffee on the counter and walked over to them.

"Hi, guys," I gave a friendly smile to Carley's cousin, who smiled back without hesitation. "Carley, are you ready to go? You get to come down to our place for a visit!"

Mara pushed the plate of fries closer to Carley and said in her baby-voice, "Are you done with your French fries? Don't you want some more?"

"No," Carley said, and she let herself slide under the table. She laughed as she popped up on the other side and started tromping for the door.

"Wait for me, kiddo," I said. "We've got to get your bag."

For the first time, Mara looked up at me. "There's some aspirin and cough syrup, because she's got a bad cold." She handed me the overnight bag. "Also, her toothbrush and fluoride rinse. You give her a tablespoon... is it tablespoon? I don't remember."

"The directions will be on the bottle. I'll check." I was doing my best to be polite, but I couldn't wait to get out of there. Carley was bouncing up and down at the door, and other customers were watching us with undisguised interest.

"Carley, your Grampa will be here Sunday to pick you up." To me, Mara said, "He went hunting, but he'll be here right at five Sunday."

"Okay, we'll be here. See you later," I said to the other little girl, who was still smiling at me.

As I reached the door and took Carley's hand, Mara called out, loud enough for the whole restaurant to hear, "Take good care of her."

Carley and I walked down the sidewalk to my car and I chattered enthusiastically about what we had planned for the weekend. Carley didn't say a word until we were buckled in and I said, "Okay, here we go."

She looked straight ahead and said without expression, "My Gramma takes good care of me."

I looked over at her, trying to guess where that came from, but only saw her blank stare. I kept my reaction light. "That's good." Then, getting back our merry mood, "You are a special little girl and deserve the best, don't you?" She nodded vigorously. "So let's go home and see what good stuff Gran'daddy has planned for you!"

At home, Spencer was waiting in the yard and she ran into his open arms.

"Gran'daddy!"

"Hey, Snigglefritz! Boy, am I glad to see you!"

"I haven't been here in a *l-o-n-g* time. I missed you *s-o-o-o* much."

"I missed you, too, sweetie." They made pretend-grunts of exertion as they hugged. "But you're here now, so we'd better get busy and start having some fun."

We had a great weekend and it passed too quickly. The only signs of her "bad cold" was a cough at bedtime. She asked for her medicine because "Gramma always gives it to me." I gave her a half-dose of cough syrup (because the label said it was for children over six) and no aspirin.

Sunday afternoon she got a little teary when she realized we were taking her back to Doolin.

"It's okay, sweetie, you'll come again. We will always be here for you, even if your Gramma and Grampa don't want you to come."

Spencer shot me a look, indicating that that wasn't the right thing to say.

"Will you come get me?" she sounded worried.

I realized that I was probably making it worse for her. "We would get some help."

Spencer tried to change the subject. "Look, Carley. Look at this funny car coming up. Wow, that's an old one."

She was not deterred. "But I like my Gramma and Grampa."

I said quietly, "Of course, you do. It's just that they don't like us so much and they don't like you to be with us."

She nodded in agreement.

"When I get bigger, I'm going to tell my Gramma and Grampa to let me see my Gran'mommy and Gran'daddy."

"That would be nice. Now, no more worrying. You're not allowed to worry. Remember?"

Spencer joined in. "That's right." He shook his finger at her and said in a mock scolding, "No more worrying."

And she laughed.

*   *   *

It was a relief for us to ignore the state agency. Don Baines called us once to say that he was glad we got our visitations back and he'd send us a copy of his report. He also said that Buck had been hounding him with phone calls; we didn't ask why. Nina Cowan sent letters reminding us that she was still working out the plan for a mediator. We didn't bother with a reply.

Our hunt for a reporter interested in exposing the failures that the state agency had made in Carley's case ended the same way as our search for a lawyer. No one wanted to touch it. Evidently, abuse without physical wounds either didn't make headlines or was too risky to print. It was another fruitless venture.

One Friday in December, Spencer and I waited at Mac's coffee counter for the Walls to come in with Carley. We were early, so we got coffee and struck up a conversation with the couple next to us.

The woman said she recognized us, and sympathized with us having to deal with Buck for these arrangements.

"Believe me, we know what a moron he is. We should; we lived next door to them for years," she said.

She and the man were sitting around the corner of the counter from us, so we could look at them as they talked. I knew them by sight, but didn't know they knew us.

The man spoke, "We see you come to pick up your granddaughter here, and it's too bad, all the trouble you've had. We watched their kids grow up, and we know that their daughter was abused so it hurts us to think that the little girl is being abused, too."

Spencer was cautious. "How do you know about their daughter?"

"She told us," the woman said. "When she was little. Of course she doesn't say it now, but I bet if she was ever on the witness stand she'd tell it."

"Abused by Buck?" I asked.

The man answered quickly, "No, by that psycho, Mara. The daughter just protects her mother because she's simple minded, accepts everything that happens to her."

"Why do you think that Buck lets Mara get away with abusive behavior?" I asked them.

"Because he's an enabler," the woman said.

The man said, "Because he's a moron."

The owner of Mac's had come to replenish our coffee cups, and asked, "Who you talking about?"

"Buck and Mara Wall," the man told him.

"That's your granddaughter's other grandparents?" he asked us.

Spencer said, "Yeah. Our daughter had a baby with their son Dewayne."

"You mean that tall, skinny guy that lives with the fourteen-year-old girl?"

I said, "With the Walls? Dewayne lives with a fourteen-year-old girlfriend in their house?"

"No," he said. "In her house with her parents. How dumb is that?"

The man and woman next to us laughed, and the owner walked away.

"That's not going to help us. Dewayne is a creep but we don't think he's the one that abused Carley," Spencer said.

The woman turned to her husband. "Do you remember when we saw Carley and Mara in here that time?" She turned back to face me. "Carley came right out and said someone hurt her. Then, when they got up to go, she came back over to us and changed it to, 'Spencer did it.'"

"She really said, 'Spencer?' Because she never calls him 'Spencer,'" I said.

The woman thought for a moment, and said, "I'm sure it was 'Spencer.' So you know it's Mara teaching her to say you hurt her," she told Spencer.

We saw Buck and Carley come in the door, and Spencer got up to get her and pay for the coffees.

"Thanks for the conversation," I said to the couple.

The man said, "Sure thing. And if you ever need us to speak up for you in court, we'd be glad to help."

"I appreciate it, but right now there's no reason to go back to court. At least until something else happens and we can afford an attorney again."

I ran to catch up with Spencer and Carley. She was happy and excited to see us both there, and she raced us to the car.

I would tell Spencer about the couple's offer later, but I knew what he would say. There was a time when we would have felt some kind of hope from their information, and put our faith in using it to our advantage. But not anymore.

CHAPTER 45

One of Don's letters stated, "Despite your frustration with our agency and the complaints you have about the way we have treated you, I feel a need to tell you that you will not make Carley safer by questioning, talking with her, etc. in situations that you should be reporting to CSD or law enforcement."

I asked my mother, my sisters and everyone close to us who knew the whole story, "Do you think we inadvertently prompted responses from Carley?" No one believed we'd said anything that might have led her in any way.

"You're both smarter than that," said our friend Lou. "I've been there when Carley talks about her Gramma and Grampa and I see how you react. Some of the things she has said makes me want to cry, but you and Spencer are very careful not to prompt her, and I've never heard you criticize them in front of her. Frankly, I don't know how you do it." She shuddered in disgust.

We were on her patio, protected and sunny with a view of the ocean. Whenever I needed to talk, we'd sit there with our coffees or our screwdrivers, depending on the time of day.

"Sometimes, I don't know if we're helping or hurting her," I told Lou.

"You're absolutely not hurting her. Just think how bad it would be for her if you weren't doing all that you're doing. Lord knows the stupid people at CSD aren't helping her. If she's getting lessons about how to tell people what they want to hear, it's from them."

We sipped our drinks, gazing out at the ocean for awhile, then Lou went on, "What else can you do? It doesn't do any good to report anything to CSD. You've done that and they've been no help. You're there for her and that's what matters."

"But," I said, "if we weren't in the picture at all, if we just let them alone, the Walls wouldn't have anything to retaliate against. They could raise her as they see fit and they wouldn't be teaching her to hate."

It was a thought Spencer and I had voiced before. My mother gave us the best advice.

"Carley has two parents," she told us. "Maybe Kim isn't able to take that role right now, but you're Kim's parents and you need to do it for her. Try to teach Carley the right things. That's all that anyone raising children, even in the best of situations, can do. Keep trying."

Letters between Nina Cowan and us continued. She wanted to know if we were refusing to attend mediated meetings with the Walls. Our reply posed questions about how it was supposed to work, what it was supposed to accomplish and what was expected of us. A lot had happened in the six months since the idea was initiated.

Cowan's main topic was the unusual privilege we were receiving, considering the state's tight budget constraints. This sort of service was intended for open adoption arrangements, a relatively new development for Children's Services to handle, and we did not fit the definition. And, she reminded us, the mediation "would not serve as a vehicle for re-assessment of past child protective services allegations."

Spencer had done some legal digging that exposed two of the lies that Mara had told to the Household Review investigator. He wrote to Cowan and reminded her of Mara's statement that her mental disorder had been resolved, and yet she was getting a monthly Social Security income for a claimed mental disability. She was also receiving Food Stamps without mentioning Buck and the income from his business.

I didn't think any of this communication was worthwhile, but Spencer said it made him feel better.

We were surprised to find out that the Walls had actually en-rolled Carley in Head Start. She mentioned "Teacher Paul" on her visits, at first hesitantly as if she had been told not to tell us. We reacted with a casualness that gave her courage to talk, and she admitted that she liked learning things at school. She especially liked one day that Gramma was sick and Grampa had to take her.

We could tell that Carley was concentrating on speaking better. She bragged about saying words the right way and we cheered her on. We could detect a Southern-sounding drawl, making two syllables out of a one-syllable word at the end of a sentence, like "I put on my ha-yat." We didn't remark. She also tried to use pronouns correctly, instead of starting the sentence with "her" or "him." Whoever "Teacher Paul" was, we were thankful for his dedication.

*   *   *

Journal entry: 12/6/97—Saturday

Last night we had our usual fun. Carley didn't talk about Gramma and Grandpa, except to say that her cough was gone but Gramma says it is still there. She reeked of cigarette smoke, but is healthy.

She went to bed willingly, but then started a phony whimpering about being afraid, she didn't know of what. I left lights on for her, and talked to her through the ceiling between our rooms. About 6:00 a.m., she was at Spencer's side of our bed, whispering stories we couldn't understand, but she was not upset. He asked her if she wanted one of us to take her back to her bed, because it wasn't quite morning yet, she said no and crawled into bed beside him. After a moment, he got up to go to the bathroom, over me to get out on my side of the bed, and back in on my side, remaining there. Carley continued talking for a short while, then fell asleep.

12/7 – Sunday

During the day, Carley wouldn't take a nap. I tried to convince her by telling her I was worried that if she got tired, she might misbehave or act a little goofy and get in trouble with Mara and Buck. She said, "I only get in trouble with Gramma and Grampa when I pee or poop my pants."

When it was time to change her clothes and take her back, she went limp and played dead. So we went along with the game and dressed her together, and that made her laugh. Heading to the car, she said, "I have to go to Gramma's and Grampa's because... Well, just because." She appeared withdrawn and lifeless on the way there, and would only respond if I asked a direct question—about Christmas lights. At Mac's, she walked instead of the usual run to Grampa.

12/19-21—Weekend before Christmas visitation

Mara and Buck both were at Mac's when we went to get Carley. They snarled at us and the only thing they said was to demand goodbye kisses from Carley. She kissed them, announced that she had a cold, then coughed to show me. I said, "Bummer," and we walked out, talking cheerfully. At bedtime, she fought us a little but we told her it was important she sleep in her own bed where she was comfortable. She tried the "I miss Gramma and Grampa" whine, but I said, "yeah, yeah," and she stopped and went to sleep.

212

Saturday we wrapped presents, baked cookies and played.

Sunday we went to Lou's house. Her grandson, Seth, was visiting and he and Carley played like old pals. Before leaving, I had trouble getting Carley to change out of her wet pull-up diaper, but I talked her into it. Then we had to joke with her on the way to Mac's to get her to smile. When we met Buck, he had his other granddaughter with him. Carley got to show-off our dog and demonstrate how to walk her. Buck tried to stop them, but he couldn't and he didn't look happy about it.

12/23-25—Tuesday through Thursday

Carley was excited when she saw Tisha with us when we picked her up. All day long she pulled Tisha around the house, delighted to have such a playmate. She went to bed easily and we got to play Santa Claus at a reasonable hour.

Wednesday, our Christmas, went really well. Carley played a little bit with everything, but mostly with the little plastic frogs. We had a big turkey dinner and she ate well. Bedtime was agreeable, except she made a game of being afraid of the "scary things." So Spencer and I talked about where everyone was—she liked that Tisha was in the room right next to hers.

On Thursday morning, she was very cooperative with having some cereal and juice, and getting dressed to go. Since it was Christmas, the restaurant was closed and Buck met us out on the street. Carley was acting very cool, kissing and hugging us all goodbye. In Buck's truck, she continued waving to us.

1/2-3/98—Friday-Saturday

When we drove up to Mac's, I saw Carley standing in a booth, playing with a plastic reindeer in the window. Mara and Buck saw us and looked away. Inside, Carley was watching for us, in a playful mood. She smiled and slid under the table, hiding. Mara and Buck looked helpless and did nothing. Spencer and I tried some encouragement, but didn't want to make a scene. When it was apparent that Mara and Buck were not going to help, we said we'd wait over by the counter. I should have dealt with Carley's behavior myself, because what they did made things worse.

Buck brought Carley by the hand and let her pay the bill at the register. Then, without letting go of her hand, he brought her to us and just stood there. Mara was there, too, asking for hugs and repeating, "Just one-two days, then you'll be back with us." At this point, Carley was clinging to Buck's leg and crying, "Grampa. I want my Grampa."

I said, "Let's go outside and head for our car." They acted the same there, looking helpless and telling her, "You have to go; there's nothing we can do about it." Mara added, "We don't always get what we want." Carley became more hysterical. Buck asked if he could have fifteen minutes to talk to her away from us. I said, "Go ahead, but not fifteen minutes. She's just very tired." He carried her a short way down the sidewalk, and Mara followed with her hands in her pockets.

He brought Carley back in a few minutes, holding her hand. She was sniffling, but got in the back seat. I got in with her to fasten the seatbelt. Buck and Mara walked away saying, "Goodbye. Just one-two days."

In the car, Carley pulled away from me and wouldn't let me do the seatbelt. She screamed, "No!" I felt her getting hot and very worked up, so I tried to get her coat off. It was slippery and padded, and she used it to hide and get away from my hold. So I let her fall to the floor, kicking her cowboy boots and thrashing her arms in that tight space at my feet. I moved things out of the way and saw that she was okay. Spencer waited until Buck and Mara had driven off, then we left. Carley cried, kicked and screamed for a few minutes, then fell asleep. We felt awful but didn't know what else we could do.

At home, she woke up and immediately went into hysterics. Spencer picked her up and carried her to the living room, where we got her coat and boots off. She threw herself on the floor and screamed for awhile. I placed a plastic cup of water next to her and told her to let us know when she needed something. We tried soothing words, but it only made her yell more. After we ignored her, she finally fell asleep.

When she woke up, about an hour later, Spencer put a pillow next to her, telling her softly, "You might like this." She smiled at us and curled up. In a few moments, Spencer got her to sit on the couch. She began talking softly and smiling shyly. I had dinner ready and Spencer told her to let us know when she was hungry. She said, "I love you, Gran'daddy," and we had dinner.

Bedtime was no problem. We read to her, explained away the "scary things," and she slept for almost twelve hours.

Sitting together in the morning, we told her we were sorry she had been upset, and that we understood that it must be hard having two homes to go to and from all the time. She said, "Gramma and

Grampa always ask me what happens here." It was very clear. I said, "Maybe you don't always have to answer them." Then she changed the subject. Throughout the day, she repeated "I love you, Gran'mommy and Gran'daddy," often.

CHAPTER 46

Being careful with our words and our reactions was a constant struggle. Where Spencer had to always be overly cautious in the way he touched Carley, I had to be careful of what I said. How should I respond when she says, "Gramma and Grampa are hurting my popo—I told them not to, but they didn't hear me"? How should I react when I see an irritation between her legs?

Sometimes I said the wrong things, the things that Don Baines warned us about. When bathing her, I saw a scratch and said, "Oh, that looks like it hurts. Can I see a little closer?"

She looked pained and said, "No! That's from where you scratched me."

"I didn't scratch you, sweetie."

"That's where Gramma scratched me."

I dropped it. Later, while brushing her tangled hair, she told me that she didn't worry about knots. I said, "That's good, because little girls shouldn't worry about anything."

Carley said, "I know that, because I listen to what people tell me. I listen to my mommy and daddy, and to my grandparents who are Gramma and Grampa, and to…."

She hesitated, so I guessed, "To your teacher, Paul?"

She said, "Yes," but without certainty.

I wondered about that list. Was she being taught to exclude us? Was it that business again about how we don't count because we weren't blood relatives?

In the morning, Carley crawled into bed with me after Spencer got up, so we talked. I told her I thought I knew what was confusing her, and that I would tell her and she could say if I was right. I tried to explain how we adopted Kim and Tisha, about mommies and daddies coming and going, and where grandparents come from. I said maybe her Gramma and Grandpa were telling her something confusing about that.

She said, "No, they don't say anything about that."

My guess had been wrong, and I should have stopped there. But I said, "That's good. They do say things to us, and—well, I just wanted you to know that we will always be your Gran'mommy and Gran'daddy. We will always be here."

"Gramma and Grandpa say I will be with you guys only a little tiny time, and be with them the rest of the time."

"Do you want to keep it that way?" Another question I shouldn't have asked.

"Yes."

"Me too, Carley," I lied. "But your Gramma and Grandpa get mad about that for some reason. They think we're doing bad things."

Carley hugged me.

"No. You and Gran'daddy are good to me. And Gramma and Grandpa are good to me, too."

"Of course they are."

I couldn't drop it. At that moment, I didn't have as much sense as Carley.

"But I'm worried if anyone is playing or touching your popo, because that is wrong."

And that's when she said they did it. I had filled her head with senseless notions and ruined any chance of helping her with this.

I blundered through explanations about serious "telling" and the need to be careful with what is true and what isn't, and about not keeping secrets inside.

I said I hoped that if she didn't want to tell me, maybe she could tell her teacher.

She was quiet for a long time, making different facial expressions as if thinking things over.

I said, "I'm sorry, Carley. I won't bother you anymore. Let's get up and go have breakfast."

It didn't end there. When getting her dressed for bed, I sneaked a look at her crotch and saw an unnatural reddishness. Without visible reaction, I asked, "Do you hurt anywhere?"

She grabbed herself, saying, "Gramma and Grandpa hurt my popo."

I showed concern in my face and voice. Looking her in the eyes, I said, "I don't like that; it is very wrong, but I don't know what to do. But you don't worry about that. I will talk to Gran'daddy and see what he thinks."

Carley said, "You talk to Gramma and Grandpa, too, when you take me back. Tell them not to do that anymore."

"We'll see, but that might not be a good idea. I will tell someone, but I'm worried about you having to be asked so many questions again."

"Yeah," she said with finality.

We would never know the truth. Our hopes that "Teacher Paul" could help were dashed when Carley revealed that Mara was always there with her.

"It's always Gramma that cleans me up when I poop my pants at school."

Then she added, "But she doesn't spank me at school. Only at home if I poop my pants."

*   *   *

On February 9th, Judge Harmon signed a Decree of Adoption for petitioners Walter Buck Wall and Mara Rose Wall. Stated therein, just before the reference to Children Service Division's Household Review that recommended the adoption, was this point:

"While the Court questions the motives of Petitioners in bringing the adoption request, the Court recognizes that the Paternal Grandparents have acted as de-facto parents for Carley for the last four years."

Then: "The Court finds that it is in the best interest of the child that some parenting stability be given to her life. She is not getting that stability from her biological parents."

We took some solace from seeing that the judge had Richard Hill, the Walls' attorney, include the Court's misgivings about their motives. Our attorney, Jason Norden, had scored points as well, with the complete visitation order spelled out. The judge stated that he found clear and convincing evidence that our visitation was in Carley's best interest, that we had a substantial relationship with her and that it did not interfere with the relationship between Carley and the adoptive family.

Buck must have seen that last part as a toehold in getting rid of us. On the Friday of our next visitation, Buck carried a sobbing Carley from the restaurant to his pickup. When Spencer followed him, thinking Carley would be handed to him, Buck said, "This happens every time. I have to start working on Carley on Tuesday to get her ready for Friday." He then showed Spencer the page from the adoption decree with the part about "interference" highlighted, and said, "See you in court." He drove away with Carley.

Other customers and I watched through the window of the restaurant. One woman said, "That poor little girl was in an extremely exhausted condition when she came in here. No wonder she was cranky." Another said, "I saw her sleeping. Her grandpa woke her up and told her, 'I know you don't want to go but you have to.' Now how did he expect her to act after that!"

On Saturday, we enlisted the help of the Doolin Police Department to get Carley from the Walls' home. She was glad to see us and came happily.

That weekend I realized the importance of keeping myself far above Buck's kind of manipulation. Carley needed to be four years old, to be spoiled with attention and to be happy. I agreed with Spencer. The best way to help her was to just give her that.

CHAPTER 47

We sent a letter announcing our plans for our two-week July visitation to the Walls, via Richard Hill. It was only February but we had to leave enough time for possible legal hassles from the Walls. Our mediated meetings were supposed to start in March, and although not enthusiastic about it, we told ourselves at least it couldn't hurt. Also, considering Buck's threat of taking us to court, it would be interesting to see how he would argue that we interfered with their relationship with Carley.

The mediator was a grim-faced, bony woman who specialized in family law. First, we met her without the Walls to discuss the expectations. She laid out the ground rules about what kind of language we could and couldn't use, and had us sign the Mediation and Confidentiality Agreement, all very professional.

Spencer told her, "We'll continue down this road as long as Buck and Mara do, but it won't last long. They won't be able to play by the rules, and if they can't get you on their side, they won't have any use for you."

"I'm not on anybody's side," she said in her cheerless monotone. "I hope you all are going into this with open minds, with the goal of giving your granddaughter the attention she needs."

"We realize the intended goal and your part in it, but you haven't met with the Walls yet," Spencer said as he shook her hand. "Good luck."

After the second meeting, Spencer and I agreed that this woman was more capable than we had expected. Buck and Mara were their usual irrational, whiny selves. They bitched and the mediator did her job by restating what she thought they meant. We waited our turn to counter their accusations, and she turned back to them. Mara looked as if she was enjoying the attention, but Buck got surly. His crossed-arm posture made the mediator scowl as she reminded us that we were all looking out for Carley's welfare, and that we were committed to return the next week.

At the third session, the Walls were missing. Spencer told the mediator, "Well, that was fun while it lasted. If you ever set up another meeting, let us know. But we're not making this trip again unless you get confirmation from them that they'll be here." The told-you-so was not spoken.

We didn't have another meeting; the mediator phoned once to say, "The Walls cannot be reached."

*　　*　　*

Our first Saturday in April, we took Carley to the beach and shot a whole roll of film. It was cold but we bundled up and she never slowed down. At home, we had a fancy dinner with candles on the table because Spencer had showed her how to use the long-handled snuffer. She loved the responsibility. The weekend passed without worry until getting ready to go on Sunday.

Carley walked into our bedroom while I was changing my shirt. When I saw she was there, I made a face at her and quickly covered up. She said something, and the only two words I could understand sounded like "sucking boobs." But when I asked her to say it again, she wouldn't.

"That damn Mara is a sick freak," I ranted with Spencer when we were alone after taking Carley back.

"You and I know that, but so what? There's not enough to prove anything to Cowan's CSD. They'd say she just saw a woman nursing a baby, or whatever. It doesn't matter. Unless Carley is whipped to a bloody pulp it's not child abuse in their eyes."

I knew. It was a continuing argument and it went nowhere. Spencer and I debated what we should or shouldn't report to CSD, knowing the risk of losing even more credibility if it was something they wouldn't call "abuse." We had to hope revelations would come from someone else, and that meanwhile Carley wasn't severely hurt.

"This is horrible. It's almost like we need for something bad to happen to her so that she'll get helped." My eyes filled as the words left my mouth. "Oh god, I can't believe I said that."

"It's okay. I've thought the same thing." He hugged me gently. "We're doing all we can, and we just have to keep it up. Try to relax and enjoy her when we see her, and don't worry about things we can't do anything about."

"I thought things improved a little bit, during the short period we had the mediation. Carley was more easy-going at the restaurant exchanges."

"Yeah, well. Buck put a stop to that."

221

"It makes you wonder what they'll do next, doesn't it?"

*   *   *

Two weeks later, I was picking Carley up at Mac's by myself because Spencer had to work late. I sat at the counter with a cup of coffee and watched the clock. It was odd that the Walls hadn't shown up by five fifteen and I started getting a bad feeling. The waitress, who had long since gotten used to this biweekly routine, chatted with me.

"You know, I haven't seen Buck or Mara in a while, and they usually come in once or twice a week. Let me go ask the bartender if he's seen them."

When she returned with a negative answer, I said, "Well, thanks anyway. It's always something with these people. I'll wait another 15 minutes."

She consoled with me while I waited nervously. We both knew something was wrong. I got up to go and said, "If anyone comes while I'm gone, would you please tell them I went to their house to look for Carley. If they're not home, I'll be right back."

I drove the mile up the highway to their house, all the time watching for one of their vehicles to pass me. At their driveway, I saw no sign of any vehicles and the garage door was closed. My heart raced as I got out of the car and slowly approached the house. My mind searched for plausible explanations for the abnormal appearance of the house. Windows were dark but the curtains were open, no lights on inside. As I passed the front window on my way to the door, I looked in.

The living room was empty. No furniture, nothing on the walls, no one home.

I stared into the stark bleakness for a long moment, taking deep breathes and willing myself to calm down and think. I wouldn't be able to reach Spencer until he got home at six, so I had to do something myself.

I got back in my car and drove to the police station. An after-hours emergency phone outside the closed office got me the 911 operator, who took my information. I told her I would wait at Mac's Café.

A few minutes later, the Doolin police officer appeared. It was the same one who had gone to get Carley for us weeks before when they had refused us our visitation. He listened politely and told me to wait there while he went to have a look. The waitress and a few customers who knew me and knew the situation expressed sympathies. I used the bar phone to call home and was finally able to talk to Spencer. By this time the shock had lessened so that I could tell him what was going on without waiting for him to react. The officer came in while I was talking.

"Wait a minute, Spencer. The police officer's here." I put the phone receiver in the air between the officer and me. "This is my husband on the line."

"Okay. The house does appear to be uninhabited. I will continue to check for the residents throughout the weekend, and on Monday I'll talk with some of the neighbors. That's all I can do at this point."

When I put the phone to my ear again, Spencer said, "Come home. We'll get through this. Just come home, and drive carefully."

PART EIGHT—RESOLVE

(April, 1998—September, 2001)

CHAPTER 48

Jason bumped the door open with the cardboard box he carried into the courtroom. I saw that it was almost overflowing with file folders and binders. He glanced at the court clerk, a pretty woman about his age, who'd stopped what she was doing at her station in front of the judge's bench. She stared wide-eyed at Jason. He smiled back, almost flirtatiously I thought.

"I know it looks bad," he laughed. "But I promise not all of it has to be entered."

Spencer must've gotten the joke because he laughed too.

I knew we had piles of evidence documents, and there had been more motions filed in the last five-and-a-half months than I could count, but I didn't understand it all. I was content to grasp that we had jumped through the proper hoops to finally sue Buck and Mara Wall for contempt of court.

The judge this time was Stephen Zoritch, a new one for us. When he took his bench, I saw that he was as short as Jason, looked to be in his forties and had a surprisingly kind smile.

He studied his papers briefly and then looked up, directly into each of our faces as he took in the whole courtroom. No surprise registered when his eyes swept past the conspicuously empty respondents' side of the room.

"You represent the petitioners today. Is that right, Mr. Norden?"

"That's correct, Your Honor."

We were allowed to sit down, and Jason and Judge Zoritch went through the required litany of motions and consents. I understood then why it had been smart to take the necessary, time-consuming steps that our lawyer had advised.

When we had contacted Jason in April, the Monday following the Walls' disappearance, we were in a vindictive rage. To us, the vision of cops searching the highways for Buck's RV, slapping cuffs on him and Mara and rescuing Carley was still in the realm of possibilities. Then the Doolin police chief had tried to get the Camas County District Attorney to help, but was told that no criminal law had been violated. Jason told us that it was clear that the Walls were in contempt for disobeying the court-ordered visitation, but first we had to find them to serve them with subpoenas. We had to do our own search.

Word circulated in Doolin about what had happened, and people talked. We discovered that the Walls had not sold their house, but had traded their boat and some of Buck's tools to a local car dealer to pay off a loan and get ready cash. The contractor who had built Buck's shop was not so lucky, and he told us his wasn't the only debt that the Walls had skipped out on. We gave that information to Nina Cowan, hoping she'd add it to the Social Security and Food Stamp fraud and change her mind about the Walls' role as responsible parents. It didn't.

That went on the list of contentions we sent to the division's top guy, Director of Children's Services. We'd heard about a grievance procedure for disgruntled clients to be heard by a citizen review board. However, when we requested a hearing, we found out that we didn't qualify. The Director informed us that we weren't "clients" because there was no record of the agency having a "plan" with us.

As I sat in the courtroom, I wished that the Director and Cowan and the naïve caseworker who'd done the shoddy Household Review on the Walls were sitting there with me.

Judge Zoritch took his time sorting through the records that documented the agonizing measures we'd taken to search for and serve papers on Buck and Mara. There was also something from an Arizona attorney, filing on behalf of the Walls, who had requested a continuance. Jason pointed out that the request was not in compliance, and the lawyer was not licensed in the State of Oregon. Richard Hill, their Oregon attorney, had officially terminated his services on April 14th, the day they left.

The judge agreed that we had a right to proceed.

Jason began with our friends who had come forward when we first started asking around town for news on the Walls.

"Are you familiar with the long-standing dispute between the two families regarding their granddaughter?" Jason asked Cindy, my hairdresser, and Mara's as well.

"Yes," she said confidently. "I know that they have been involved in numerous court battles over Carley."

"Would you tell us what transpired on January 9th of this year?"

Cindy was prepared and knew what she was going to say, and did so without hesitation.

"According to my appointment files, Mara Wall came in to get her hair permed. This type of appointment takes approximately two hours, and we talked a lot, mostly about her granddaughter. She told me that she and her husband were in the process of adopting the child and once it was finalized, they would be moving to Arizona. A couple of years ago, Mrs. Wall had been in as a customer and told me that she and her husband had purchased some property there. She said that they wanted to go as soon as they sold their Doolin property in order to get away from Carley's other grandparents."

Satisfied, Jason said, "I have no more questions for this witness, Your Honor."

I knew that Cindy was being careful not to show any bias as she left the witness stand without making eye contact with me. I hoped she knew how grateful we were. She'd taken unpaid time from her business to do this for us.

Next up was a fellow inspector from my office. Dale had been inspecting a project on the highway that ran in front of the Walls' house in Doolin. During the seven months of the project, Buck had been one of the sidewalk supervisors that Dale had had to contend with.

After answering the same introductory questions as Cindy, Dale was given the go-ahead to tell it in his own words.

"On 28 February 1998, I initiated conversation with Buck Wall regarding two mailboxes near his driveway entrance."

I had to duck my head to hide a smile. I knew this sounded like a canned speech, but it was how Dale talked, at least for authority types. At our desks, out of managers' earshot, he and I joked like bar hounds.

"We also discussed the Ford Thunderbird in his driveway with a For Sale sign in the window, his welding work and the construction of his shop. He asked me what office I worked in, and when I told him, he asked if I knew Gail McGhee." Dale nodded in my direction, and continued.

"I told him that she worked in another part of the office and I only had contact with her once or twice a week. Mr. Wall then said that Mr. and Mrs. McGhee were the source of all his problems. He said that they made his life a living hell, especially Gail McGhee. To quote Mr. Wall, 'She is a fucking bitch. She's falsely accused me of child abuse, and she can't be trusted.' He then continued to say that he was planning on moving out of Oregon to get away from them. He said that his house, boat and cars were for sale in preparation for the move. He said that he owned property in a small town in

Arizona, and he was taking his granddaughter there so that he would not have to see the McGhees anymore. He then went into his shop and brought out some color photos of the property. I remember commenting that his pictures, showing only pine trees and brush, didn't look like what I knew of that area."

I wasn't sure what purpose Dale's testimony served, but I was glad the judge heard it, and I know Dale enjoyed saying it.

Spencer then took the stand to describe what we did to try to find them.

"I researched Arizona county assessors on the Internet," he explained, "and found the property, a small, undeveloped lot in an extremely rural area off of Highway I-40. I found a private investigator in Prescott, and I flew there to meet with him. I hired him on a per-hour plus mileage and expenses contract to locate the property and verify whether anyone was there.

"When he found it, he reported that it was what people around there called JSP, nothing but junipers and scrub pines, and not much of those. He had to drive down seven miles of rutted dirt road to find their driveway, and didn't see any sign of anyone having been there. He described it as the kind of place where 'survivalists' live. No electricity, no phones. People haul in water over bad roads."

Our lawyer said, "What other efforts did you make to find your granddaughter?"

"We notified Childquest.org, an Internet search website, but found out we couldn't register a lost child without law enforcement involvement. Oregon State Police told us they would discuss it with Nina Cowan at CSD."

The week that Buck and Mara left, we had phoned CSD and reported that Carley had made a strange remark about "sucking boobs" when we last saw her. Cowan left a message for us that she would investigate, but we hadn't heard from her since.

Spencer continued, "I also tried the sheriffs' departments in two Arizona counties. Deputies there said they would keep an eye out for them. We got descriptions of Mara and Buck and their vehicles and distributed them, with a photo of Carley and a plea to 'help us find our granddaughter,' to RV parks and campgrounds in the area. I enlisted the help of Arizona's Fraud Unit, because of discrepancies in Mara's Food Stamp and Social Security claims. And we tried two other on-line data search companies looking for Buck Wall."

Spencer paused to take a breath. Jason let only a few seconds go by before he prompted him again.

"Where else did you look for the Walls?"

"In Nevada. Our daughter, who's living in Utah, got a call from Mara Wall in late May. She said Mara told her they were staying on tribal land north of Reno."

I thought back to the shock we felt when Kim phoned us in April, shortly after the Walls left Doolin. It was the first we'd heard from her since the November phone call asking for help getting Carley back, and she acted like she didn't remember that. Then my mother told me about a long letter she'd received from Kim. She wanted my mom's help getting through to us because, Kim said, all attempts to talk to us ended in a fight. This time it was close to the truth, because I told Kim if she really wanted to be part of the family again, she could help us find Carley. Four weeks later she called to say that Mara had called her. But all she would tell us was that Mara said they were having a nice time.

"And did you file papers with the tribal court there, attempting to serve the Walls if they were located?" Jason asked.

"Yes, but we were told there was no sign of them. We checked with them repeatedly, as we did with the Mukilki tribe and the BIA in Oklahoma. "

"Did you have any mailing address for the Walls?"

"Oh, yeah. The Doolin Police found a neighbor who had a forwarding address in Texas for the Walls, but it turned out to be a mail-collection site and couldn't give us the forwarding address. We attempted to serve the hearing notice that way, but it was returned unopened."

All this was to show Judge Zoritch that we had the right to serve notice by publication, meaning the local newspaper. Jason added an exhibit of our investigative costs and attorney fees. He'd told us that with "contempt" cases, you had to ask for a money judgment; it gave the judge somewhere to go in order to satisfy a remedy. What we wanted was to get Carley back, hopefully for good. Against Jason's advice, we'd asked him to include a Petition for Custody or Visitation. We argued that we had enough to meet the statute defining a child-parent relationship with Carley. The Visitation alternative was a safe back-up and we left that worded the same as the existing order.

Judge Zoritch asked us to stand. "I've heard testimony and received the exhibits, and I find that Mara Wall and Walter Wall have intentionally and willfully withheld visitation from the petitioners, who have expended substantial amounts of time and money attempting to locate Mr. and Mrs. Wall.

"Mr. Norden, you will write the judgment ordering the respondents to pay the attorney fees and costs incurred by the petitioners, and to pay $100 per day from the date of entry of this order until the contempt ceases and visitation is restored, or the passage of three weeks, whichever occurs first. If the contempt continues for more than three weeks, that will increase to $250 per day.

"Visitation exchanges shall continue at the premises known as Mac's Café in Doolin, Oregon, and transportation incident to visitation shall be at the expense of Walter Wall and Mara Wall.

"I am not convinced, however, that the petitioners satisfy the definition of 'child-parent relationship' under the ORS...."

I lost track of what he was saying then. The disappointment crushed me. It didn't make sense that he thought justice was served by fining the Walls, money we'd never see anyway because they could just file another bankruptcy, and not change the situation for Carley.

Spencer reached for my hand and I heard the judge say, "You shall include in the contempt order, Mr. Norden, that the petitioners will have eight weeks continuous visitation with Carley Wall during the summer of 1999 as recompense for their loss of visitation these past months."

At least that was something.

CHAPTER 49

Jason Norden explained to me that winning the money judgment was beneficial, even though we knew the Walls couldn't pay it, because it forced them to come back to Oregon. When they received the judgment order, through their Arizona attorney who promptly withdrew, the Walls responded with notarized template documents, apparently prepared by themselves, asking for a continuance. We cringed when we read their whining excuses, lies and accusations. The only recourse was to go back to court, costing us more attorney fees.

"I keep wondering how any of this helps Carley," I said to Spencer on our way to Jason's office.

"Yeah, I know. But what else can we do? Kidnap her and disappear?"

It wasn't the first time we had asked ourselves that question. The answer was always that we didn't want to give her a life of running, of deceit and paranoia, evading the law and, by doing so, losing all touch with our family. Carley's life was off to a rough start, and chances were that it would remain so. Our choice was to stay and fight. By keeping our life stable, we would be giving our granddaughter the best future we could provide, however long it took to realize.

The jumble of paperwork that the Walls had filed eventually amounted to a Motion for Reconsideration and Clarification of Order, and a Motion to Continue. Jason had fought Judge Zoritch over their right for a continuance, but the judge had given them two months.

"Damn it! How do they do it?" Jason huffed. "Zoritch couldn't possibly believe their sob story—Mara's unemployed... Walter has a new job but bad weather's delayed it... leaving might get him fired... it would be disruptive to Carley in her new school. And this is bullshit!" he yelled at the faxed letter in his hand. "'...we repeatedly called Mr. Norden and left messages requesting that he stipulate to this continuance but he never took our calls.'"

Spencer laughed. "What's the matter with you, Jason? You didn't want to negotiate with them? You know Buck was just trying to be reasonable. After all, a $250-a-day contempt charge was only a *suggestion*."

"Yeah, right. The contempt ruling doesn't mean anything. It was in Oregon, for Christ's sake, and they're in Arizona. They can ignore it."

Their cynical humor was a short-lived release from the frustration we all felt.

In December, Buck and Mara appeared in the Camas County Courthouse. I hated the sight of them. Because they didn't have a lawyer, Buck was allowed to question us as witnesses. When he asked me if I was going to take Carley to a psychiatrist and give her drugs like we did to our daughter, I was fed up.

"No," I said, projecting my hatred into the one syllable.

Buck obviously wasn't getting the response he wanted. "Do you think Carley needs a psychiatrist?"

"No, do you?" I almost smiled, seeing Buck sputter in confusion, but the judge immediately ordered me to let Mr. Wall do the questioning.

It was soon over, and their motion was denied; contempt was still in force. The judge ordered Jason to explain everything to Buck and Mara, and obtain a workable visitation schedule from both parties. A new hearing was scheduled for February 22nd.

Out in the hallway, Buck said, "We'll allow you visitation, but you have to go to Arizona to get her. That's where she is now, with some friends. We had to drive all this way…"

Jason didn't let him continue. "The judge's order holds you responsible for transportation costs for all visitation." He was pacing in short semi-circles between us, as if he could not stand another minute with these idiots.

Mara spoke then. "The financial burden is too much. If this keeps up, we'll give her away. We'll just give her to the Indians."

The remark stunned us. If Mara was embarrassed by her own heartlessness, it didn't show.

I reacted first. "What about Christmas? Can we have our awarded Christmas visitation if we come get her? It's supposed to start at nine Christmas morning, and end on December 27th."

Buck said, "If you come get her, you can't come on our property. You can pick her up at our church."

Jason told them, "If we can get a trip worked out at this late date, you'll get notified at the post office address that you gave us."

He motioned to us, and the three of us turned away. We couldn't get out of there fast enough.

*   *   *

As the judge had directed, we tried to comply with Carley's new school schedule. All we had to go on was a typed letter from a "Gospel" academy, addressed to "Whom it may concern," and the name of the pastor. Spencer called the county sheriff's office there, who didn't have information about the church, but they obligingly sent an officer to check on Carley for us. The deputy called and said he'd seen Buck at the foot of their driveway where a "Keep Out" sign was posted. The deputy learned that the Walls were living in a fifth-wheel trailer, hauled in water and gas, and had a cell phone. Buck was supposed to call us and let us talk to Carley.

When we got the call, Buck had to first tell us how all their problems were our fault, and we could see Carley more often if we would just leave them alone. In the background, we could hear Carley asking to talk to Gran'mommy.

Finally, "Hi, Gran'mommy." She was excited, but shy.

"Hi, sweetie. I miss you so much. So does Gran'daddy. Do you want to talk to him, too?"

"No," she said softly.

"Oh. How come?"

Slowly, she answered, "Because he hurt me."

Shocked to learn that they were still preaching that story, I asked, as tenderly as I could, "When did he hurt you?"

"When you weren't there."

Spencer, listening on the extension, bowed his head, reflecting the sadness we heard in Carley's voice.

I put a smile in mine and said, "Oh, I think you're kidding me. Maybe someone is putting ideas in your head. It's probably very confusing for you."

Her response was an abrupt giddiness. "Are you coming to see me? And will you play some games with me?"

"Would you like that? Because we would really like to come."

"Yes. Come see me."

"Well, we're trying to work things out. As soon as we can, we'll come."

"Good. I want to play with you, and with Gran'daddy. I miss both of you."

The moment of truth. The words that broke through all the bullshit. Spencer and I grinned at each other from our extensions across the room.

Mara got on the phone then, and said, "Your daughter needs you. You should feel bad that you don't talk to her."

I was surprised to hear that she was still in touch with Kim. "She knows where we are, Mara. You should stay out of it."

"We just want you to know that we love you."

"What? You love us?" I laughed. "Your behavior sure doesn't show it."

"I love you. I love you," she repeated crazily.

"Why, then, did you leave town without telling us? Why do you tell lies about us to Carley?"

Mara pleaded, "No. No. No"

I couldn't take any more of her lunacy. I said, "I have to go," and hung up. Spencer picked up the conversation, apparently with Buck.

"We're not sure we can make plane reservations for Christmas, Buck. There are some problems, but we're still trying."

I waited to see where the conversation would go next.

"Buck, we need to cooperate. The visitation can still work over long-distance if we…"

A pause. "No, we didn't do that. Why would we have turned you in for a zoning violation on your shop in Doolin? We liked that you had a home and a job. We had regular visitations with Carley and she was happy. It wasn't us that forced you to Arizona, Buck."

I wondered how we were ever going to come to a reasonable solution to visitation logistics. And how much harder things could get for Carley.

CHAPTER 50

It was impossible for us to arrange the trip so quickly. We told ourselves that an abrupt, two-day visit with Carley after our long absence might be hard for her to handle anyway. A longer stay could be arranged in January. We called the Walls to explain our idea.

"We're sorry we can't see her for Christmas, but if it's alright with you we'll come after the first of the year," I said.

"It's up to Carley," Buck said.

I didn't understand what he was getting at. My only thought was that he wanted time to teach Carley to say she didn't want to see us.

"Well, it's not really fair to make a child make these kinds of decisions. Maybe you should talk to somebody about Judge Zoritch's ruling."

"I'll talk to Carley."

Spencer spoke from the other phone. "We'll call you back in a few days, after you've had a chance to think it over."

The next time we called, Mara answered and put Carley on the phone right away. For a minute I thought they were really going to have a six-year-old control their legal obligations for them. But Carley was playful and happy to talk to both of us for about thirty minutes, singing songs and telling us how to make a snowman. Before Mara took the phone again, Carley said she loved us.

Our plan was to fly down in late January, go pick up Carley and bring her back home with us. Then Buck and Mara would get her back when they came to Doolin for the hearing February 22nd.

"You wouldn't have to pay for her trip, and it would show Judge Zoritch that you're cooperating with us by giving us some make-up visitation." Spencer was using his most diplomatic tone, something I couldn't do.

"That means she'd miss school," Mara said.

Carley was in kindergarten in a three-student bible school, and Mara was one of the teachers. They'd already told us they were planning on bringing her with them in February. If, instead, she left a few weeks earlier, Spencer and I thought it could hardly have much of an impact on her education.

"She could go to kindergarten here. Or, have the pastor send her school work with her. There are some details to work out, but we're just asking for you to think about it."

"Yeah, we'll think about it. Call us back on the weekend, because I'm working weekdays," Buck said.

"Okay, fine. Can we say good-bye to Carley?" Spencer asked.

"Well, okay. But only a second. These long phone calls are costing us."

I couldn't figure that one out, because we had dialed them. But Spencer told me they probably had pay-by-the-minute cell phones. Anyway, logic was useless when dealing with them.

In the end, we didn't get what we wanted. The best they offered was to allow us to pick her up February 13th, turning Carley back over to her aunt in Doolin two days before the hearing. They were going to drive up in their RV, camp out at the aunt's house for a couple of days and drive back to Arizona with Carley. Letters telling us their demands emphasized that Carley should spend time with her aunt and cousin, not be left with a strange babysitter. The implication was that that was our usual practice. They added that the trip would not be for pleasure. "Our vacations do not consist of going to court over visitation of our daughter."

*   *   *

We found the little church that was the designated meeting place at noon. It was a deserted, ramshackle pre-fab building in a dry, desolate scrub land. After an hour wait, we drove the four miles back to town and called the sheriff's office, but were told the only deputy was out. No one answered when we tried the cell phone number we had for Buck and Mara.

Back at the church, we found two workmen dismantling an outbuilding.

"The Walls' place? Yeah, I think that's six or seven miles more. You'll see a "No Trespassing" sign on the right."

It was three o'clock.

"We don't have much choice," Spencer said. We braved ourselves for a confrontation, and aimed the rental car down the washboard dirt road.

When Buck saw us, he charged out of the open doorway of the trailer yelling, "You're trespassing on private property! Now get out!"

We saw Carley at the door, and she smiled at us.

"We're here to pick up Carley. We called for the deputy to help us, but he's not available," Spencer explained calmly.

"Call the cops if you want to, but I'll charge you with trespassing."

"Look. We'll go back to the church and wait if you want us to, but we're going to get Carley."

"We were there at nine like our letter said," Buck argued. "We waited forty-five minutes and you never showed."

I took the letter out of my bag and handed it to him. "Buck, there is no mention of time in your letter. We wrote you that we'd be there at noon."

With no more discussion, Buck agreed to have Carley at the church in half an hour. They arrived forty minutes later, with Mara and two other women that were there to witness the signing of duplicate copies of release letters. These were better written than what they usually produced, and stipulated that only Carley's aunt had authority to seek medical treatment for Carley during our visitation.

Carley was shy for about two minutes. Then, when we had driven out of their view, she started chattering excitedly about seeing us at her driveway. Then we saw the deputy's car, and stopped to tell him what happened.

"Sorry for the delay. I'm glad everything worked out," he said, smiling at Carley. We thanked him and headed out of town.

Carley said, "My Gramma and Grampa want their cops to listen only to them and not to you guys, so that you will be arrested and thrown in jail."

I was sitting next to her in the back seat while Spencer drove.

"That's not going to happen," I said definitively. "We haven't done anything wrong, Carley, so don't worry about it."

"I know you and Gran'daddy are not doing wrong things, because I want to be with you."

"Well then, that's that," Spencer said, trying to get off the subject.

"I want to stay with you for a long time," she continued.

"That would be nice," I said.

"But my Gramma and Grandpa said you would hurt me."

"What do you think about that?"

"I am sad about that. I know you and Gran'daddy would not hurt me."

"You're absolutely right. I'm glad you know that."

"You're a pretty smart Snigglefritz. Do you know that?" Spencer said, still trying to be playful.

Carley's face took on a mischievous expression and she shouted to Spencer, "Yeah, 'cuz I'm on your side and I want your team to win!"

Oh brother, I thought. This was not a game we wanted to encourage.

"There aren't any teams, Carley. A judge listens to everybody and decides what's best for you."

She nodded with apparent satisfaction, and said, "I will tell the judge when he asks me that I want to stay with you."

Spencer said, "I don't think he will want to bother you with questions. But he will do the right thing for you."

He finally maneuvered the conversation to the scenery, the plane trip we'd be taking, and the motel with a pool. I realized that I had been in an anxious state of mind for hours, and I allowed myself to relax. Watching Carley as she laughed and talked with Spencer, I appreciated how she'd grown. She was probably two inches taller and her face and body looked leaner. Her speech was still slightly impaired, but better. When she smiled, she looked just like her mother.

But the ugly circumstances surfaced again later at the motel, and Spencer's heart was once again broken. Carley told him he was not supposed to be in the room while she dressed, he could not tuck her in bed, and she was not even supposed to take a bath while staying with us. He lowered his head and politely left the room.

"Are you afraid of Gran'daddy? Afraid he might hurt you?"

"No. But my Grampa and Gramma said to tell you guys that."

"What do you want?"

"I want Gran'daddy to tuck me in. Grampa and Gramma are wrong. He never hurts me."

"You know he loves you very much. Me, too."

Carley threw her arms around me. "I love you, too, Gran'mommy. And I love Gran'daddy. When he comes back, I will tell him."

*   *   *

That's how it went all week. Like a poison she couldn't get out of her system, she worried that her Gramma and Grampa would have us arrested and thrown in jail. Whenever friends asked us, "How was Arizona?" Carley said, "Tell them how fast my Grampa shooed you off his property." We had to promise repeatedly that we

240

would take her to Aunt Shelly's house on Saturday. She worried because Mara and Buck told her we would try to take her away forever.

Still, there were the spontaneous hugs and I-love-yous. Her sense of humor showed in the way she could play word games and running gags with Spencer. She loved to tell stories, but assured us that she understood when telling the truth was important. Because she wasn't the least bit fragile when it came to rough-housing, I was nervous when she and Spencer were wrestling.

"You'll tell us if he gets too rough, won't you? If he holds you too tight?"

"I will," she insisted.

"Her? What about me? Ow!" Spencer cried as she hurled herself at him.

She thrived on his attention and explanations of how things worked, like teaching her to drive the lawnmower-tractor to carry hay to the cows, which she took very seriously. She asked all the normal "why" questions and had a quick grasp of complicated concepts. The only thing slowing her down was her speech. If she were in a real classroom with other kids her own age, we believed that difficulty would go away. But she wasn't.

*   *   *

The court hearing consisted of putting a date on the completion of the contempt order, thereby ceasing the assessment of fines. Judge Zoritch said that as of January 1st, 1999, the Walls had been in compliance with the visitation order. Now, he said, it was up to us to fashion a new visitation schedule that did not interfere with Carley's schooling.

Jason, Spencer and I got to work. Our attorney's official request of a schedule from Carley's "school" generated a response of dubious validity. The letter from the "Grace Academy Administrator" had no letterhead, had grammatical errors, was unsigned and faxed from a real estate office. The typed surname of the writer was the same as the church pastor's, presumably his wife. She professed that, including summer sessions and enrichment programs, the school operated year round. Any interruptions, even more than two days, she wrote, would cause hardships for Carley because she was a gifted student. It was an obvious put-up by the Walls, who must have forgotten that they'd testified that Carley simply went to tutors when she wanted to because school was not in session.

Spencer's research turned up the fact that no one in Arizona's Department of Education or Health Department had heard of the Grace Academy. A second letter from the Grace Academy Administer, signed this time, explained that they were a private school and not required to be accredited. We found that there was a Christian school accreditation program, but no one there had heard of them either.

By searching the internet, I found that the so-called church and academy had changed their name several times. My e-mail contacts in the area reported horror stories of a known "Christian" cult with some of the same names, a cult that had been exposed as child-abusers in another state. I wanted to find the link that showed this hokey school for what it was, but I didn't find one. All I could do was give the judge what we knew, and hope for the best.

*   *   *

Letter to Judge Stephen Zoritch, March 23, 1999:
Your Honor,

There is more to the matter of Carley's situation than the letters from the Arizona church suggests. We are very concerned with the substance of the school. When she visited with us, we noted that she needed help to count to twenty, that she did not recognize the alphabet, did not speak clearly or use simple words correctly. She had also stopped using normal hygiene habits that she knew before.

Carley could not name any other students, and told us she didn't go to school because her grandma taught her at home. She told us she couldn't sit still for very long, so she wouldn't like school. When we told her what kindergarten was like, she said that sounded okay.

When we were in Arizona, we saw that the church property consisted of a small church with no air conditioning, heat or water. The Arizona Heath Department and the building permits office had never heard of the church under any of the names associated with that pastor. The closest thing we've come across in our research is a "cult" called Grace Fellowship Church.

We've tried to phone the Walls, at the two cellular number they gave the Court, several times. We get only a recording of "not in service."

We ask for your consideration to allow Carley to stay with us for part of the normal school year, to give her the benefits of attending school with other kids her own age.

*   *   *

In March, he wrote his ruling. Judge Zoritch maintained that he had reviewed all the material and therefore ordered that the visitation conform to the current school schedule. He pinpointed gaps in the academy's non-mandatory sessions that gave us a three week period beginning in late January, and a four week period in late July, the two parties to share transportation expenses. He allowed a minimum of two phone calls per week and unlimited letters while the child was with the other family, specifying that none should be monitored, edited nor withheld. There was the usual instruction that parties not disparage the other parties in front of the child, and he wanted it noted that we would allow reasonable visits with Carley's other Oregon relatives.

We celebrated only the stipulation that we would get our eight-week make-up visitation starting July 1st.

CHAPTER 51

For the next three months, Buck and Mara made communicating with Carley nearly impossible. We'd received the judge's ruling in a letter in March, but we didn't get a copy of the signed court order until late May. And that's the only thing that Buck and Mara paid attention to. At various times and days, we tried phoning the cell phone numbers they'd given us, but without success. We sent cards and Easter gifts to Carley but received no acknowledgment. One letter to the Walls got a curt reply that their phones were cut off because they had to pay court costs, and because of the garnishment of his wages.

They wrote, "Despite your best efforts we are still able to provide a healthy, loving, caring environment for Carley, but this does not include the luxury of having a cell phone."

Back in January, we had started legal actions to claim some of the financial judgment awarded us in the contempt of court case, an amount of $23,795 when all was said and done. Because Buck's employment was hard to pin down, he didn't start losing wages from his mechanic's job until March, at which point he quit. Then he filed an objection in their county court, but lost. We had received a total of $227.20; they hadn't made any attempt to negotiate further payment, and we had the additional burden of paying an Arizona lawyer.

Spencer let me write the reply.

"Two courts have ruled that Carley's care includes regular contact with us, despite your best efforts. Your financial difficulties that stem from the denial of these rights are not our responsibility." I gave them a toll-free number they could use to phone us, and specific days and times we were available.

Again and again, we were confronted with their illogical reasoning. They insisted on adhering to the letter of the law when it suited them, and blurring it or misinterpreting it altogether when it went against them. Buck used the fifteen-minute minimum phone call, as ordered by Judge Zoritch, as a strict maximum limit; we actually heard a timer go off before Carley's hurried "good bye." Zoritch's "reasonable visitation" with Carley's Oregon relatives was read by Buck as his right to know exactly where she was every day, and we had to stay at home so that "her family" could see her any time they wanted.

We began taping our phone conversations with Carley when it became obvious that she was being coached. Oregon law allows recording phone calls when one party knows about it, and we believed there was a chance that someday we might need that documentation.

We could hear Mara's voice during one call, prompting Carley to ask us why we don't contact our daughter.

Spencer told Carley, "Kim knows where we are. She can call us if she wants to."

"My Mommy doesn't like you because you hurted her."

He ignored that and switched to talking about our pets.

The next time she called, the first thing she said was, "My Gramma is my adopted mom and my Grampa is my adopted dad."

For a while, Carley started calls by saying she didn't want to talk to Spencer. She made growling or static noises into the phone, but he joked with her until she forgot about it. When she started calling us by our first names, I asked her why.

"My Gramma and Grampa want me to."

"What do you want to call us?"

Carley whispered, "Gran'mommy and Gran'daddy."

There were many days that we didn't get a call at all, or they were taken up by Buck's ranting or were shorter than fifteen minutes. Sometimes the coaching Carley received went haywire.

"Hello? Hello, Carley?" Spencer asked. "Is that you?"

Silence. Spencer teased, "I can't h-e-a-r-r-r you."

Carley giggled.

"Ah-ha! I knew it was you."

"I was just playing," she said.

"Oh, okay. But next time, before playing the game say 'hi' first so I know you're there."

"Okay. But you ruined our day," she said with affected annoyance.

"What?"

"You ruined our day because we wanted to go fishing but we had to call you and it is a butt in the pain."

It wasn't hard to guess where that message came from.

After a few minutes of fun talk (her dogs, the wild turkeys in our yard that she wanted to see, and going swimming when she got here), we asked if she was excited about coming this summer.

She whispered, "Yes."

Then we had to talk to Buck about details of the pending trip, and he complained about the twice-weekly phone calls.

Spencer said, "If you want to request another day for phoning us, just tell us the changed time and day. We're flexible."

"We always have things to do and then we have to go and call you, and my phone is shut off so we have to go to town."

"I'm sorry about that, but it isn't our problem. Maybe you could make some kind of arrangement…"

"It is your problem."

"Buck, it's not fair to tell Carley that."

"Well, it's the truth. And we always tell her the truth. It's the way we live our life."

Sometimes when she called from their house (evidently when their cell phone was working) she was distracted. They would call us when they had her favorite TV show on, or when "Daddy" was visiting.

"I don't want to talk now because my Daddy is here and we're going on a bike ride."

"Oh, okay. That's sounds fun," I said. "I'll only keep you a minute."

We talked for ten minutes then Dewayne started tickling her. We could hear his taunts and her giggling, then she said, "Good-by. I have to hang up now."

We said, "Good-by." Then we heard her running away from the phone and yelling, "Wait for me." She had forgotten to disconnect, and from what we could hear, Dewayne had gone off without her.

*   *   *

The trip to Arizona went smoother than the previous one, and after we picked Carley up, we flew to Maryland to visit Spencer's family. Thanks to Spencer's determined diplomacy, Buck finally understood our itinerary and contact information. On the days they were expected to call and talk to her, we reminded Carley and tried to keep her available. But they didn't always call at the agreed hour, and Carley's attitude fluctuated; sometimes she was sleepy, sometimes playing. She liked to wander around while on the phone, to be in the same room as us or near where her East Coast cousins were playing. She tried to politely tell Buck and Mara about her new

246

friends and the fun things she was doing, but it didn't sound like she got very far with that topic. Once, I heard her repeat, "I'll let you go now" eight times but the call continued twenty minutes more.

Sometimes she cried and murmured apologetically. I sat with her afterwards, and she said talking to them made her miss them. I told her I understood. When I asked her if she wanted to be left alone when they called, she said no. The next time, she talked from the stool in the kitchen, making eye-contact with me every few minutes whenever she said, "I miss you, too." She didn't cry, and afterwards went merrily off to play.

That's how communications continued after we returned home. If they didn't call at the right time, we went about our business and took Buck's wrath when he eventually got through. He accused us of not letting Carley call her aunt in Doolin, until Carley told them she tried to call but there was no one home. I heard Carley telling them that she couldn't find the note with the lawyer's number on it that they'd given her, but, yes, she would call 911 if we gave her any trouble.

I don't think they knew she was sitting right next to me when she talked to them, but that was the way Carley wanted it. Sometimes, because Carley held the phone away from her ear, I heard part of what they were saying. When she told them we had pizza for dinner, Buck said, "Somebody doesn't know how to cook, huh?" The few times she tried to tell them about our activities, she was stopped until she repeated that she was bored and missed them, and ended the call in tears. They always told her how many days until it would be over and they'd be "a family" again, reminding Carley to tell us she wanted to go home. She never did.

Once during the eight weeks, I took Carley with me to talk to a counselor. I explained to her what I liked about it, and told her she could talk if she wanted to. Within a few minutes of meeting the woman, Carley said she would like it, so I left them alone. They seemed to hit it off and I hoped it would give Carley someone all to herself to talk to at more meetings. But when I admitted that I didn't have legal authority to take Carley to professionals, the counselor declined.

During the Walls' next phone call, Carley wanted to tell her Grampa about the talk.

"I went to a house to see a lady," she said with some excitement.

Buck was suspicious immediately. "What kind of lady? Did they call her a doctor, or a therapist?"

"It's a good lady."

"They don't have permission for any kind of treatment," he said loudly.

"It wasn't treatment," Carley pronounced the big word precisely. Then she put her head down and turned so that I couldn't hear Buck anymore.

She began, "My Gran'mommy turned me in…" I think she meant *took me in*, but it got confusing. "No, nobody turned *her* in … I went in…"

Poor Carley was getting frustrated with their questions. When she was finally able to finish a sentence, she said, "But I want to talk because she can stop my hurt feelings."

Wow. It had been tough to listen to, but she finally got it out and I was proud of her. Then she lightened the mood by playing a song on her toy piano for them. I was surprised then when I heard her ask them, "How long do I have to stay with you guys?"

Then, "No. How long do I stay there before I come back here?"

It would've been interesting to hear how they handled that one.

CHAPTER 52

The eight-week summer visitation went by too quickly, and we packed as much fun as we could into it. Carley got to be a flower girl for her aunt's garden wedding in Maryland, and swam in the pool there almost all day everyday. Back home, we went camping, threw a kids' party, had visits from my family and from Tisha, and got a kitten.

After she returned to Arizona in late August, our sporadic phone contact with Carley went the same as before. But it was only a brief wait until our two-week visitation started in January.

When the time came, the Walls drove her to the Las Vegas airport and she flew as an "unaccompanied minor" to Portland, where we greeted her with a huge, ladybug balloon. It was the first of many airplane trips she would make as a two-family kid, and we started a tradition of balloons and an overnight stay at a motel with a pool.

On this trip, Spencer's brother and family from Seattle joined us. They hadn't seen Carley since she was an infant, so watching her play with their six-year-old son was especially fun. At home, we stayed active doing Carley's favorite things: going to the beach and throwing sticks in the waves, visiting George and Lou, playing with our dog, Rosie, and the new kitten, Sweeney, and doing the farm chores that Carley got such a kick out of.

Our neighbor had a daughter that liked Carley, and at six years old they both had what it took to keep a friendship going over long, extended intervals. So Jenny went with us for four days to play in the snow. We rented a cabin in what Carley called "the Snowy Mountains," and it was so successful that we decided to make it another tradition for Carley's winter visits. The girls had their first try at Nordic skiing, made snow sculptures and had many snowball fights. Inside, we played board games and poker for beans, and the girls put on shows for our evening entertainment. On the sledding hill, we took turns taking videos of our rides, either in a train of three sleds or dog-piled on Spencer. We all came home in one piece, exhausted and happy.

Then it was time to take Carley back to the airport. For the first time, we believed this was something that could really work, this long-distance visitation. We should've known it wouldn't last.

Before we could plan our summer with Carley, the Walls filed a petition in the Arizona court to change the venue of litigation concerning visitation modifications. Spencer drafted a response, with a little help from Jason Norden, that explained the Walls' history of "forum-shopping" and the suspect nature of their timing. To their complaint of the "burdensome travel obligations to litigate issues affecting the child," we argued that they were entirely of their own making; the petition was just another effort to subvert the orders made in Oregon courts. We filed the response *pro se* and the case was dismissed.

Little changed in the following months. The contentious hostility from Buck and Mara surfaced in every contact we had with them, and became more pervasive in Carley's demeanor. We did our best to counter it with uncomplicated rules that we made for ourselves: stay positive, don't bad-mouth Mara or Buck in her presence; explain the contradictions in her life as simply as possible, but never lie; be consistent in our discipline for misbehavior; give her huge amounts of encouragement and praise; show her how many people in our part of the world love her; let her be a kid.

When we were with Carley, it wasn't hard for us to keep the faith that our presence in her life was having a positive influence. The stressful times were when she was in Arizona and we either didn't hear from her or the phone calls were disturbing. She would sometimes say hurtful things like, "I never want to go to your house again," or things that scared us like, "Every time I come back to Gramma's and Grampa's house, after three days I throw up." Our reaction was to downplay the Walls' obvious coaching and talk her into a playful mood, but sometimes she just hung up on us.

Spencer and I worried that because they kept themselves so isolated, there was no one to see how Buck and Mara treated Carley, regardless of whether the harm was physical or emotional. But there was nothing we could do to help her.

Troubling revelations kept cropping up. During the summer visitation in 2001, Carley and I were going somewhere in the car and talking. She told me her daddy was living with them sometimes. I had figured as much, since he had left Oregon after being jailed for a third-degree rape conviction. The father of an underage girl had

250

turned him in, and Dewayne did thirty days before violating his parole by leaving the state.

"My daddy is nice," she told me.

"I'm glad about that, Carley, but sometimes he isn't so nice to other people and it got him into some trouble here."

"I know about that. That's why he's in Arizona, so he won't go to jail," she said matter-of-factly.

"Tell me something, Carley. If he ever scared you, or hurt you in any way, would you be brave enough to tell somebody?"

"I would tell my Gramma and Grampa."

"Could you tell somebody besides them?" I said, careful to keep my tone conversational, like I'd seen the counselors do.

"Yes," she said.

"That's good, because if they ever did something bad to you, you could tell someone."

She nodded in agreement. I knew I was on thin ice. How could I give her the tools without pushing her to try them without reason?

"I know they love you, but I know that sometimes they have bad moods."

Carley said, "Whenever Gramma gets weird, I try to leave her alone and stay close to Grampa."

"What does 'weird' mean?"

"Whenever Gramma doesn't take her medicine, she just gets weird-acting."

I was working hard at staying neutral, and said, "Does your Grampa ever get weird?"

"Yes, sometimes, but for a different reason."

"Oh, what reasons?"

"He has a different medicine he forgets to take."

I took a calming breath. "What do you do then?"

"I run and hide in the wash. My dog, Buddy, goes with me and we snuggle and keep warm, and then I go back when I'm done crying and it's dark."

We talked about the wash, the dry creek bed in the back of the property. She told me it wasn't too scary because Buddy would protect her, but one time she saw a rattlesnake. "We know what to do, and if there are cougars around, too."

I realized that some of what I was hearing could be made up, and there was no way of knowing for sure, but I kept the conversation going.

"Do they say anything to you when you come back in the house?"

"No, they don't see me. They just keep yelling at each other. I go to bed."

She had already told me that they all sleep in the same room, so I asked her how that works.

"My Grampa usually goes to bed first, then I go, then Gramma. Sometimes the door is shut and I sleep on the couch. If they are yelling, I leave them alone and go to bed."

Spencer and I thought this was enough to get somebody at the Arizona children's services agency interested. After Carley returned to Arizona, I reported the conversation to a social worker there. When I told him where they lived, he said, "I know that some people out there have dogs. Do they have dogs?"

"Yes, but I don't think they're vicious or anything."

"Well, this isn't enough for me to go out there."

I said, "I was hoping you could at least take the report as history, because we believe there is a case building."

"No, it's not enough."

CHAPTER 53

When I started telling this story, I didn't know how it would finish. I couldn't just make up an ending, though I wanted to. I wanted it to end with fulfillment, an encouragement to those in a similar situation.

The truth is that I didn't feel happy about the circumstances when I started writing them down. But I told myself that changes do happen, sometimes for the better, and life does go on. Sometimes, hope is the only consistent thing in our lives.

I've usually got a sound spirit, so I'm not devastated when bad things happen. But it's much more intolerable when they happen to other people. The fact that the horrors of September 11, 2001, touched so many lives is inconceivable to me. Like imagining the universe, I can't do it.

Yet my family members and I lost no one that day. Instead, we found someone.

I had awakened that morning with flu symptoms, bad enough to need bed rest, so I called in sick. The office could survive without me. Spencer left for work as usual, and it was shortly after that when the news I was watching on CNN changed everything. It was almost too incredible to take in , but I remained calm. I called Spencer at his office so he could turn on his radio. He told me no one in his family was traveling, and no one we knew was in New York or near the Pentagon. I understood that people do that in times of emergency, look out for their own first. So, with an unnatural sense of separation as the horrifying events unfolded, I lay on the couch watching from safety.

I was not thinking of our daughter, Kim, who hadn't contacted us in three years, and that had been a painful phone conversation. The futility of our efforts to communicate, to reach that part of her that made any sense to us, had dwindled in the eight years of her estrangement and we had given up. So when I answered the phone that morning and realized it was Kim, my mind reeled. In the midst of distant turmoil on the television, it became personal.

In a wavering voice, she said, "Hi, Mom. I'm watching the news, about the crashes, and I'm scared that our relatives living on the East Coast might be involved."

"Kim. No, no one is hurt. Where are you?"

"At home. In Arizona."

The coincidence of her being in the same state as Carley struck me, but it wasn't important.

"Are you all right? Who's with you?" I asked.

"I'm all right, just anxious about what's happening. John, that's my husband, is gone and I didn't know what to do, so I went to my friend next door. She asked me who I really wanted to talk to, and I said you." A pause. "She told me to phone home."

That friend gave remarkable help. Persuading Kim to overcome the emotions that separated us and to call us was the first step towards the happy ending I wanted. The getting there is rough, though. A few months later, Kim was heartbroken when her friend died suddenly from a brain tumor. I never met her, or thanked her, but she was a hell of a friend. I hoped she had known how much good she did.

In time, we worked through the many levels of hurt, big ones and little ones. The barriers crumbled, familiarity returned; we finally had our daughter back. She had worked hard to get well and make a new life for herself. She had started a family with her loving husband, and she is a terrific mom to two little boys.

The proximity to the Walls was, after all, a convenient coincidence. It was a day's travel between them, and Kim had been able to see Carley once; they told Kim they would keep in touch with her as long as she had nothing to do with us.

Still the growth continues. As a thirty-year-old woman, Kim searched for and found both of her biological parents. It took a tremendous amount of courage for her to make contact with them, and I heard the excitement and pride in her voice when she told us about it. When I realize how strong Kim is, I am glad knowing her again, in being a part of her life. I think she knows herself now, and will be happy.

We know there is hope for Carley's happiness, too. Seeing and understanding Kim's long struggle and success in breaking the cycle of abuse that began her life, we hang on to our belief that it can happen for Carley. I am glad knowing her and being a part of her life, too.

CHAPTER 54

In December, 2001, we filed a contempt of court suit against the Walls for denying phone calls and disrupting visitations. After two hearings were rescheduled, a judge, was finally appointed. We proposed a modification of visitation in March, 2002. In November, the attorneys for both sides argued by phone for three hours from their respective offices, with clients present. In the end, the arrangement for phone calls with Carley was improved, but visitation days were lost.

It was not a fair settlement. I hated it when we made it, but we believed our lawyer when he said the circuit court judge we happened to draw was famous for her "split-the-baby-in-half" decisions. That, and having to listen to the monotonous whining from the Walls and their sanctimonious attorney; I just couldn't take any more. They used the term "welfare of the child" quickly enough when we asked for anything that affected their conveniently invented routine, but they had no real thoughts for Carley. Their hatred of us was and still is all-consuming, to a point that blocks out seeing the pain their contentiousness causes her.

In an effort to end the turmoil, we agreed to six weeks visitation every summer, and one week during Carley's Spring Break in odd-numbered years only. In addition to paying for the airplane ticket, we agreed to provide $150 in advance for each trip the Walls had to make to the airport. The Walls said they were too old and sick to make the four-hour one-way trip in one day so they needed to stay overnight. When we asked if they couldn't get a friend to take her, Buck said, "We only know old people and Mexicans."

So, once again, we gave in to their demands so that we could get out of a long, horrid contempt of court battle that would punish Carley in the long run, and we salvaged what we could of our long-distance relationship with her.

In December, 2002, we received official notification that Buck and Mara Wall had filed bankruptcy.

"Isn't this the third time they've gone bankrupt?" I asked Spencer. "How many times can people legally do this?"

"As often as every seven years. All of their debt disappears like magic. Again. Including our lien on their property."

"We don't get anything out of them? The monetary judgment that was supposed to punish them for running away with Carley, for ignoring the visitation order in the first place, cost them all of $227? What about the house in Doolin?"

"It was already foreclosed upon and sold at public auction in 1999."

"Oh, I forgot. Shit." I raged. "We should've foreclosed on the Arizona property and had them evicted."

"Well, it's too late now. The bankruptcy law protects them. And besides, what would that have done? They would have gone who-knows-where, lived on the road in their fifth-wheel trailer?" He continued softly, "We don't want that for Carley."

"No. Then we'd be like them—making Carley suffer just to get back at them." I had to give into the exhaustion I felt. "So, what now?"

"We stay in Carley's life. We're the only constant for her." Spencer reached for my hand and gave it a soft kiss. "You know we're doing the best we can."

"Yeah. I know," I said. "As always."

Spencer continued, "And Mara and Buck will continue their fucked-up paranoid lives, and maybe someday it will catch up with them."

*   *   *

Carley comes once a year for six weeks, and every other Spring Break for seven days. Her body changes shape and gains a few inches in height each time we see her. I'm not concerned about her baby fat, but she says kids call her "Fatty." She says she's learning about nutrition at school and works at eating a balanced diet, which is commendable for an eleven-year-old. It's a definite improvement from the white-bread diet she's been raised on. She's a big kid for her age, already beating the mark we made on our kitchen wall for her mother at the same age. But she goes outside a lot, playing with the animals or bike-riding, so I think her body will develop healthily enough.

Her poor teeth aren't getting much better, but aside from reminders to brush well, there's nothing we can do. I'm sure the

Walls won't let us help get her braces, even if we could afford it; they don't take her to a dentist, let alone a specialist.

"I go to a doctor at the clinic once a year, and she says my teeth will grow in okay when my twelve-year-old teeth come in and push these out of the way," Carley once told me. I hope it's true. She's got a beautiful laugh.

The annual doctor visits must've increased, because now Carley is talking about changes made to her medication doses. Of course, we always wonder whether what she says is the truth, or some crap that the Walls fed her for our hearing, or her imagination.

"Actually," the clue word that usually warns us of impending make-believe, "I've been on medication for a long time, and the doctor just took me off it."

"You were taking pills right up until you came here?" I asked.

"Yes. The doctor wants me to be off of them for the summer so she can see how I do, and then see what I need for regular."

"Well, what signs do you have that it's either working or not?"

"My tics will come back," she said.

Ah, yes, the tics. I remember something about that at Spring Break, when I told her that her constant throat-clearing was annoying.

"Do you have something wrong with your throat?" I asked.

"No, it's my torr..rrr...something-or-other syndrome. I forget what it's called."

"Tourette's Syndrome?" I was stunned. The Walls were always coming up with these exotic illnesses. The last one was the "inverted extra nipple" on Carley's chest, which had been there since birth and looked to me like an accidental birthmark made by forceps.

"You were told you have Tourette's Syndrome?"

"Yes. My daddy has it, too." First time I'd heard that.

"I've never noticed you stuttering, blurting out things or anything like that. How does it affect you?"

"That's the reason I have to clear my throat a lot, and I don't even know I'm doing it. Another thing is I have to burp, or it sounds like little burps. And like when I'm staring at the TV for a long time, my chin sort of drops and my eyes roll back," she answered.

I thought of alternate explanations, but knew that arguing wasn't a good tactic.

"You know, I've read a little bit about that condition, and I'm not sure that's what could be bothering you. So I hope the doctor does some more work with you."

I let it go. Nothing more has come of it, until now, but I did begin to speculate on the possibility. Since talking age, Carley's had a habit of repeating the very last sound she made when searching for the next word. Not a stutter exactly, but a very clear stop and start, as if she took a pause to regroup then backed up one beat to begin again.

Carley would say, "I was running down the driveway… (pause)…-ay, and then I turned and slipped on the grass…. (pause)…-ss, and that's how I fell."

What else? She does drop her head from time to time, but I thought it was an imitation of her daddy, because she looks just like him when she does that. Oh no, don't let that happen to her.

Now she's making puffing noises, like she's blowing wisps of hair away from her mouth. It doesn't get on my nerves and I'm not mentioning it. I don't know if this stuff is real, psychosomatic or what. But I do know she doesn't need any more reasons to feel abnormal.

Yesterday, a particularly hard day for us, she said as much. She and I had a breakdown right after she finished breakfast. I had started out in such a good mood, with plans of sightseeing, lunch out, buying her some new shorts. It wasn't asking too much, I thought, to get her moving at nine o'clock and leave the house by ten or ten thirty. But she couldn't get it together. She was distracted by anything and everything, and got angry and sulky when I reminded her of what she was supposed to be doing. Almost every day of her visit so far has been like this, taking two hours to do a ten-minute task like picking up her clothes or brushing her teeth. I had had enough.

"I can't do this," I told Spencer on the phone. "We aren't going to Camas City today. She just won't move. I've tried everything, and I give up."

My frustration scared him, I think. It felt to me so much like when we were raising our kids, only then it seemed he wasn't paying much attention. But we both learned. So he knew now that I was really calling for help. He talked to Carley on the phone while I cooled off out in the garden. When she joined me, she was full of apologies.

"Okay," I said. "But I need to see something in your actions, not just words. Can we still go to Camas City? It's up to you."

"I want to go," she said.

"Then show me. You have to get socks and shoes on."

She moped up the stairs. Ten minutes later, I followed. She was sitting on the floor, staring out of the window, her shoes dropped in the middle of the room.

"Carley, you haven't done anything!" I was exasperated. "You're eleven years old. I refuse to baby you. Do what you want, but I'm not getting disappointed again. I'll believe we're really going when we're actually walking out the door."

Later in the car, finally on our way, I tried to talk about it calmly.

"Are there things you want to change, so that this doesn't happen again?"

"Yes." I could barely hear her.

"Like what? What would you change?" I tried to coax her, but it was hard work. "Can you say that you would like to be more something, or you would like to be less something?"

"Yes," she said, barely audible with her head hanging. "I would like to be less ignorant."

This floored me.

"What makes you think you're ignorant? You're far from it, you're smart. If you were ignorant, it would be easy. You would be treated differently. We would give you only simple tasks, like getting out of bed and getting dressed, but we'd put your clothes out. We'd make all decisions for you."

She was quiet, and I knew I was losing her. It felt like I was deciphering a code. I tried another way.

"What else? Can you think of something you would like to be more of?"

She spoke with more emotion now, as if she had her strategies worked out. "I would like to be more normal, where I wouldn't have to go back and forth to two places all the time."

There it was again. Her standby excuse for all bad behavior. What can we do? It was true; she had a disjointed, sometimes contradictory life. Yet not a good reason for rudeness, sloppiness, refusal to follow basic household routine. It makes me think of criminal defenders that try to justify anti-social behaviors, allowing bad choices to go without consequences. But not us. We never let our kids carry on about being adopted.

Were we wrong? Was there something more we should've done, and is there something more we should do for Carley? If she really suffers from Tourette's or any other learning disability, is there a way to help her?

But I struggle with the daily routine. How do I get her up and going without treating her like a baby? I want to do things with her. I

259

want to have fun playing. Laugh and talk about silly stuff in an eleven-year-old's life. I want her to be happy. I want her other grandparents to stop teaching her to hate. I want to have her more than these six weeks. I want it to stop raining.

I want to be more normal.

EPILOGUE

The McGhees' correspondence with legislators, both Federal and State, were answered with polite sympathy. In February, 1998, they learned of an Oregon Legislative Committee that was seeking public input on, among other issues, the creation of an oversight committee for CSD. They responded with written testimony supporting a bill to create an open board of review, instead of the current, ineffective Ombudsman Office which doesn't investigate complaints from citizens, and doesn't have access to confidential records. The bill died in committee.

Nina Cowan was eventually bumped up to a top job with the agency in the state capital. Before leaving her position as Branch Director in Camas County, however, she had continued to wield remarkable power.

Spencer McGhee registered and trained for a volunteer position as a Court Appointed Child Advocate (CASA) in Camas County. Days before being sworn in, the director of volunteers rejected his application. He was told that Nina Cowan had given the order.

Months later, Spencer McGhee was turned down for a position with the Victim Assistance Division of the Camas County District Attorney's Office. An insider said he was the best suited for the job, but Nina Cowan had told the D. A. that she would not work with any case McGhee touched.

Emily Sanchez, and later Irma Pierce, transferred to the state correction agency for teenage offenders. Some of the children they work with are the same children whose cases had been terminated, at Cowan's direction, from their previous caseloads at CSD.

In 2001, Oregon's child welfare division published its Services Review to the U.S. Department of Health and Human Services. Six out of the seven "outcome areas" analyzed for safety, permanency, and well-being were identified as not in substantial conformity. [www.acf.hhs.gov/programs/region10/ extra/orefsrrpt.pdf]

As recently as October, 2007, the *Oregonian* reported that six years after the dismal federal review, the state's system had made little progress protecting children. And in April, 2008, a headline read, "Abuse cases still in shadows."

After some personal exploring, Tisha McGhee returned to her hometown and has become a successful office manager in her father's business.

Gail and Spencer McGhee have continued their relationship with Kim, enjoying the usual parental trappings, including bragging about their grandsons. On rare occasions, Carley gets to visit her mother; they share common interests and can carry on as if they just saw each other the day before.

The author would like to encourage interested readers to learn more about their state's child welfare policies. Locate, join, and contribute to organizations that protect and advance the interests of children.

Made in the USA
Monee, IL
28 December 2022

23789507R10151